Darkness
of Slumber

By ROSEMARY KUTAK

WILDSIDE PRESS

CONTENTS

CAST OF CHARACTERS
IN THE ORDER OF THEIR APPEARANCE

PART ONE

BARBARA MINARY
June 8, 1943

1.

THE NOTE was propped against the telephone. Barbara saw it as soon as she entered the rear hall, and her anomalous foreboding curdled into quick fear.

On closer approach she recognized Julia's scrawny handwriting. The message was a single sentence. "Dr. Castleman from the hospital says to tell Mr. Minary the time is changed to five o'clock."

Puzzled, Barbara picked up the note and read it over a second time. The mention of a doctor touched a buried association. Not the usual sick-bed sort of thing—something else, a vague and frightening memory that did not quite come to the surface.

However, a doctor could need legal advice as well as anyone else. And the oddness of the hour fitted in with a physician's schedule. This Castleman was probably a client of Phil's.

But her pulse was a tocsin beating out alarm. At first sight of the note she had known, beyond reason, that this

1

was IT. The mysterious something behind Cissie's manner and discreet insinuations at lunch. The thing she had felt coming closer to her all afternoon.

In the midst of her rising agitation, she heard footsteps on the back stairs, and pulled herself together quickly, as Julia walked in from the kitchen. Tall and loopy in her afternoon uniform as the letters in her handwriting, she stared with a curiosity that seemed to Barbara almost gloating.

"This message isn't very clear, Julia. Was this all that Dr. Castleman said? What hospital did he mean?"

Julia did not reply immediately. In the time since Barbara had come to the house, Julia had never spoken to her without first going through a little facial ritual. With an outward thrust of her lower lip that sent disapproving creases down the sides of her chin, she would express her resentment of the woman who had taken Eve's place. Then, in resignation to the inevitable, her upper lip would smooth her rebellious expression into forced truce.

Today for the first time in three years, she omitted her preliminary pantomime. She did not smile, but her thoughts twinkled like small malicious stars in the depths of her eyes.

"I don't know, Mrs. Minary. That was all the doctor said. Just to tell Mr. Minary the time was changed."

"All right, Julia."

The cook turned back to the kitchen, the triumphant set of her retreating shoulders making it plain she was not telling all that she knew. Barbara looked after her, apprehensively.

First Cissie, and now Julia! Cissie commiserating and Julia maliciously complacent. And with it all this premonition of something terrible about to happen, this growing fear steadily pushing her to the edge of panic!

With the note in her hand, she sat down on the filigree iron chair Eve had brought from Italy. Placed beneath a wall bracket of hanging ivy, it gave the aqua-tinted back hall the feeling of a garden.

Coming events can't throw shadows before them. There is no such thing as premonition, Barbara thought to herself. I'm frightened because there is something really going on. I've been warned subconsciously by something that happened—although I didn't notice it at the time.

She scented danger near her, and like a primitive man reading the message of his senses, she thought back over her day, trying to interpret the frantic signals coming from her intuition.

Breakfast had gone off as usual, except that, as she now recalled, Phil, on leaving, had turned back to say abruptly that he would be home late—might not be back in time for dinner.

Now that was unusual—for him to be so noncommittal. And it all tied in, she realized, with this note of Julia's.

Ordinarily he would have said, "I have a new client coming in this afternoon—a Doctor Castleman. He can't get down until four and he may take a while. If we're not through by six, I'll have dinner in town."

Instead, he had told her nothing at all about this appointment. She had made a mental note of his words, as she used to do when she was his secretary, but, preoccupied, she hadn't paid much attention. For she had some very special plans of her own. She had been thinking about her appointment with Mr. Nagle.

Now she saw that Phil's reticence was significant. But his secretiveness alone was not enough to have touched off her train of fear. There must have been something else along the line.

Breakfast over, she had run up to the nursery to find her young daughter splashing in the bathinette. "Why, Christine, are you giving Debbie her bath, already? I was going to help you get started. I didn't mean for you to go ahead all by yourself."

The little nursemaid looked up with a shy smile. "Oh, I didn't have any trouble at all. I knew you were dressed for town, and she'd get you all wet. I could give her her bath every morning, if you wanted me to."

Barbara laughed. "What's the use of having a baby, if you can't have the fun of taking care of her? . . . Well, good-by, darling." She leaned over to pull the washrag from her baby's mouth, and kiss a chubby cheek. "Don't let her suck on this cloth, Christine. I wouldn't be surprised if there isn't a first tooth coming through." And she started off without a cloud on her horizon.

The events of the morning passed through her mind in a succession of vivid scenes. She saw herself, in a pink booth in Pages' beauty salon, with her hair, curly from a recent permanent, standing out in a damp brown halo, and Charles, poised with an atomizer of wave-set in one hand, hopefully suggesting a new, upswept hair-do.

"It is not every face that can wear a pompadour, Charles."

"True, madame, but for every woman there is a coiffure that is at the same time becoming and fashionable. Now, if we part the hair far on the side, and sweep it across . . . so . . . with just the *feeling* of a pompadour . . .?"

She looked in the mirror over the dressing-table, and in spite of Charles's sensibilities, she had to laugh at the sight of his sophisticated swirls topping her wide-cheeked, stolid face. She had her usual wave after all.

Certainly she had felt no slightest premonition, no signal from her subconscious while she dreamed away the time, waiting for her hair to dry, luxuriating in the mid-morning leisure like a cat in the sun.

That welling contentment stayed with her when she went on into the drapery department and Mr. Nagle. Cissie had told her about him, and he turned out to be a jewel. He entered into her plans with enthusiasm, pulling forth great swatches of chintzes, twills and hand-blocked linens for her selection.

It was past noon by the time she finally concluded her shopping. Highly satisfied, her mind filled to the brim with details for slip covers and valances, she was starting for Pages' restaurant when she ran into her next-door neighbor, Cissie Humber.

They had their lunch together. With that odd inconclusive conversation! And when Cissie left her, her contented, carefree mood was gone. She was filled with foreboding and deep misgivings.

There it was. That meeting with Cissie had been the turning point of the day. It had started the whole thing. And yet, she did not understand even now, just what it was that had happened.

2.

BARBARA was leaving the drapery department when she had her strange encounter with Cissie Humber. She had just tucked Mr. Nagle's samples into her bag, and on looking up saw her friend step from the elevator and glance searchingly around the room.

Cissie, a fullback in a Parisian frock, caught sight of Barbara and made first down in one across the crowded floor. The interference turning to watch, noted avidly the details of her chic. Then covetously, they deplored that all that smartness should be wasted on such a woman.

For Cissie was one of nature's seconds. She was an oversize, and the awkward way she was put together enlarged her actual bigness. Her eyes, hair and skin were so nearly the same shade—a sort of pongee color, that her face, without definition, seemed merely an extension of her body. Only her nose had identity. That and her long forelip gave her features, when in repose, the look of a sad-faced mule. But Cissie was seldom in repose.

There was no compromise with such a physiognomy. With it, a woman must go through life either crushed or dauntless, and Cissie was dauntless. She loved dashing and expensive clothes, and wore them, not with the hope of improving her appearance, but purely to pleasure herself. However, the zest and bravado of her garments triumphed to an extent over her person. When Cissie entered a room she brought with her an exciting potpourri of Cannes, Mayfair and Park Avenue.

She came down the aisle now toward Barbara with unleashed urgency, green hat flaring, tiny white figures dancing across the black of her dress. "Well, here you are, Barbie. Julia said you were at Pages' and I have been scouring every floor for you. What have you been doing?"

Barbara glanced at her friend in surprise. Cissie knew perfectly well this was the morning she was going to select the new things for the living room. In fact, Cissie had been as interested and enthusiastic as Barbara herself, and yet here she was, vague and oddly excited, having apparently forgotten all about it.

"Mr. Nagle?" A look of startled dismay crossed Cissie's face at the mention of the drapery department. She recovered quickly and hurried on, "Oh, yes, of course. How did you like him? You must tell me all about it. Are you ready for lunch? We might as well eat here, although the crowds are awful. If we hurry, maybe we can snare us a table."

Barbara agreed with alacrity. It was always fun to be

with Cissie. She had the knack of converting the simplest social encounter into an occasion. One could not so much as drink a cup of tea with her, without a heightened sense of the drama and latent possibility of life. In fact, Barbara thought as she hurried along toward the restaurant, Cissie made a career of friendship.

The two friends found a table in their favorite corner, near the big fountain. Without glancing at the menu, Cissie ordered shrimps Arnaud and coffee. "Make it a double order of shrimps. I lerve the little things and it is heartbreaking to see five lonely pink rascals brought in on a great heap of shredded lettuce."

Barbara chose chef's salad with Roquefort dressing, and removing her gloves, pulled a handful of samples from her purse. "Cissie, we chose the loveliest pale, creamy yellow for the walls, and Mr. Nagle found this red—it's so dark it's really mahogany—for the wing chair," she began, extending the little square of twill toward her companion.

Cissie fingered it absently, and Barbara, as she continued with the description of the striped linen for the chesterfield, and the chintz for the window curtains, became increasingly aware that there was something different about her friend today. Cissie, who was always intensely interested in all the Minary arrangements, was paying only surface attention, while she concentrated inwardly on some hidden, absorbing thought.

When the waitress arrived with their lunches, Barbara gathered up her samples, pushed them decisively into her bag, and asked forthrightly:

"What is the matter, Cissie?"

"Matter?" Cissie tried to make her little eyes look round and innocent. "Why, nothing is the matter." She squeezed lemon juice over the ten pink shrimps on their mound of lettuce.

"I thought you had a lunch on at the League of Women

Voters. Why did you come down to Pages' looking for me instead?"

Cissie buttered a crusty roll before replying too lightly, "My dear, in this heat? I just couldn't face eating tomato-surprise wedged elbow to elbow between two Leaguers—with a report on juvenile delinquency for dessert. The fact is I am playing hooky from my civic duties, but I'll drop in for the board meeting afterwards."

She ran her fork through a shrimp, pushed it about vigorously in the paper cup of sauce, and leaned forward to thrust it into her mouth. "I don't know why I keep on with the League. It has been beyond resuscitation for years. It used to be different, when Eve was president and the reform campaign was on. Things were zipping then. More fun and games for the little girls at the Club."

Barbara winced, and involuntary reproof slipped into her voice. "The fun didn't last very long for Phil. And Hal Crane found the game had murder in the prize packet."

Cissie's face lost its sprightliness. "Yes, I know. I shouldn't have joked about it. You were pretty close to it all, weren't you?"

She glanced restively about the room and suddenly exclaimed, "Do you see what I see over there by the door? Slacks in this restaurant! I guess there is a war going on after all, but I didn't know it made people quite so desperate. That woman's rump looks like a trailer bumping along behind a four-door sedan. Now me—I wear slacks—but not at Pages' and though I am big behind, it's all solid bone."

Barbara shifted her glance to the door and her thoughts from the past. It was hard to keep pace with Cissie's disjointed thoughts. Her conversation that noon was like the early movies with constantly changing focus that used to come at you clear and too close one moment, before fading into a blur the next. Cissie's gusto was forced, and now and then she forgot it altogether as she receded into a mental distance.

It filled Barbara with vague disquietude. Especially the way Cissie's little mule's eyes yearned at her from under the big green hat. She looks at me, she thought, as though I were about to have a dangerous operation.

She felt disappointed, too, as she ate steadily through her chef's salad. It was annoying of Cissie to be so absent and withdrawn just when she had so much to discuss with her.

For that morning she had crossed a Rubicon. It was a very minor Rubicon, but even thinking of doing over Eve's silver and gold drawing room made her feel like a trespasser bent on sacrilege. However, it was all settled. Thirteen successive spring and fall cleanings had depleted beyond repair the fragile loveliness selected by Phil's first bride.

Barbara had never felt very comfortable with those silvery gray walls and gold-threaded Rodier fabrics. She preferred warmth and color in a room. But she had had no experience with such things and was afraid to trust her own judgment. So Cissie had recommended Mr. Nagle.

And Mr. Nagle had been most helpful and sympathetic. Her living room was going to have the desired homelike atmosphere—with sturdy fabrics and cheerful patterns. Everything was to be different.

Except the former keynote. The poetic, pastel portrait of the first wife. There, in her gold frame over the mantel, she would be as alien to this new room as Barbara had felt in its original exquisiteness.

"Someone is stepping on your grave." They used to say that in her childhood when she shivered on a hot day. But that little chill that just chased down her spine came from the past. From the memory of loveliness and a horrible fate.

She looked up and met Cissie's fixed and watchful gaze.

She shivered again. Cissie's eyes were queer. Barbara had never noticed those green sparks in their dun coloring before.

Uncomfortable under that enigmatic stare, she plunged into nervous chatter. "Charles wanted me to try one of those new, complicated hair-do's this morning. Can you imagine it with my face?"

"Why, there's nothing wrong with your face, Barbara. It's a very nice one—so fresh and wholesome-looking."

"Oh, please—Cissie, don't!" Barbara implored, laughing. "That was what my mother's friends and my teachers always said. 'Barbara is such a wholesome girl.' They used to make me feel like a great loaf of graham bread."

She transferred a second helping of salad from the serving bowl to her plate. "But I learned a long time ago that you can't turn graham bread into French pastry. There is nothing I can do about my face. My cheeks are too wide, my eyes are too earnest and I look too chockful of vitamins to be exciting. No one has ever seen anything interesting in me. . . Except that red-headed boy, Hal Crane," she added in sudden after-thought. "He said a funny thing to me one day, Cissie.

"He was lounging around the office waiting for Phil, when out of a clear sky he told me my face was an anachronism behind a typewriter. He said that I didn't belong to this century. That I had a medieval look—a look of 'timeless endurance and ancient tenacity.' Something Rembrandt painted into his pictures of peasants and mystics."

She gave a little laugh as she forked up some salad. "I think Hal meant it for a compliment, but, as I recall, peasants and mystics are not conspicuous for feminine charm. And the old Dutchman always painted such stolid-looking women. I can't say I'm very thrilled at being taken for a Rembrandt."

"I'd rather look like a Rembrandt than a flying buttress

off of a Gothic cathedral." Cissie remarked dryly. She ran an appraising eye over her companion. "Why *don't* you try wearing your hair on top of your head, Barbie? I think it might be quite becoming."

"I did try it this morning, and I looked like a scrub pine trying to pass for a Christmas tree. High fashion is not for me You know, Cissie, it would give the Ladbrookes quite a laugh if I were to step out of Page and Page looking like a *Vogue* cover."

"Why the heck shouldn't you go in for *Vogue* styles, Barbara? You have married into the smart set, you know." Her instinct for clothes awakened, Cissie leaned forward with enthusiasm. "Now, I would like to see you in— "

"No, Cissie," Barbara interrupted seriously. "I'm not the type; and it is a good thing that I'm not. When Charles was trying to glamorize me this morning, I realized something. Don't you see, it is just *because* I am not beautiful, or glamorous, and have no social background that they have accepted me? Now, if Phil had picked out a debutante for a second wife, they would have resented her intensely. But with me they feel . . . well, they could see when we married that Phil needed someone to look after him, and that little Jonathan would be better off . . . and they didn't feel that I would really take Eve's place, that is, I wouldn't be a rival . . . even to her memory."

Cissie looked uncomfortable. "Now Barbara, don't tell me you have an inferiority complex. You're just imagining . . ."

Barbara's laugh was free and genuine. "But Cissie, I don't mind at all. I'm really glad they feel that way because it makes everything so much easier for Phil. Do you think it matters to me what people think? I have what I want. I have Phil . . . and," she added hastily, "everything."

Over Cissie's face there came that same odd look she

had had when Barbara talked about Mr. Nagle and her new slip covers. But this time there was also a penetrating sympathy, and something else, not quite definable. She asked softly, "It's the real thing between you and Phil, isn't it, Barbara?"

Flushing hotly, Barbara looked down at her plate, as shy as a child, a little embarrassed smile on her lips. "I thought perhaps you had guessed, Cissie." She looked up. "The others have never realized. You know, we didn't intend to deceive. It wasn't deliberate—the impression we gave. Phil and I—we never discussed it together, but from the very first we always treated each other in a matter-of-fact way when other people were around. I guess we both just felt that it would have been . . . well —sort of unseemly, to have acted like a pair of lovers— even with Eve gone for seven years."

Still embarrassed, she picked up her glass and swallowed some water. "As I said, the whole thing just happened that way. But if we had sat down and calculated it, we couldn't have been more exactly right."

That odd expression of Cissie's, with its queer mixture of emotions, deepened. "You have been very happy with Phil, haven't you? Three years of love! That is your capital of happiness." Her tone deepened with portent. Like Cassandra intoning Troy's fall in the midst of feasting, she added with finality, "You can draw on it the rest of your life. You have had enough to last you out."

Barbara stared at Cissie. "What a strange thing to say! You sound as if . . ." she faltered, unable to put into words the sinking feeling of disaster evoked.

Cissie pushed away her empty plate and poured herself some coffee, but did not light a companion cigarette. Instead, she picked up the cup with both hands and gazed into it thoughtfully, as she turned it about.

She had been backing and filling all during their hour together, and now Barbara realized, she was preparing to reveal the purpose of this forced meeting. That there was something back of Cissie's conduct, she had felt from the first, and the knowledge was becoming increasingly disturbing. All her pleasant small preoccupations of the morning rose like bubbles to the surface of her mind, and evaporated leaving her flat and empty And in their place a nebulous apprehension began to gather.

Cissie broke the silence. "Did my remark seem strange to you? Well, it was just a little chip off my philosophy of life. This is a world in which terrible things can happen to human beings, you know Everyone needs to build themselves some sort of armor . . . One can never tell what is going on behind that quiet façade of yours. Have you a philosophy of life, Barbara? What is your armor against the slings and arrows of outrageous fortune?"

As Barbara, baffled by the unorthodox question, hunted about in the blankness of her mind, Cissie answered her own question. "I know how you would meet trouble. The stoical way You would bury grief, set your jaw, and go on with the day's work.

"But stoicism is not enough, Barbara, nor religion. either, any more. We moderns need something different. Einstein has pointed the direction. People in this age need to realize that time is a dimension of life."

"Einstein, Cissie? How on earth could he help people like us? Only twelve men in the world know enough to understand him."

Cissie set down her cup. "What I mean is something very simple. When you look up and see the stars twinkling in the sky at night, they appear to be really up there, don't they? But some of them aren't there at all any more. They have passed beyond sight ages ago. You see it takes light so many eons to travel through the vast inter-stellar distances, that the sparkle those stars made before there was life on this planet is only just now coming through to us."

"Cissie, is that really so?"

"It is true. And it is just as true, that whatever has happened to each of us in our lives, whatever pleasant experience, whatever love we have had once, we have always. In spite of change—or death—or loss. It is always there, a part of us, if only we grasp the reality of time. Time is not a passing stream, carrying events away. It is cumulative, forever adding and storing up."

Cissie leaned forward as though through the sheer intensity of her feeling she could transmit her vision to her friend. Barbara looked at her in amazement. Of course, she had heard Cissie called a "tower of strength" by friends in trouble. But she had not suspected that her gay, swashbuckling neighbor could be like this—philosophical, almost mystic. Never before, during their three years of companionship, had she had a glimpse of this secret Cissie. She realized that only a crisis could force her to expose her inner self this way.

And in this realization, all her gathering uneasiness changed over into alarm. She recognized the signs. Cissie was laying the ground, was preparing her for something.

Cissie pushed aside her cup. "I'm not talking a lot of sentimental theory. Believe me, I have been taken over the bumps in my life. What I want to give you is the fruit of my experience because I know it works."

She hesitated a moment, and then asked awkwardly, "You never met my husband, Freddie, did you?" It was amazing to see Cissie embarrassed.

"I know what people thought and said after my divorce. 'It is wonderful how Cissie has risen above her troubles. Cissie has made a wonderful adjustment.' Well, I didn't do any rising or adjusting. I just went on keeping what I had."

To hide her diffidence, she had begun playing with the crumbs on the tablecloth. She built them into a little mound with her big longshoreman's fingers, courageously tipped by Revlon's latest shade, before she remarked abruptly, "Freddie was in love with me. Don't look so incredulous, Barbie. It is hard to believe, I know, but I have never been one to deceive myself about myself and I tell you he loved me. We were really very happy for quite a while. . . . I have never told anyone what happened . . .

"There was a woman . . . a close friend of ours. She was beautiful and she made Freddie realize what a woman should mean to a man. What he needed then I didn't have to give. She didn't either. She loved her husband, not Freddie. But it was the end of our marriage. . . . He has been living in New York for more than ten years, now. He married again. Someone he met in the East I hear that she is very pretty."

Cissie brushed away her edifice of crumbs with a swift gesture and looked up to meet her friend's eyes. "But Freddie has never left my life. He is as much with me in the present as that star is we see shining at night—the star which has passed into another universe a million years ago. Do you understand?"

Barbara had been listening with only half her mind. Convinced that Cissie was laying the ground for something, her frantic thought ran along her life-line of happiness . . . Phil . . . Debbie . . . Jonathan, the stepson who was almost as dear. Which one?

"What is it, Cissie? Has there been an accident? Is it Phil? Tell me. I can take it. Only tell me . . . tell me."

"Good heavens, Barbara! What is the matter with you? Of course there hasn't been an accident. Your precious family is all right. I had no idea you were so emotional."

"But you were leading up to something," Barbara protested, near tears, and still in the grip of uneasiness. "Why were you talking like this? Why should I need armor and philosophy now?"

Cissie laughed, but her eyes were evasive. "Why shouldn't a lonely female unburden herself to her best

friend if she wants to? I admit that Pages' restaurant is
an odd place to take down one's back hair, but then
haven't you realized that I am an odd person?"

She picked up her cup and took a hasty swallow of cold
coffee. "Seriously though, Barbara, I guess I felt an impulse to talk as I did because you seem so vulnerable
in your happiness. Hang on to it, Barbara, no matter what
happens. You can, you know. And don't forget that I am
your friend. Remember I can help you when . . . if you
ever need one." She set down her cup.

"And now unless I run, I won't get in on even the tail
end of that board meeting. I'll have to get on my horse."
She rose and gathered up her gloves and huge black pat-
ent leather purse.

"Stop looking like a little pot of purple ink, Barbie. I
liked your samples. That red twill is gorgeous, the stripe
is perfect with it and Mr. Nagle is a wizard. I'll run over
tomorrow and see the rest of your selections."

She waved gaily as she started off, but Barbara saw
flickering in her eyes somber knowledge of something she
would not—or could not—disclose.

3.

HEAVY, HEAVY hangs over thy head, what shall thee do
to redeem it? The refrain was a chorus to the frightened
suspense throbbing in Barbara's pulse as she drove her
coupé through midtown traffic. She was a child again,

it was her turn in the game, and she was waiting to learn what her forfeit was.

Her childish apprehension came not so much from what Cissie had said as from that odd look on her face when they mentioned doing over the house, and again when they spoke of Phil. As though it were all make-believe, an elaborate whistling in the dark, and Cissie were humoring her even as she saw the end coming steadily closer.

But nothing except unexpected death could threaten her happy married life, Barbara thought in perplexity. There wasn't even a chance of Phil's going into service. He was thirty-eight, the father of two children—and the army wouldn't have him anyway, because of that old stomach trouble. Those ulcers were all over long ago. They had been brought on by the terrible time he had gone through when he was in the D. A.'s office, and Crane was murdered. But if you had ever had anything wrong with your stomach, the army wouldn't take a chance on you. So she had absolutely nothing to worry about.

Barbara came to the crossing at Barret where she meant to turn off for Strauss's grocery. But forgetting her marketing, she drove on past. For she had just thought of that other one . . . of Eve. She, too, had been unworried. She, too, had had her hair done at Pages', had lunched with Cissie, and driven happily along this street to her home. Many times . . . unaware even on the very brink of catastrophe.

Barbara stopped for the red light at the boulevard without consciously seeing the signal, deep-sunk in the mood Cissie had bequeathed her. It was still with her when she turned into the tree-lined road to Hillways. The grassy lawns and shrubbery of the bordering estates shimmered in the afternoon heat, telegraphing an uncoded message.

Her short hour with Cissie had shifted the world into another focus. Everything looked different to her—even the sun. Its glare now had a frightening quality. It made her think of the vast empty spaces in the soulless universe, of thousands of light-years of inter-planetary distances— all inanimate, indifferent to human values. This was a world in which terrible things could happen to human beings.

She thought again of those words of Cissie's as she drove between the low stone posts marking the entrance to Hillways. The heavy summer foliage of the trees permitted only fleeting glimpses of the three houses ahead on the ridge, the ivy-clad Georgian home of the Ladbrookes, Cissie Humber's somber gray mansion, and nestling between them the little jewel box Judge Ladbrooke had built as a wedding present for his daughter on her marriage to Phil. Certainly terrible things *had* happened to the little cluster of people living on the saddle-back hill. . . . Evelyn's tragedy, the wreckage of Phil's career, Cissie's broken marriage, and later Judge Ladbrooke's death . . . young Hal Crane, too.

There was no movement or sign of life from the three houses, their windows shuttered against the heat. As Barbara approached them, they receded from the present and from her. They became a faded lithograph on a page torn from a book of the past.

Unreality closed in on her. She was stepping into the fourth dimension . . . into time-space. The house before her was not the home warmed by domesticity she had left that morning. This was a house that had lain empty and silent for ten years . . . a tomb enclosing a memory.

After the sunlight, the hall was chill and very silent. It was like stepping into a secret place. She was a stranger, lost from the things of her own life—a wandering trespasser venturing into a forsaken and haunted spot.

Hat in hand, Barbara paused in the archway of the living room and looked at the face over the mantel. In the dim, slatted light filtering through the Venetian blinds,

the vague grays and golds of the room were like the ghosts
of outworn charm.

It had been a long time since she had looked at Eve.
She had closed her mind to the presence of that image
over her hearth, just as she had closed off that room upstairs. She had been in Eve's bedroom only once, the day
she looked through the house on her return from her wedding trip.

One glance into that shell-tinted bower of love, hung
with filmy white, evoked such vivid recollection of Eve,
the charmer, that Barbara closed the door again quickly,
and she had not opened it since. That room represented
the past. That door was closed on a chapter of her husband's life, and Barbara lived in the present. But now,
with a plain woman's awareness, the second wife studied
the beauty of the other.

The portrait had been painted in Paris in a twilit,
Marie Laurencin mood. One of those impressionistic treatments in which nothing was distinct. The immature figure in the yellow dress blended without clear outline into
the background, so that one could not quite distinguish
the woman from the hazy enveloping light. Only Eve's
eyes stood out clearly—large and dark, with a hint of
tragedy. . . .

In life they had been gay and vivacious, but perhaps
the artist had perceived an underlying sadness no one
else had seen there. Or maybe he had had a prophetic
sense.

What was it, Eve? What happened? Barbara found
the old question insistently rising to mind again as she
looked at that shadowed face. What forced you to turn
away from husband and baby and withdraw into the
dark?

But the soft young face in the gold frame gazed back at
her with the half-smile it had bestowed on a forgotten
artist in a Paris atelier years before.

The little French clock on the mantel suddenly tinkled out the hour. The musical ping broke into the quiet resoundingly, and Barbara came out of her revery with a start. Was it mid-afternoon so soon? Then she remembered the groceries she had meant to pick up on her way home. This hour of the day and nothing in the house for dinner! If she got her order in quickly, she might catch Strauss's last run. She hurried toward the phone, planning as she went. Lamb chops and new peas, a shortcake for dessert. . . .

As soon as she entered the rear hall, she saw Julia's note propped against the phone.

Barbara sat on the chair beside the telephone stand, the events of the past few hours passing through her mind in quick review. Phil's reticence, Cissie's odd look and her talk of a need for armor against catastrophe, Julia's malice, and her own mounting sense of impending disaster— these impressions flowed through her and coalesced with the present.

She looked again at the note in her hand. One implication stood out clearly. Phil had an appointment with a doctor . . . a mention of a hospital. Taken together with the secrecy shrouding the whole thing, it pointed in just one direction . . . although Phil seemed perfectly well.

There were symptoms that came on suddenly, though— diseases that were not immediately obvious, terrible things like brain tumors, she thought in panic. Could Phil have noticed something wrong with himself? Was he going to have a consultation, a critical examination at the hospital this afternoon? He must be planning to keep it from her until he knew for sure.

He might even be going to have an operation, something terribly dangerous.

But she wasn't a delicate flower that had to be protected from harsh facts. In quick decision she picked up the phone and called her husband's office. The familiar voice of the girl at the switchboard informed her that she was talking with Ladbrooke, Halsey and Minary.

"Amelia, this is Mrs. Minary. Is my husband there? . . . Do you know where he is? . . . Let me speak to Mr. Ladbrooke then. . . . Oh, dear— Well, if either of them comes back, have them call me. Thank you." Barbara dropped the phone onto its cradle.

Maybe Cissie is back by now, she thought. I'll make her tell me what she knows about this. Heedless of the sun, she ran out the side door, across the baking grass and through the unlatched screen into Cissie's morning room. The house appeared deserted. She walked through it, calling out frantically, "Cissie, Cissie!"

There was a movement on the stairs and in a moment a housemaid appeared, in a kimono, her hair bristling with bobbie pins under a net.

"Mrs. Humber is in town, ma'am. She said that she didn't know if she'd be back for dinner tonight."

"Oh, all right, Lucy. Thank you."

Barbara wandered back into the morning room, feeling cut off from everyone. Surely, she thought in desperation, there must be someone I can find to tell me.

She considered Madeleine Ladbrooke. Madeleine would probably know, but she was seldom at home in the afternoon, and anyway Barbara felt reluctant about asking Scott's wife.

Then she thought of Jeff Halsey. It would be natural to ask Jeff. In the days when Scott and Phil were first starting with Ladbrooke and Halsey, they were always telling her to ask Jeff about this case or that procedure, and Jeff was always ready to help.

She hurried to the phone and got Amelia again. In a moment the senior partner's reassuring voice came to her across the wire, shaming her nervous fears.

"Hello, Barbara. How are you?"

"Jeff, I have a message for Phil, from Dr. Castleman. Do you know what it is all about?"

"Why, yes . . . I do." Constraint was in his voice now, and her apprehension flared up fresh. "Nothing to worry about, Barbara. . . . Just a little piece of business."

"But I *am* worried about it. There have been a number of funny things. . . . Jeff, I want you to tell me the truth. Is something wrong with Phil? Is he going to have an operation—or something? It isn't right to keep it from me." She could not quite keep her voice from breaking.

"No Barbara, there is nothing the matter with Phil." He was silent so long, she thought they had been disconnected. Finally he said, "I am going to tell you about it. Phil thought it would be better to wait until we saw how things turned out, but you are worrying yourself sick as it is, and you might as well know now. . . . Dr. Castleman is one of the psychiatrists out at Oaklawn. They are going to try a treatment with metrazol. . . ."

At his first words, her relief was so great that she did not catch the rest. Dr. Castleman was from Oaklawn. That meant it was something about Eve. . . . Poor Eve, who for so long had been beyond all knowing. Even if she were ill, needed special treatment, she wouldn't suffer. Nothing more that could happen to Eve would really matter now.

Then Barbara realized that Jeffrey was saying something more to her, and at the guarded note in his voice she became suddenly alert. "What do you mean, Jeffrey? I am afraid I don't understand. What is this metrazol treatment?"

"I was just telling you, Barbara. They have had some good results with it in other cases—but it's still pretty experimental."

"But, Jeff." Barbara was unbelieving. "You don't mean that they have a treatment for dementia praecox? For a case like Eve's?"

"Well, they have used it successfully in other parts of the country. About Eve's case—we don't know at all. They are going to try. . . . But metrazol is a very dangerous drug. They inject it into the veins, and sometimes the shock is too much and the patient dies under treatment. Then, on the other hand, it sometimes has no effect at all. The whole thing is a gamble. We don't know what is going to happen this afternoon. . . ."

"But Jeff, what is it they are trying to do? If it goes off as they want, what do they expect from it?"

"They are hoping for an improvement in her condition, of course. But it will be a long-drawn-out process. Even if they get a favorable reaction, it will be months before we know where we stand."

". . . Jeff? . . . What? . . . Is there a possibility? . . . Is metrazol a *cure?* Do patients ever get really well again?"

"Well—yes. There are a few cures on record. Of course Eve is in a very advanced stage, and it is such a long-standing case. McKeith and Castleman, the psychiatrists, aren't promising anything, but they think it is worth trying. . . . Barbara? Are you still there? Now listen, Barbara, I hope you are going to be sensible about this. There is no use getting worked up over it, you know. The whole thing is so uncertain. . . . Barbara, are you all right?"

"Yes, Jeff, I'm all right. . . . I'll be all right. . . . Thank you."

THERE WAS only one break in Oaklawn's secretive encircling wall. The gate at the front entrance yawned wide with a sinister invitation. Since it was a barrier only to those not at liberty to leave, all incomers were admitted freely, and the attendant waved on Barbara's approaching car without question. She drove through quickly, apprehensive as to what lay ahead.

But there was nothing forbidding in the tree-dotted lawns spread about the main building of the hospital, a Colonial structure with gracious pillared portico. On the grassy terrace a nurse was chaperoning a group of men and women in summer clothes. They lounged about in deck chairs, drinking something from tall, frosty glasses. A couple in shorts were batting a ball back and forth on the tennis court. It was a deceptive picture of luxurious ease, an ironic invitation to those for whom there was no peace anywhere.

Among the cars parked in front of the portico, Barbara recognized Phil's gray sedan, and nosed her coupé in beside it, taking brief comfort from the vicarious proximity. Then, with a trembling in her midriff, she walked up the steps and through the door.

The lobby, abloom with chintz slip covers and garden flowers, tried valiantly to counterfeit the atmosphere of a summer hotel. There was a blond-wood desk near the door, and a young woman with matching hair sat behind it. She rose and came up to Barbara with the smile of a professional hostess.

"Good afternoon. Is there someone you would like to see? . . . Mr. Minary? Oh, yes. He and the others are in the waiting room on the fourth floor. You can go right up."

Walking over to a wall panel, she pushed it open to reveal an automatic elevator. "Just close the door and push the button for the fourth floor."

She smiled as though her visitor were en route to a cocktail party.

Barbara hesitated. She wanted the support of an impersonal presence when she broke in on the group upstairs.

But the receptionist, leaving Barbara stranded, was already walking away, her swaying hips saying that this was the best of all possible worlds.

The elevator stopped noiselessly at the fourth floor and Barbara stepped out to white walls and a faint smell of drugs. No effort was made here to disguise the essential character of the institution. The linoleum-floored corridor stretched ahead some distance to a heavy-looking door on which DISTURBED WARD—NO ADMITTANCE was printed in large letters.

Halfway down its length, the hall opened into an alcove, equipped with the wicker table and chairs indigenous to hospitals. Here Barbara discovered her party. Phillip, Scott, Madeleine, Cissie,—and Jeff Halsey was there, too. A little group, close-knit by long association and mutual devotion to Eve, they were making her, the second wife, an outsider, excluding her from this crucial experience.

She was frightened now at her temerity in coming here unasked and unexpected. But she had not been able to face that waiting alone at home—those hundreds of minutes before she would learn the outcome of the fateful experiment.

Barbara's approach had been so quiet none of them was aware of her presence as she lingered uncertainly in the corridor looking at them.

Madeleine had that usual crisp look of hers—of a cellophane-wrapped gardenia that had just been taken from the icebox. Even at the end of this hot day, she was immaculate in a yellow turban and simple black linen dress, cut to reveal her narrow waist and the fullness of her throat and bosom. She made Barbara acutely aware of her own unpowdered face, of her wrinkled chambray suit and that her hair, which she had forgotten to recomb, lay in flat, rigid waves from her hair set.

But Madeleine, for all her careful composure, was not

at ease Her eyes, filled with intent watchfulness, never left her husband, who sat with his head in his hands, his back a bow of nervous tension.

Phillip, looking more than ever like a granite statue of Lincoln, seemed lost in a world within himself.

They were all in the grip of a great tension. Cissie, silent for once, was turning mechanically the pages of a magazine she did not see Jeff Halsey, who was standing, leaned against the wall fidgeting with an unlighted ciga rette. Except for the sprinkle of gray in his hair, he seemed, despite his ten additional years, no older than Phillip.

It was Jeffrey who saw her first. His restless glance discovered her, hesitating near the elevator. "Why, hello Barbara. Come over here and sit down. I told Phil you had called me and that I decided I'd better tell you what it was all about. Phil, Barbara is here."

Phillip, with obvious effort, pulled himself back from the far reaches of his preoccupation. He stood up and looked at Barbara as she walked doubtfully forward. For an instant she saw some emotion rise to the surface . . . love? . . . pity? . . . encouragement? He pulled up a chair for her. "Sit down, Barbara. It won't be long now."

He rested a hand lightly on her shoulder, whether to reassure her or himself, she could not be sure. Then he withdrew again into that abstraction her arrival had interrupted.

She sat down to wait with the others. No one made an attempt at conversation. The waiting, charged with immediacy, seemed to Barbara even more painful here than it had at home. And then these sterile walls, the pervasive drugs—so inimical to human values . . . so foreign. . . . It occurred to her that all this was familiar enough to Phillip, and she thought how strange it was that she had never been here before, never wondered even what this place was like that now loomed so importantly in her life

—that, she realized, had always been there in the background of her marriage.

But for so long she had thought of Eve as of one dead. They all had—even Scott. He still made those daily visits, with his pointless little gifts, but it was as though he were taking flowers to his sister's grave. When Dr. McKeith made his hopeless prognosis ten years before he told them it was not "worse than death," but just the same as death. And in time they had all accepted his point of view.

Phillip, pulling himself together, had made it the basis of his adjustment to the future. It was the premise on which he had finally sought a divorce—using that technicality.

But McKeith had been wrong. Now he was going to resurrect the dead, and Eve, a strange living ghost, would return to haunt the scene of her former life. Or would it be the other way, Barbara wondered distraught, would Eve's coming to life turn her, the usurper, into a ghost? . . . a forlorn, living ghost.

Already she felt stripped of her place,—almost disembodied—uncertain what she was. She looked at her companions. Their faces transformed by strain were like masks. The contagion of the atmosphere infected her, too. Even the insistent question of her own future slipped from her mind in the face of this awful expectancy.

A medical miracle was to be attempted. They were going to try to bring a dead mind back to life. So must the watchers have waited around the grave of Lazarus, each isolated from the others by the imminence of an impending mystery, face to face with the deepest secret of nature!

Yet, even the recall of Lazarus was less terrifying, in a way, than this thing which confronted them now. For Lazarus, dead only a few hours, had been brought back from a journey to the next world. But what had become of Eve during those long years in which her body had lived on soullessly? Had her mind resolved itself back into its

elements, turned into nothing? And were these doctors going to summon consciousness up out of the void?

Two men in white coats appeared in the doorway. Their
loud voices broke shatteringly into the hush as they casually entered that emotion-charged room. Everyone rose
and there was a chorus of exchanged greetings. The lean,
older man, who seemed acquainted with everyone there,
shook hands all around, introducing the other, the quick
dark young one. "This is Dr. Castleman. He is our expert
on metrazol. He'll be in charge of the treatment this afternoon."

Barbara felt Phil's hand on her arm, pulling her forward. "Barbara, I want you to meet Dr. McKeith. . . .
Doctor, I don't believe you are acquainted with my wife."

The gaunt man with the ascetic lines in his face, looked
at her with interest. When he took her hand, she felt his
gray eyes probe with kindly questioning, as though he
understood about her troubled heart and were asking
"And how is it with you?" But when he spoke, he merely
said, "Mrs. Minary, I want you to meet Dr. Castleman.
. . . Mrs. Minary, Marc."

As the young man, incurious and hurried, acknowl-
edged the introduction, there was a stir among the others.
Barbara turned and saw a nurse wheeling down the hall a
white-draped figure on a stretcher. When she was abreast
of the alcove she stopped, and McKeith said gently, "Here
is the patient."

With a catch in her breath, Barbara moved forward
with the others, for her first sight of Eve in more than
ten years.

She was lying on her side, her limbs curled in a curious
position. Her eyes were open. Large and dark they stared
sightlessly. Barbara had heard her condition described,
but even so, she was not prepared for this,—this rigid
effigy of a woman.

She crowded closer, noticing other details. The passage

of years had left no trace on Eve's youthful face. She still had the smooth creamy skin of a girl in her twenties. There was even a delicate pink flush on her cheeks.

Although she created the illusion of beauty, Eve had not been beautiful. She had been too thin, with a nervous, hollow look. But while her mind slept during her long trance, her body, released from tension, had matured into a rounded loveliness. She had received meticulous physical care, Barbara remembered. It had given Scott consolation, in his unending grief, to describe to them the exercise machines, the massages, the sun lamps, the hot baths and needle showers that were used in Eve's treatment.

At a gesture from McKeith, the nurse, wheeling the stretcher quickly forward, brought an end to the hushed scrutiny. Dr. Castleman had already gone on ahead through the door marked DISTURBED WARD.

"We won't be gone long . . . perhaps about twenty minutes. I'll let you know immediately how it turns out," McKeith told them.

"But, Doctor . . ." Scott was quick to protest. "I thought I was to go with you . . . be in there with her. She might . . . If anything happened . . . I wouldn't want her to be all alone . . . to pass away without any of us with her."

McKeith looked troubled. "There is a certain risk involved, as you know. But we would send for you at once. It is only a step from here. There is no reason why you shouldn't be present, if you insist. But I don't advise it. It would be a most painful ordeal, for you, Mr. Ladbrooke. The reaction to metrazol isn't a pleasant thing to witness."

"I know that, Dr. McKeith. But I don't want my sister to go through this alone. The least I can do for her is to stay in there with her."

"Well, come ahead, if you insist. But you'll wish you had stayed out here."

McKeith turned away and Scott followed him down the

hall. Madeleine quickly caught up with her husband, and, slipping her hand through his arm, walked along by his side. But he seemed heedless of her presence as he trailed after McKeith and the nurse.

Without a word Phillip started after them, walking like a man holding on to himself with great effort. Barbara, after a moment's hesitation, found herself moving along behind him.

They went through into the ward for disturbed patients. This section, Barbara learned later, was soundproofed and fitted with immovable windows. The corridor was lined with closed doors. As she passed one of them, she heard a low-pitched, horrible moaning coming from within.

The last door along the hall was open. When Barbara reached it, she found that Eve had been lifted onto the bed. Two orderlies were strapping her to it. Dr. Castleman had just finished washing his hands at a basin in the corner. He walked over to the bed. McKeith pulled up a chair on the opposite side, and, sitting down, placed his fingers on Eve's pulse.

They moved with quick, silent precision. Castleman raised Eve's arm and swabbed off a spot in the hollow below the elbow. He reached back without a word, and the nurse placed in his hand a hypodermic syringe she had picked up from the sterile-dressing tray on the side-table. She broke off the head of a glass ampule and passed it to the doctor. He filled the syringe slowly and carefully. Then, holding it in his right hand, he pinched up Eve's flesh with his left until the vein stood out blue and swollen. With a deft movement he plunged in the glittering needle.

Barbara flinched at the sight, but there was no slightest movement from the figure on the bed. Very slowly, the doctor pressed down on the plunger, feeding the drug gradually into the blue blood traveling toward Eve's heart. For a few seconds she continued motionless. Then there was a faint trembling of her eyelids, before she doubled up tighter in the beginning of a convulsion. She screamed,—a paralyzing, unearthly scream, and threw her limbs violently outward. The bed rocked with her struggle, and the two orderlies threw themselves over her, trying to press her back.

Barbara closed her eyes and crouched against the wall, pressing her hands over her ears. But she still heard those awful screams. They were far worse than the cries of a suffering, sentient human being. Those screams were inhuman, as though wrenched from inanimate matter, like the shrieks of agony from stone and earth at the creation.

Barbara did not know how long she huddled there, trying to close out the sounds in that room. There passed through her mind, memory of a superstition of early mankind, about the mandrake. The plant that shrieked when uprooted, and brought death and calamity to any mortal who dared disturb nature's secret plant. Those screams of Eve's . . . that must be how the mandrake root sounded when torn from the enveloping soil! A protest from nature itself!

Finally Barbara was aware of silence, of a change in the atmosphere of the room. She opened her eyes. Eve was lying on her back, her head turned slightly on its side, her long dark lashes shadowing her cheeks, and her limbs straightened out at last. She was relaxed, breathing deeply as in a heavy drugged sleep.

Dr. McKeith rose, and, bending over her, lifted one of her eyelids. He looked closely into the pupil for a moment. Then, straightening, he turned to them with a smile. "The treatment has been most successful . . . so far."

PART TWO

IAN McKEITH
October 27, 1943

5.

Iᴀɴ McKᴇɪᴛʜ, ducking his head against the wind, hurried across the grounds from his house to the hospital. He entered through the rear door, walked over to the hall radiator, and stood close to it shivering with cold. As he warmed his hands he glanced down the empty passage avidly.

He had been home with flu for two weeks. A long sere stretch, reflected in his deprived expression. One of those lean, gray-eyed men of Scotch blood who combine wiry toughness with a look of sensitivity, he had a face that was both intellectual and virile. Now, as he took in the familiar atmosphere of Oaklawn, the bleakness drained from his look.

Sticking his gloves in his pocket, he picked up the folder he had laid on the radiator and started for his office. But on passing the entrance to the south wing he hesitated, and after a brief uncertainty, turned down the corridor.

This section contained the women with milder cases who were allowed to visit back and forth and receive guests from outside unsupervised. However, a nurse was always present in their recreation room, and one was stationed at the desk in the corridor to keep an eye on comings and goings.

The young redhead on duty in the hall jumped up at the psychiatrist's approach. "Why, hello, Dr. Mac! It's simply wonderful to see you back." She beamed at the middle-aged doctor, her glance lightly laced with flirtation. "We've just been limping along without you."

His mobile mouth took on an ironic curve. "Yes, I know, . . . you've been utterly desolate." His answer was deprecatory, but he was smiling with a gratification only slightly cynical as he walked down to the recreation room and stood looking through the glass doors.

They had just given out the after-lunch ration of cigarettes, and the patients were scattered about in animated social groups. A hum of conversation, mixed with the strains of a Viennese waltz, seeped through the closed doors. McKeith's seeking eyes hunted through the room and concentrated on a detached figure by the radio.

Eve Minary was listening to the gay music with obvious pleasure. But even a layman would have noticed the naïve quality of her attention and the peculiarly childish way she sat, with her head tipped to one side. Her feet were parallel on the floor and her hands lay on either side of her like a doll or a baby placed in a chair. The immaturity of her pose and expression was in contrast to her smartly cut frock. a pinkish wool that brought out high lights in the chocolate curls dressed high on her head.

At sight of her, McKeith's eyes brightened with a surge of pleasure, then became professionally critical. When she turned at a burst of laughter near her and glanced curiously in the direction of the sound, the doctor smiled.

But almost immediately some thought turned his face haggard.

He started to open the door and then checked himself when he saw he had attracted the attention of an elderly woman sitting with a group near the entrance. When she leaped up with an exclamation he turned away hastily. But Isobel Shively, clutching her ample maternity dress in bunched-up folds, rushed out into the hall followed by a bevy of excited ladies.

"Oh, Dr. McKeith, are you well again? Has Dr. Castleman told you the morning sickness is gone now? . I'm so glad you're back. I just *couldn't* go through it without you. . . ." Her shrill voice high-noted the clamor of the others, some timid, some insistent, but all vying for the doctor's attention.

Resignedly he turned back and chatted with them, careful to distribute his interest equally. After promising each of them an early interview, he extricated himself with practiced proficiency and retreated down the hall.

"So the Greek chorus were on hand to welcome their hero!" Marc Castleman, who had just come up the stairs from the staff dining room, grinned derisively at his chief-of-staff. "Did Shively tell you she is 'expecting it to happen any day now?'—You know it's been about nine months since the delusion started, and Isobel keeps her eye on the calendar."

McKeith laughed. "It looks as though we'd better brush up on our obstetrics."

Castleman stuck a cigarette in his mouth and fished for his matches. "Well, the dear ladies aren't the only ones glad to see you back. . . . I'd hate to have to get Eve Minary ready for her treatment by myself."

The older man smiled. "I'll have her upstairs for you at five." Since Castleman had been experimenting with metrazol for some time, McKeith had given him the responsibility of the treatments with the drug, while he himself concentrated on the patient's emotional development.

McKeith shifted his hat and parcel to his left hand and reached inside his overcoat.

"Here, have one of mine." Marc offered an open pack of cigarettes, struck a match and held it until they both got lights.

McKeith exhaled and frowned somberly at his cigarette. "I don't like the way this case is shaping up, Marc. That damn flu has left me with precious little time to prepare for what's coming. . . . I wish we didn't have to go ahead with that next injection this afternoon."

"I wish we didn't either. If it proves decisive—and by all indications it should—I know it's going to force our hand. But I can't risk a longer interval." Castleman leaned against the wall, smoking in quick draws.

He was a slight young man with black hair, dark blue eyes and a narrow intent face that was always charged with a keen interest—if not in the people about him, then in thoughts about his research or the problem of life in general.

His eyes were sharp with his usual keenness as he asked, "Did you see Minary last night?"

"Yes. He came out to the house and we had a long talk. But he says he hadn't an idea anything was wrong with Eve until I was called in. He'd been mixed up in a mess down at the D. A.'s office and hadn't been home much those last months."

"Well, it sounds damn queer to me," Marc said. "I don't see how a woman could develop a dementia and her husband not notice anything wrong with her until she was in the final stage. . . . Surely somebody in her family must know what happened?"

McKeith loosened his coat and pushed it open. "I've made appointments for this afternoon with the Ladbrookes, Barbara Minary and Cissie Humber. I ought to find out something from them. But . . ." He left the sentence unfinished, weighing some thought heavy on his mind. After a moment of troubled abstraction he asked, "Have you noticed anything unnatural in these people of Eve's? . . . Something . . . not quite right in their attitude?"

"Why no . . . I haven't." Marc was surprised. "As a matter of fact I haven't paid much attention to any of them. While you were sick I made it a point to be there several times when they visited Eve. She'd been so much more alert since that last injection I thought she might show a new reaction to them. But she was as indifferent as ever. No questions—no interest in going home. I was concentrating on her behavior all the time, but her family struck me as acting just about as you'd expect. . . . What's the matter with their attitude?"

"It isn't easy to explain," McKeith answered slowly. "But when I've been with those people lately I've gotten a sensation . . . a feeling of something suppressed that's banking up . . . not just normal anxiety over the outcome of the case, but a tension that's somehow all wrong." He saw the incomprehension on Castleman's face and pondered how to make his perceptions understood.

"One of those thrillers you brought me last week was about a time bomb coated with chocolate, fixed up to look like a pastry, and delivered to a dinner party. There it sat, ticking inaudibly away, all set to go off at a certain moment,—and all the time the people around the table were busily eating and making plans and looking forward to dessert.

"Do you get what I mean?" he asked, looking urgently at Marc. "Now these people connected with Eve—they're covered with icing an inch thick. They express all the proper sentiments, they're devoted to her and to each other, everything is light and love on the surface. But I've sensed that under the chocolate there are tensions and motivations I don't understand, coiled emotions working toward a climax. But I don't know what direction the explosion will take . . . or who's going to explode . . . or why."

Castleman was still puzzled. "I'm afraid I've missed getting anything of all that. I realize that the family's attitude, everything that happened to Eve before she came here, is becoming important now. But I guess I've been focusing too exclusively on her reaction to metrazol. That part of it has been pretty absorbing in itself. I've been thinking of writing up the case for the A. J. P." He stopped and glanced down the hall, as the doors of the recreation room were thrown open.

A nurse came out followed by a stream of patients. When she began to urge them toward their rooms for the afternoon rest period, the two doctors moved quickly out of sight onto the stair landing.

Marc dropped his cigarette on the concrete and ground it out. "You know this case has a fascinating side, quite apart from its professional interest. It's like putting together pieces of a puzzle without knowing what picture you'll get. We started with just a body. We taught it how to walk, and talk and feed itself, and now a personality is beginning to emerge. . . . I wonder what sort of woman we'll get."

"Didn't I tell you that I'd met her before?" McKeith walked over and glanced out the window at the side of the landing.

"Why no—I didn't know that!" Marc looked curiously at his colleague. "You've never mentioned it before! It ought to be a big help to you now. What was she like?"

McKeith turned slowly from the window. "I saw her only once or twice at a committee meeting. It seems rather ironical now—she was on the board of the Mental Hygiene Clinic. It was several years before her illness. I didn't see any indications of instability then. . . . She was a pretty thing—romantic looking." He looked out the window again, his voice reminiscent. "She had a sort of flair, very enticing—a delightful person."

There was a moment of silence, a little strained. McKeith abruptly extinguished his cigarette and glanced at his watch.

"Well, I'll see you at five then."

"Okay." Castleman moved over to the flight of steps. "I guess I'd better get upstairs. Potts is probably champing around up there now waiting for me."

"How is he? Still apathetic?"

"Oh, no. Potts is very much interested, Potts is." Grinning, Marc turned back, his hand on the rail. "He's been having a series of significant dreams. He is an Oedipus all right, with some fancy trimmings. He's quite excited about it. Just counts the moments until he can go to bed and start dreaming. He dreams steadily all night and remembers every detail. He's caught on to my method of interpretation and has everything all worked out for me when I get there. He's practically analyzing himself. . . . Doing a good job, too," he added, laughing.

McKeith joined in the laughter as he turned away, and then his face clouded with that deep pity he had retained through the years of dealing with twisted human emotions.

He walked along the emptied hall, turned down a side passage, and entered his own quarters by way of the surgery.

A newly lit fire crackling in the marble fireplace greeted him when he opened the office door, and he blessed the efficiency of his Miss Evans. He laid down his folder and looked around the pine-paneled, chintz-hung room like a returned exile.

The disarming character of his office was part and parcel of McKeith's therapeutic method, and every object and its arrangement had a clinical significance. The prevailing blues were soothing to disturbed personalities, and touches of red and primrose yellow stimulated without exciting.

The two wing-chairs by the oriel window made a "conversation piece," an intimate spot where the doctor liked to sit and chat with a patient he wished to put at ease. The deep couch by the fire was used in a later stage of therapy, the psychoanalysis.

The whole atmosphere reflected McKeith's personal, understanding approach and was immediately reassuring to new patients. The familiar associations of the room were subtly appeasing today to the doctor himself. He put his coat and hat in the closet and with an air of contentment sat down at his leather-topped desk. His secretary had brought him his mail during his convalescence and there was nothing waiting for his attention except the folder he had brought in, a gray-cloth binder marked, "Minary—Evelyn Ladbrooke."

He opened it and turned over the pages. The case history began with a printed face sheet filled in with routine data, followed by several carbons, duplicates from the files of Eve's family physician and from the records of her obstetrician. McKeith flipped through these and came to the first entry.

Dated in April, 1933, it consisted of a transcription of interviews with Eve's family and associates. McKeith glanced through these pages and then riffled through the succeeding sheets, reports of periodic physical examinations covering a period of ten years. The record of a body in perfect health while the mind slept away its life.

When the doctor came to the date, June 9, 1943, he paused and read musingly the entry dictated by Dr. Castleman. "At 10:00 A. M. the patient opened her eyes, blinked when light struck them, and turned her head voluntarily. Eyes do not focus. No response to sound or other stimuli, except light and pain. Flinched and cried out at pin prick. Became restless at mealtime and moaned, but could not be induced to eat. Given tube feeding and slept until 6:00 P. M. Indicated response level of day-old infant."

McKeith leafed slowly through the remaining pages, stopping to read bits here and there from Castleman's entries after each injection of metrazol. Marc's dictations were interspersed with McKeith's findings and later with transcriptions of his conversations with the patient. It was all familiar to him from previous study and he skimmed through it absently as though unable to settle down to anything else.

After a few moments he closed the folder, walked restlessly over to the window, and stood staring out at the winter garden, dismal under an overcast sky. There was a distant, threatening rumble of thunder and McKeith looked up at the clouds. Although the sound came from overhead it had a muffled, subterranean quality—"like this case and these people of Eve's," he thought.

There was a knock on the door leading to the anteroom, and McKeith turned as his secretary came in. Her smile told him how happy she was to have him back, but she said, merely, "Mr. and Mrs. Ladbrooke are here, Doctor. Are you ready for them now?"

His answering smile told her that he, too, was glad to be back in teamwork with her professional competence.

"Yes, send them in." He walked over to his desk and switched on the concealed dictaphone.

6.

McKeith was at the door when the Ladbrookes swept in, redolent of the sleek handsomeness advertisers like to pose against royal palms and nightclub interiors. "It's good to find you up again, Doctor." "I've been wanting to have a talk with you." They greeted him with the friendliness, familiar yet restrained, which comes from prolonged association on a professional level.

McKeith had frequently encountered Madeleine Ladbrooke coming and going with the others on visits to Eve during the past months. Although she was a beauty, and he was appreciative, there was a peculiarly negative quality about her lovely features that canceled their appeal for him. Her manner with its gracious smile and appropriate remark was always as smooth as an airflow curve, and as conventionally predictable. She played her rôle like a formal actress going through a routine part, incapable of an impulsive gesture or spontaneous expression.

The doctor was better acquainted with Scott who had seldom missed a daily visit to his sister during the time she had been at Oaklawn. Five years older than Eve, he was a dark Anthony Edenish sort of man who gave the impression of moving through life with the ease of the practiced aristocrat. But the psychiatrist had observed a fine-drawnness about him, indicative of an intense and emotional nature.

Today his poise was in discard. Talking nervously while McKeith assisted Madeleine with her fur coat, he walked

over to the fire as jittery as a thoroughbred on the way
to the post. "Well, it looks as though this is It!—I hardly
feel prepared. It's come so suddenly after such a long
wait." He sat down abruptly on the edge of the couch beside his wife, pressing a finger against the lower rim of
one eye, which had begun to quiver in brief spasm.

"Over-mobilized," was McKeith's silent diagnosis as he
seated himself beside the fireplace. Pulling a pad from
his pocket, he scribbled a few lines while replying, "Yes,
we hope this next injection will be decisive. But don't forget we still have a long way to go." He tore off the sheet
and handed it over. "Here is a prescription I wish you'd
get filled. Take a couple of tablets after dinner and get a
good night's sleep. You want to be in shape for whatever
develops tomorrow when Eve comes to."

"Thank you." Preoccupied, Scott accepted the prescription and stuck it absent-mindedly into his pocket as though
dismissing the whole incident. McKeith laughed and
turned to the lady. "Will you see that he follows my orders, Mrs. Ladbrooke? You're going to have to play nursemaid for a while. This fellow needs looking after."

Smiling, Madeleine abstracted the slip from her husband's pocket and put it in her handbag. "I'll get this
filled on my way home and see that he takes two with his
postprandial brandy."

Scott, heedless of the little by-play, leaned forward intent on his purpose. "Do you realize what a damnable
situation we're in if Eve wakes up tomorrow with her
mind clear? . . . Of course Barbara should have gone to
Reno as soon as we started with metrazol. If she'd taken
up residence last June, Phil would have had his divorce
by now. But he thought they should wait to see how
things turned out. And of course, there was some uncertainty then. But now, even after that last injection, Phil
still thinks they should wait. God knows why! There is
no time to lose!"

His lower eyelid began to twitch again, but he seemed not to notice it. "Phil can't seem to appreciate the effect all this delay is going to have on Eve. It's bad enough for her to have to learn of his marriage. She can't stand the strain of waiting around for him to get a divorce after she's ready to come home. Can't you make him realize how disastrous that would be for her?"

McKeith let out a short exasperated sigh. "But Mr. Ladbrooke, talk of a divorce now is decidedly premature. I've told you that even with the most favorable results from metrazol, we'll still have months of analytical therapy ahead. If Eve wakes up in the morning with her mind unblocked, we'll be at a crucial stage. That's why I wanted to talk with you this afternoon. In order to give proper treatment, I must know about all the circumstances that led up to her dementia."

Angry protest flashed into Scott's eyes at the doctor's veto of a divorce. Then, apparently unable to detach his thought from his own urgent objective, he withdrew all signs of interest.

McKeith stopped and waited. When Ladbrooke looked up with stubborn, troubled eyes that became reluctantly attentive, the doctor began again, speaking incisively. "You've got to understand what we're up against. Your sister is suffering from a dementia that is invariably rooted in terrible mental conflict. Ten years ago she must have found herself in a situation so unbearable that escape from reality was the only way out. Something intolerable—an utter frustration, a harrowing sense of guilt, or some other irreconcilable factor in her life—forced her to deny the present, to retreat into the past, to withdraw from all conscious life clear back into the subconsciously remembered existence before birth. When you called me in I found her in a trance-state, a condition we call the intra-uterine stage of retrogression.

"Now," he continued, "for the last months, with a series

of metrazol shocks we have been blasting away at the
mental insulation, stirring up the buried consciousness,
and bringing Eve back, step by step, toward the present.
But in doing this, in breaking down the protective mecha-
nisms of the subconscious, in tearing away the mental
anesthesia dropped over unbearable pain, don't you see
that we're taking a terrible risk unless we have a treatment ready?"

Scott, who had been listening with growing excitement,
started to speak, but McKeith went on inexorably. "Eve,
in her present state of retrogression, is living back in her
early childhood with no memory of her adult life. But if
this next treatment lifts her over the last hurdle, she'll
wake up tomorrow right where she left off ten years ago.
And when all those old personal difficulties that drove her
insane come flooding back into her consciousness, the pain
and the struggle will begin again. If she finds it too much
to face she may slip right back out of things before I get
a chance to work with her. It is important for me to hit
straight at the heart of her trouble, to hold her attention
in those first moments . . . and I'm completely in the dark.
I've never had access to the conscious experience of my
patient. I haven't the faintest idea when her trouble began
or what led up to the dementia. You have to tell me about
that."

"Good God! Don't you know I would have told you
long ago . . . if there were anything to tell? Eve means
more to me than anything in this world. There is nothing
I wouldn't do for her. I've tried to help you in every way
I could."

Scott's thickened voice broke. His fervid brown eyes
looked black.

McKeith glanced quickly at Mrs. Ladbrooke, who sat
detached from the conversation. Her fashion-ad face was
impassive as she watched the flames in the fireplace, indifferent to what was said. Her husband's voice was less

vehement, but crusted with impatience when he continued.
"Frankly, I think there is nothing to this theory of yours
about a dementia. Eve never showed any sign of a mental
conflict. She wasn't in any sort of difficult situation. I
don't understand why you're bringing this up again. You
talked to all of us at the time, and we all told you the
same thing. Eve acted exactly like the normal, happy
woman she was, and always had been, right up to the day
of her collapse."

McKeith slumped back in his chair, rucking his gray
tweed jacket about his shoulders. "Yes, I know I talked
to all of you when I was called on the case. And I didn't
get anywhere. But you remember you were all distraught.
. . . And then, too, I thought perhaps there was some reason . . . something you didn't care to discuss . . . especially as I'd told you her case was hopeless. I wasn't satisfied, but I let it drop. After all there was no point in pushing my inquiries, then. . . . Even after we began with
metrazol, I didn't press you because we were doubtful
that we'd get this far along. But now that there is a good
chance for her recovery, I expected you'd tell me more,
give me some sort of guide, at least."

"But there was nothing in my sister's life for us to conceal. We told you everything we knew. Don't you believe me?"

"Yes . . . I have to believe you," McKeith answered
slowly. "Unless you're all in a conspiracy of silence," he
added with a wry smile. His face with the ascetic eyes and
virile mouth was weary. "I believe you are telling me the
truth as you see it, but haven't you closed your mind to
the issue? Dementia praecox is a disease that comes on
slowly, usually developing in adolescence. In your sister's
case, there must have been symptoms over a long period.
At the time, you didn't recognize their significance. But if
you would think back, review her behavior in the light of

what we now know, I feel you could make a different interpretation—give me some indication. . . ."

Scott's eyes remained adamant. His lip curled slightly, in the grimace of a man forced to listen to nonsense.

"Of course," McKeith went on after a moment of silence, "regardless of what the underlying factors were, a new element must have come into the situation to precipitate her sudden withdrawal. Something must have happened when she was in a weakened condition after the baby's birth. A shock, a profound disturbance, coming at this time, could have induced a rapid development of her dementia."

Scott tossed up his hands in a gesture of exasperated futility. "But nothing in the slightest degree upsetting occurred. From the time of the baby's birth until the moment of her collapse, Eve was either in the hospital or convalescing at home. Except for the one time she went down to see Gray, her obstetrician. Cissie Humber was with her and Gray told them both that she was making a remarkable recovery from the Caesarean. He attributed it all to her splendid frame of mind—and it was that very night that she broke down. So, you see?"

"Wouldn't you consider murder an upsetting incident, Ladbrooke?" McKeith's eyes were appraising. "Wasn't it around that time that that young assistant of Minary's was killed? And as I recall, Minary himself was severely criticized over it. Was, in fact, held to be partly responsible. Wasn't all this disturbing to Eve?"

"Not at all." Scott dismissed the suggestion with an impatient shrug of a shoulder. "In fact, Crane was killed the very night little Jonathan was born. Eve didn't even hear about his death until several weeks later. By that time the publicity had died down, and it wasn't until after Eve was up here at Oaklawn that the thing flared up again and the politicians forced Phil's resignation."

"But it must have had some effect on Eve," McKeith probed cautiously. "Wasn't she acquainted with Crane, at all?"

"Oh, she had known Hal casually for some time," Scott conceded. "As a matter of fact, they were in the same class at high school. He was one of a bunch of youngsters hanging around Eve in those days. But she was easily the most popular girl in school and Hal was just one of a crowd. After graduation she was away at college, and then, when she and Phil married and settled down here, they didn't move in the same social circles as Crane. I doubt she ever saw him from the time she left high school until he wrote up the reform campaign."

Scott shifted his position and hurried on impatiently. "Of course Eve was shocked over his death. We all were. But it didn't concern her personally. Crane was trying to expose a ring of political grafters. He got too close to the truth and was murdered. That sort of thing has happened before. His murder was shocking and regrettable, but I can see no possible connection with Eve's illness."

He got up in agitation and stood with his back to the fire, his hands thrust into his pockets. "There was nothing wrong with Eve, mentally. I'm convinced her condition was the result of a physical breakdown. You're the one with a closed mind—insisting on some mysterious, non-existent circumstances, in the face of substantiated evidence to the contrary. You've no basis for your suppositions except your own diagnosis, and as to that—it isn't as though analytic theory were really scientific."

He broke off at the look on McKeith's haggard face and said, flushing, "I beg your pardon, Doctor. What I meant was that psychotherapy is still experimental, theoretical . . . that is, you can't diagnose with X-rays and that sort of thing. You and Castleman have done a fine job with metrazol and I'm deeply grateful to you. But our immediate problem is insuring Eve's recovery, seeing that her adjustment to everything is made as easy as possible. Phil should start divorce proceedings right away. If you are really concerned over Eve's welfare, I can't see why you won't tell him you agree with me."

Years of dealing with disturbed personalities enabled McKeith to control most of his resentment, but there was an edge to his voice when he said, "My diagnosis is based on unmistakable symptoms. And unless I can find the cause of Eve's disease, I shan't be able to cure her. However, since you can't, or won't, help me, there is no point in continuing the discussion. Now as to this matter of Minary's divorce, that lies entirely outside my province as a psychiatrist. I have never sought to play the rôle of God in the lives of my patients. My job lies with Eve, in helping her re-integrate her personality and adjust herself to whatever circumstances she faces. It rests entirely with Mr. Minary whether or not he seeks a divorce."

Scott walked over and sat on the arm of the couch, his face stormy. "It seems to me it's not outside your professional duty to advise Phil that delay might have an adverse effect on the patient, especially as it's not a question of whether he gets a divorce, but only of when he starts proceedings."

Ignoring Ladbrooke's truculence, McKeith studied him thoughtfully. "Are you sure Minary intends to get a divorce?"

"Why—yes, certainly." Eve's brother was somewhat taken aback. He considered the matter as if for the first time. "It's not as though Phil were in love with Barbara. This second marriage was just . . . I suppose you could call it a marriage of convenience. There's been no question in my mind that Eve comes first with Phil. It's just that he's wanted to make sure of her recovery before acting. I haven't understood why he's still delaying, but I see now. You've been filling him with this poppycock about a dementia and months of analysis ahead. . . . Well, I've had enough of waiting. I've been in to see Cunningham. We're prepared to institute proceedings to have Phil's divorce from Eve declared null and void."

The doctor dropped the pencil with which he'd been fiddling and sat up astonished. "I'm not conversant with the law, but I was under the impression that once a divorce had been obtained in the United States, even fraudulently, and a subsequent marriage had taken place, it was next to impossible to upset the divorce."

The tic below Scott's eye was twitching again. He brushed his hand over it in annoyance, as he answered, "Well, you're right, Doctor. The court is extremely reluctant to reconsider the validity of a divorce, if one of the parties has remarried. But my purpose in bringing action is to force Phil's hand. He would never let this thing be dragged through the courts. I can't get him to see the urgency of the matter any other way."

"What grounds do you have for your action?" McKeith asked, curiously.

"Well, the divorce *was* obtained with fraud, and with the court's and my own connivance, I regret to say. At the time it seemed fair enough. Under the laws of this state, insanity is not considered grounds for divorce, as you probably know. And yet divorces for such cause are granted constantly. The claimants get around the difficulty by claiming mental cruelty *prior* to the onset of the insanity. It's just a form of procedure, a technicality. In Phil's case, the judge knew all the circumstances. The whole thing was handled very quietly and everyone understood.

"I realize now we were wrong. It was a crime against Eve. But you had told us there was no hope for her whatever. If she had died and Phil had remarried, I wouldn't have objected, and it was just as though she were dead.

Phil had been alone for seven years, and Jonathan
needed someone like Barbara."

He sighed in contemplation of the error of the past,
then shrugged lightly. "Well, it's water over the dam.
The thing now is to consider the future." He was interrupted by a knock on the door, and the entrance of his
senior partner, Jeffrey Halsey.

"How do you do, Doctor? How are you, Madeleine?"
Halsey nodded to Mrs. Ladbrooke and turned back to
the psychiatrist. "I hate to interrupt this way, but I
promised to pick up Ladbrooke for a business appointment. Are you about finished, Scott? We're due out at
Inglewood at three, and it is twenty of now. I looked in
on Evelyn for a moment, Doctor. She looks wonderful,
almost like herself again. I understand you're counting
a lot on this next treatment?"

"Yes," McKeith answered equably. "We're quite hopeful. We're expecting very interesting results when Eve
wakes up in the morning. ... I won't keep you any longer,
Ladbrooke, but I wonder if I could have a little talk with
you now, Mrs. Ladbrooke?"

"With me?" Madeleine asked, in mild surprise. "Why
—I am afraid there is nothing I can tell you about Eve,
Dr. McKeith."

"There are some things I would like to go over with
you, if it won't inconvenience you to stay awhile longer,"
McKeith insisted.

"I *do* have a foursome at three, but I can let them
wait awhile. It is just that I really can't add anything
to what Scott has told you. However ..." She seated herself again gracefully, as her husband and Halsey started
out.

Scott paused at the door. "I hope you can let me see
Eve when she wakes tomorrow, Doctor. I'll be here in the
morning, before ten . . . waiting."

7.

Now THAT Scott had departed with his turbulent emotions, McKeith hoped for an intimate little tête-à-tête with Madeleine. But he knew it was not going to be easy. He closed the door and stood for a moment considering her. In size and coloring she was curiously like her sister-in-law. But she had a polished worldliness very unlike Eve's remembered natural grace. However, ten years ago when her character was still unformed, the resemblance must have been close.

Today Madeleine was doing her hair a new way, brushed straight back and net bound in a big loop, as dictated by the latest mode. She had picked up a cigarette and was holding it unlighted in a hand with orange-red fingertips. The varnish on her nails and her matching lipstick were her only touches of color. She was all in beige, excessively smart in a Jersey dress and abbreviated headgear—something called a half-hat of the same fabric. Even her gold and silver earrings and necklace were a neutral tone.

As McKeith flicked on his lighter for her, he wondered why it was that ultra-fashionable women always avoided healthy colors and picked out what they called subtle tones, or more frequently yet, drab grays and tans, the most emotionally depressing of all shades. And the most unbecoming, too!

However, Madeleine's black velvet eyes and white skin emerged triumphant over her colorless clothes. She drew on her cigarette, looking at him in that detached way of hers, and he was reminded of a mannequin he had seen in a Fifth Avenue window on his last trip to New York. The thing, made entirely of platinum-colored metal, had appalled him. Even the hair and eyelashes were of some fine-spun metallic substance. And the worst feature of the grotesque figurine was the intention. For it was not a caricature, but an interpretation of feminine sophistication. Only a woman as streamlined and metallic as the mannequin could wear properly the clothes it displayed.

"And so this," he had thought at the time, in horror— "this complete negation of femininity, is the ideal of the twentieth-century woman." He had since found the same negation in the faces of the models pictured in smart magazines, and here it was now, exemplified in Madeleine Ladbrooke. The doctor knew the psychological cost involved in this complete reduction of the emotions, and wondered if under the lacquer of her poise Madeleine concealed a mass of repressions. But he decided that perhaps she had had bred out of her all the errant impulses that are the source of neurasthenia—and also of so much of human happiness.

He dropped his lighter into his pocket and smiled, remarking as he pulled his chair closer to the figurine on the couch, "Well, it seems your husband and I both have closed minds."

"Isn't that to be expected? After all, you're both men."

Chuckling, McKeith crossed his long legs and rested his head against the chair in a relaxed attitude. He thought of this as his chatty position, conducive to easy, gossipy talk.

He was a psychiatrist noted for his skill with women. And although he had made significant contributions to the theory of abnormal psychology, his colleagues attributed his special success to a personal quality. His sympathetic appreciation of feminine nature was a sol-

vent that usually melted inhibitions and drew out con-
fidences irresistibly. But Madeleine was not responsive.
Even her chaffing remark had been offered, without
sparkle, merely as correct repartee.

"But even we men can't afford to keep our minds
closed now," he said. "We've reached a critical point in
Eve's treatment. I need to know when her trouble first
started and what was connected with it. I expect you
observed many little things—emotional upsets, moods,
troubles—that a woman would perceive and that your
husband didn't notice at all."

"But I scarcely knew her, Doctor." Madeleine raised
her eyebrows in delicate arches. "My home was in Boston. I wasn't acquainted with Eve before my marriage
and it was only three years after I came here that she—
had to be sent to Oaklawn.

"Of course," she explained smoothly, "I lived next door
to Eve and naturally we were thrown together a good bit
. . . but somehow we never became very intimate. You see,
Eve was terribly civic-minded, and I'm afraid I couldn't
get excited over the League of Women Voters and that
sort of thing. And then, too, they started the reform campaign and she became so taken up with that."

In spite of her noncommittal manner, McKeith caught
a faint hint of depreciation when she mentioned Eve.
Possibly something more intense than depreciation. He
wasn't sure, but he thought he detected indications that
Madeleine was concealing a violent emotion connected
with her sister-in-law. His senses quickened like those of
a miner beginning to pan gold. But he proceeded, carefully, casually.

"I take it that you weren't active in the reform movement?"

"Scott was on one of the committees and I used to at-
tend the meetings with him. I did what I could to help,
of course, but I felt rather out of place in the midst of

politicians and electioneering. I could never get as
frenetic over the thing as the others did. Frankly, it all
seemed rather silly and futile to me."

McKeith decided to act like a man amused at the
vagaries of a pretty, frivolous woman. "Just why did you
feel it was silly for these people to try to get a better city
government?"

"Well, it was foolish for a group of amateurs, without
political experience, to think that they could outfight sea-
soned, professional politicians at their own game. And
the whole thing was futile. Look how it ended. Judge
Ladbrooke tried to warn Evelyn, but she wouldn't listen."

McKeith's interest was sharp. "I thought the Judge
was one of the leaders in the movement. Do you mean
he was opposed to his daughter's taking part in it?"

"He wasn't opposed to her taking a part, but he didn't
want her to get so completely wrapped up in it. He felt
she was bound to be disillusioned and bitterly disappointed. He said it was a matter of bread and butter to
these officeholders to keep their party in power. They
worked at it, not just at election time, but every day, year
in and year out, while the members of the Citizens
League couldn't afford to make a lifework of politics. So,
although they might have a temporary success, they
would soon go back to their other interests, and the
political machine would be in the saddle again. And
that was just what happened."

"You think, then, that Evelyn was more disturbed
over the way things turned out than Mr. Ladbrooke
realizes? All the criticism of her husband?"

"No," Madeleine weighed the matter judiciously. "As
Scott told you, Eve missed the first wave of criticism. . . .
But even if she had heard all the slander, she wouldn't
have brooded over it. She was so afire with her ideals,
she would have seen herself in the rôle of a martyr. Like
these conscientious objectors. I think they positively en-

joy going to isolation camps, and all the attendant fuss and furor."

"But the murder of this boy Crane? How did she take that?" the psychiatrist pressed.

"She was shocked of course. But she accepted it as a casualty in a righteous battle. I'm sure she felt no responsibility for it."

The bitterness and more than bitterness in her voice was unmistakable this time, and McKeith, feeling he was on the verge of discovery, probed deftly. "Wasn't it rather . . . strange . . . for a sensitive young woman like Eve to remain unaffected by the tragic death of an associate? And it certainly wasn't natural for a newly married wife to be so zealous, so wrapped up in an interest outside her home. Didn't you feel she had an abnormal personality?"

Madeleine took a deep breath. "Eve's personality . . ." she began, and then hesitated. Abruptly her careful lacquer of poise cracked up, and suppressed emotion flooded to the surface. She gazed at McKeith without speaking. Her dark eyes, dilating and narrowing, wavered as though she were shivering deep inside.

McKeith froze to attention. The horror in her eyes, the profound inner shudder, revealed the force of a haunting memory. He realized that Pandora's box was slowly opening, and braced himself for the dreadful hidden things that would emerge.

But abruptly as it had lifted, Madeleine's noncommittal mask came down over her face again, and she said, "Eve was different in many ways from the average girl, but I didn't consider her abnormal. That is she wasn't . . . pathological. Her personality was wholly admirable."

Disappointingly the lid of Pandora's box had banged shut, and McKeith wondered in sharp dismay how he was going to pry it open again. "I know Eve's motivations were admirable," he tried, "but wasn't her zeal fanatical?

Mightn't she have been driven by a compulsion? . . . or was she seeking an emotional outlet . . . maybe because of frustration in her marriage?"

"Oh, no, there was nothing like that at all. Eve and Phil were an ideal couple. Perfectly happy. And although Eve was idealistic, she wasn't a fanatic." Her face was closed, and McKeith knew the revealing moment had passed. He had had that one brief glimpse of something as yet unguessed, something dark and sinister, and carefully concealed. But Pandora's box was locked now.

He sighed and glanced at his watch. He felt increasingly the pressure of that rapidly approaching final test with metrazol, and talking with Madeleine now was like gathering handfuls of mist. He straightened up in his chair and asked directly, "Didn't you notice anything at all unusual in Eve's behavior during her convalescence?"

"No, she seemed just the same as ever to me. We were with her the evening . . . before that last day. She planned to go into town the next afternoon and was looking forward to getting out again. We went over to her house the following night as usual and Phil told us she had come home exhausted and gone right to bed without eating. The next day Dr. Gray prescribed complete rest, and she wasn't allowed to see anyone, not even Phil. Then, after a few days you were called in and your diagnosis was an absolute surprise to all of us. We hadn't had the slightest inkling that anything was wrong with Evelyn's *mind*. I'm sorry to seem so unhelpful, but I can't tell you about something if there isn't anything to tell, can I?"

There was a strange expression on the doctor's face as he closed the door after the departing Madeleine. He had learned nothing definite to help him with Eve, but he had discovered a human emotion stirring in the platinum mannequin. For although he could not guess its significance to the case, or the reason for its presence, one

thing was unmistakable, it had pervaded the whole conversation—the fact of Madeleine's dislike . . . and fear
. . . of her sister-in-law.

It had grown too warm by the fire. McKeith crossed
over and sat in his desk chair, with his head against the
back, and his eyes closed. A conspiracy of silence? he
wondered.

He gently massaged his temples. A psychiatric interview could be as delicate and nerve-straining as a sur-
gical operation, and the Ladbrookes had taken it out of
him. Scott with his single idea was like a sealed rocket
bound for the moon. And as for Madeleine—he'd been
wrong about her. She lacked the three-dimensional character of a mannequin. She was as flat as a paper doll.
Perhaps Barbara Bachman Minary would be an antidote
to Madeleine's pallid elegance, he thought, pushing the
buzzer that notified Miss Evans he was ready for his next
appointment.

The second Mrs. Minary, in a brown suit and bitter-
sweet blouse, brought into the office the feeling of autumn
leaves blown along country soil. Her cheeks were pink,
too, he noted with approval. But when he had led her toward the twin chairs in the bay, and light from his oriel
window fell on her face, he saw that her bloom was ap-
plied and that her features were taut with strain.

He lifted the lid from a blue cloisonné box on the side table, "Care for a cigarette?"

"No thank you. Not now." She brushed aside the offer almost brusquely, impatient of the amenities, eager for him to come to the point immediately. To his surprise she sat in his chintz-covered Queen Anne chair as though it were a dentist's chair and she were braced for the moment when the drill would strike.

"It's that damn divorce talk of Scott's monkeying up the works again," he thought, eying her in consternation. "She's come here expecting me to order her to Reno."

He lit a cigarette for himself. "I want to talk to you about some things that happened a long time ago." He smiled at her in his friendly companionable way. "I hope you won't think I'm just a gossipy doctor prying into things that don't concern me. It's very important for me to understand Eve's background, and, so far, her family haven't helped me very much. Too close to the woods to see the trees, perhaps. Maybe looking from outside you had a perspective different from the others."

He could see that she was tremendously relieved by the direction he had given the conversation. "I understand. I'll be glad to tell you anything I can." She faced him with earnest eyes and wide apple cheeks, like an attentive secretary ready for his bidding.

"First of all, Barbara—you don't mind if I call you Barbara?—I always call my patients by their first names and it becomes a habit with me . . ." She nodded and smiled, oddly pleased. He saw her apprehension had left her, and suggested, "How about a cigarette now?"

"I believe I will." She selected one from the Chinese box and leaned forward for a light in the careful, deliberate way she had. McKeith had noticed before her manner of holding herself and of speaking, as though she were conscientiously following some self-prescribed rule of deportment. Not like Madeleine's careful poise,

the hard shell enclosing a vacuum. Barbara's poise, Mc-
Keith thought, came from schooled emotions, from competence and deep steadiness. She would be a balance
wheel in the emotional machinery of family life.

"Well, first of all, then, how well did you know Eve?"
he asked.

"I came to know her pretty well. Much better than a
secretary usually knows her employer's wife." She considered the question carefully, relaxed and fully at ease
now. "You see, when I went to work for Phil, he was
fresh out of law school. Scott was, too. They were both
learning the ropes and I was just window dressing.

"We were pretty informal. The boys used to have me
make tea for them around four o'clock. The Judge would
drop in, sometimes, and if Madeleine or Eve were in
town, they would stop by, too. I saw a good bit of Eve
that way and then after the campaign started, I worked
with her every day. I suppose you know all about the
campaign, Dr. McKeith?"

He made a wry grimace. "Politics are a little out of
my orbit, but no one who lived here at the time could
help knowing something was going on." He smiled. "I
guess we just went through an inevitable stage in the life
cycle of the American city. Grumbling, but busy, citizens had put up with a machine-ridden government for
years, until finally things got so bad even the tax-paying
worm finally turned, and a reform campaign was
launched. Right? And the Ladbrookes were in the thick
of it."

"Yes, Phil gave all of his time to it. He was assistant
to the executive secretary, and Eve was chairman of the
Women's Committee."

"The Reformers put on quite a show, I remember,"
McKeith remarked. "But in spite of it all, they got just
one candidate elected. What happened? Did they over-
shoot their mark?"

"But that was our strategy—to put up just the one candidate," Barbara explained quickly. "You see we weren't strong enough to elect a whole slate, so we concentrated on one key position, the office of district attorney. If we had that, we could prosecute the grafters and break the machine by putting the leaders behind bars."

"That makes sense. But why on earth did you choose Hugh Nelson as your candidate?" McKeith's eyes were amused.

"Do you know him?" Barbara asked, surprised.

McKeith laughed. "I've heard him make a few after-dinner speeches!"

She laughed, too. "We knew he was an awful stuffed shirt, but he was well-known and belonged to a prominent family, and we couldn't find a really able man, who would give up his practice for the job. So we ran Nelson as a front. He'd decided to appoint Phil assistant district attorney and it was Phil we were banking on to really dig up the evidence of graft."

"Just how did Hal Crane come into the picture? Was it on Evelyn's suggestion that Phil took him on as his assistant?" McKeith had slipped into his chatty position, with his legs crossed and his head resting lazily against his chair.

His question sounded only casually curious.

"Evelyn?" Barbara looked surprised. "No, I don't think so. Hal was a reporter. He covered the campaign for *The News*, Judge Ladbrooke's paper, and he became interested in what we were doing. Sort of converted. And after the election he wanted to play along with Phil, undercover. You see, he'd been on the police beat and he used to pal around with the politicians in the speakeasy across from City Hall. He was a typical young reporter, sticking an inquisitive nose into everything, and he'd gotten a kick out of knowing the big shots and picking up the inside dope and rumors going around. He thought he could use his connections to pick up tips and pass them on to Phil."

"Then Crane wasn't on the D. A.'s payroll, he had no official position?" McKeith had taken his pipe from the table drawer, and was tamping tobacco into the bowl. "He was working just for the love of it?"

"That's right," Barbara agreed. "At first Phil didn't think anything would come of it, but Hal was terribly en-thusiastic and he thought he saw a shortcut to the long, tedious investigation Phil was working up. He knew that Sam Tilton, the city purchasing agent, was jittery. The other members of the gang were not worried. They thought if they just sat tight, the thing would blow over. But Tilton was a weak sister. He was shaking in his boots from the first, and Hal thought if he worked on him, he'd turn state's evidence."

McKeith had his pipe going. He lay back puffing at it, watching Barbara with half-closed eyes. She was a brunette, but a very different type from Madeleine and Eve.

Their coloring was exotic, ebony and snow-white, while Barbara was a "nut-brown maid," with a fertile, earthy look. The doctor guessed that she was farm reared, of a long line of country folk.

She was quite unselfconscious, talking along easily now. "Hal would drop in at Mike's, Tilton's favorite speakeasy, when he thought he would find him there, and would pass on information he pretended he had picked up sub-rosa. He would say, 'I hear Minary is going to investigate that cement deal' and sure enough in a week or ten days, the D. A.'s office would subpoena the records on concrete purchases. Then, later he'd say, 'Minary is nosing around that Oakland playground appropriation,' and of course in a little while Phil would look into those contracts, too. Do you see how he worked it?"

McKeith nodded. "If Tilton was emotionally unstable

and fear-ridden, I expect Crane's line scared the pants off him."

"It did. Then Hal began a new line. He'd say, 'You know, I think the boys are underestimating Minary. He has lit the end of a time fuse. One day the bomb is going off and break things wide open and a lot of guys are going to wake up behind bars. You ought to get out from under while you can. If I were in your shoes, I'd make a deal. I bet Minary would trade immunity for the right sort of evidence.'"

"Crane was a pretty good psychologist," the doctor remarked, removing his pipe. "But what about Nelson? Did you keep him as much in the dark about this as he contended later?"

"Yes, we did." Barbara said, her eyes troubled. "You know Nelson. He was the sort who liked to stand up in front of the fireplace at the Club and tell his friends how clever he was. If he had known about Crane, he couldn't have resisted dropping a few broad hints, telling his pals with a wink that subpoenaing records wasn't all he was doing, that he had a spy in the enemy's camp. . . . We couldn't afford to take the risk. Of course, later we realized we were wrong—it would have made all the difference if he had known that night."

For a moment, McKeith's gentle sucking at his pipe and an answering sibilance from the fire across the room were the only sounds in the quiet of the office. "You mean, the night Jonathan was born?" McKeith prompted. "I wish you'd tell me exactly what happened that night. You were down at Phil's office, weren't you?"

"Yes. Eve was very sick and Phil hadn't been in the office much for several days. Things had piled up and I was working late. It was about eight o'clock when Hal came in. He said Tilton was ready to spill everything. That he had been boasting at first, had said more than he meant to, and then the bravado left him and he was ready to take any way out. If Phil brought him in now for questioning, he would tell everything he knew.

"I phoned the hospital, but the nurse said Phil couldn't take the call, that Eve had just come down from the operating room. I left word for him to call his office as soon as he could. It was all I could do, but Hal was wild. He said Tilton was likely to take a powder. That we would never get another chance like this. He suggested I call Nelson, but I knew that was hopeless. The D. A. didn't know Crane from Adam, and Tilton was an important person. Nelson would never order him brought in on my say so."

She hesitated, and looked at McKeith in distress. "Maybe I made a mistake . . . but I don't think Nelson would have acted, and it would have been going over Phil's head. I thought Phil would call back in a little while . . ."

"And he didn't?" McKeith asked, sharp with interest.

"No. The nurse forgot to give him my message. But Hal didn't wait. He decided to go right back to Mike's bar, where Tilton was, and stick with him. He said to have Phil order Tilton picked up as soon as possible. He rushed out of the office like a one-man army, . . . and that was the last I saw of him. . . . His body was found the next morning in his car, parked in an alley downtown. He'd been shot through the heart."

"Yes, I remember. The papers were full of it at the time," McKeith remarked. "And of course it gave the opposition a chance to jump Minary."

"They claimed he'd muffed the whole thing," Barbara said bitterly, "and of course Nelson was furious over it."

McKeith laid his pipe on the table and shifted in his chair, looking at Barbara full face. "I didn't follow it closely at the time, and the papers confused the issue as much as they could, but I recall there was a good bit of innuendo,—hints Phil had double-crossed the police. What was back of that?"

"There wasn't a word of truth to it," Barbara asserted vehemently. "They were terribly unfair. You see, when Crane's body was discovered, the police had no leads at all. It was just a 'mysterious slaying of young reporter,' until Phil told them of Crane's connection with our office and with Tilton. Then of course they went after Tilton, but he was gone by that time. He was indicted for the murder, but has never been apprehended. They blamed Phil because he didn't put them onto Tilton as soon as they found Crane's body. But Phil didn't even hear of the murder until I called him about it around seven in the evening. He'd never left the hospital, and I didn't see a paper until I went out to dinner. I'd had lunch sent in from the drugstore that noon. I called Phil at once and he went to the police with our story, but Tilton had a head start, and they couldn't pick up his trail."

"That was the end of the whole reform movement, wasn't it? I suppose Minary quit, because he couldn't get support?" McKeith asked.

"No, Phil isn't a quitter. He wanted to go ahead with his investigation. He had gathered a lot of data, but he needed more time, and Nelson wouldn't give it to him. He requested his resignation, about a month later. Just after Eve . . . was sent here."

"He got a raw deal all around," McKeith said sympathetically. "He was in pretty bad shape at the time I was called in on Eve's case."

"He barely avoided a nervous breakdown," Barbara told him. She added proudly, "But after a rest in the East he came back to Ladbrooke and Halsey and he's proved he has one of the best legal brains in the state." She flushed, embarrassed at the intensity of emotion she'd shown, and said quickly, "But I'm afraid I've wandered off the subject. You wanted to ask something about Eve?"

"How did she take Crane's death?" McKeith clasped

his hands over his knees, sitting up a little straighter, looking directly at Barbara with sharp interest.

"I went to see her once during her convalescence, after she came home from the hospital. We talked about Hal's death, and I was surprised she was so unconcerned—almost callous about it. But, I understand now, since I have had my own baby." An amused little smile softened her face. "When a woman has just had her first baby, everything else sort of moves off—nothing else matters very much for a while."

"But obviously there *was* something else that mattered—that disturbed her so much she withdrew even from her baby Something that must have come up during her convalescence," McKeith pointed out. "Did she seem upset when she dropped in to see Phil, that day she went into town?"

"I didn't see her. Cissie said Eve had stopped by the office on her way home from Dr. Gray's, but I had been in and out all afternoon and she must have run in when I wasn't there. Don't you remember? You asked about that when you took over the case. Phil had been in a conference and didn't see her either."

She looked at McKeith with serious, candid brown eyes. "I know you're trying to find out if something went wrong with Eve's personal life—but she was completely happy—and always seemed to me as normal as could be."

The doctor stretched out his long legs and clasped his hands behind his neck. "The trouble is you people are all laymen, Barbara. You've missed something significant in Eve's behavior, because you are looking for the wrong thing. The symptoms of incipient insanity are not always overt—hysteric depression and erratic behavior come later. It is the little oddities that give us the first clues."

Barbara's intelligent face was animated with interest, and the effort to understand. McKeith smiled, and explained. "I had a patient not long ago, a manic-depressive. For a long time before her insanity became obvious, her behavior was perfectly normal except for one thing She had a queer phobia about buttons."

"Buttons?" Barbara was incredulous

"Yes, buttons. One day she started to sew a button on her husband's shirt. Suddenly, she looked at it as if it were a snake, threw it down and ran out of the room crying. Her husband tried to find out what was the matter, but she just cried as if her heart would break and wouldn't explain. After that he noticed that the children's clothes were all fastened with hooks and eyes, that she had no buttons on her own dresses, that she wouldn't look at or touch a button, that if the word were mentioned she became upset.

"Eventually, she developed hysteric depression and was brought to me. I tried everything to get at the seat of her trouble, analysis of stream-of-consciousness and dream content and so forth, but I didn't make any headway until her husband remembered her odd behavior with buttons. That gave me something to go on, and I probed and probed until I got the association."

"You mean, this business with buttons wasn't important, in itself, but it gave you a clue to something else?" Barbara asked, fascinated. "You sound like a detective in a murder mystery. And you really solved the case by finding out why she was afraid of buttons?"

"Yes. When the patient was a child, she had a little playmate who lived on Button Street. She had a—shall we say—Freudian experience?—with this child and developed a crushing sense of guilt over it. When she grew up, her conscious mind forgot the whole experience; but deep inside of her, like a cancer, this unacknowledged feeling of guilt spread and spread until it broke through the crust of her inhibition in an inverted form."

Barbara wrinkled her forehead in concentration. "And you think that Eve . . . ?"

"It was a little thing that gave me a clue in that case, and I am looking for some little thing about Eve that you've all overlooked. Did she have any personal idiosyncrasies? Did you ever notice any little oddities of behavior? . . . Things that didn't fit, loose ends, unexplained circumstances?" He saw a queer expression come over Barbara's face. "You do remember something!" he fired at her triumphantly.

"No. I—! That is, I remember something,—unexplained. But it didn't have anything to do with Eve. It was about Hal Crane, something that happened after his death."

"It might be pertinent. Anything that happened during that crucial time may have a bearing," McKeith pointed out.

"But this couldn't possibly have had any effect on Eve," she was embarrassed and reluctant. "And it's something I learned—confidentially—in the course of my work."

"Won't you let me be the judge of its importance?" he urged. "You know anything you tell me will be considered a professional confidence."

"Well, I suppose it doesn't matter now, anyway," she conceded doubtfully. "But it can't help you. Phil hoped Crane had left some notes or memos that might help in his investigation. He had Nelson subpoena Hal's personal effects, the contents of his pockets, desk drawers and so forth. I listed everything turned over to us and signed a receipt. Among the things was a packet of letters tied with a gold cord.

"I put Hal's things in the office safe and after Phil went through it all, he told me to return everything to the D. A. When I checked against the list, the packet of letters was missing, and Phil said he hadn't seen them. We never learned what happened to them."

"Who had access to the safe?" The doctor was intent.

"Just Phil and I."

"What sort of letters were they, did you get any idea?"

"They were in their envelopes It was the sort of stationery a woman would use, white with a blue border."

"And the handwriting? Was it familiar?"

"No—but it looked like a woman's."

"Would you recognize Eve's writing?"

"Why . . . no, I guess not." Barbara was taken completely by surprise. "She always dictated her memoranda to me. But I'm sure the letters weren't Eve's She couldn't have been involved in any way with *Crane*."

"Not with *Crane*," the doctor repeated, catching her inadvertent emphasis on the name. "But she was involved with someone else?"

"Oh, no—no! Not at all! I didn't mean it that way You haven't any right to draw such a conclusion." Barbara was dreadfully upset.

McKeith assumed full professional gravity. "Barbara, Eve's sanity, her whole future depends on my knowing every detail that can help me in her treatment If you withhold this information, you will be deliberately obstructing her recovery. It would be the same as murder."

"But I don't know anything really," Barbara cried in desperation. "You're making a mountain out of a molehill." She saw the skepticism in his eyes and floundered on miserably—"It was just a vague idea I had, something Cissie Humber said to me last summer. I never even met Freddie Humber. . . ."

"You think that Eve and Freddie . . ." McKeith began, mercilessly insistent, but Barbara, almost crying, interrupted at once.

"No, I'm sure Eve never looked at anyone but Phil. Cissie told me her marriage broke up because her husband fell in love with a beautiful woman, a married woman, who was a close friend of hers. . . . It could have been entirely one-sided—and I just wondered if . . . ! Eve was very beautiful—and she was Cissie's closest friend."

9.

"I'm GOING to be a great disappointment to you, Doctor!"

"Oh, come now, Mrs. Humber, must you be so utterly discouraging? Even before you know why I want to talk with you?" McKeith protested, smiling at the apparition confronting him.

Cissie's silver-fox cape, thrown over her chair back, provided a dramatic frame for her gold-colored wool dress. She wore with it a black turban, shot with metallic silver threads, repeating cleverly the coloring in her furs. Out of this background of magnificence, her big face loomed at him, her little eyes sprightly amused.

"Why, I thought I was being most cooperative, Doctor. Isn't it considered helpful to put a 'no thoroughfare' sign in front of a blind alley? You're chasing down one, you know, in trying to unearth some mysterious cause for Evelyn's dementia. I knew her as intimately as anyone could, who wasn't married to her, and there is not one single solitary fact to support your thesis. Scott agrees with me, and we both grew up with her."

Without allowing McKeith a wedge in her barrage of words, she suddenly darted off on another track. "Did you know Scott is going off half-cocked, trying to toss

poor Barbie out, without a by-your-leave? He has a reg-
. ular red-queen complex, shouting 'Off with her head, off
with her head.' at the least provocation."

"Yes, I know about this idea of his. It is decidedly
premature."

"Not only premature, but perhaps unnecessary." Cissie
leaned forward portentously. "Did it ever occur to you,
Doctor, that Evelyn might not want Phillip back?"

McKeith looked at her with quickened interest. "What
makes you think that?"

She delayed her answer, while she slowly and deliberately lighted a cigarette. The large, semi-opaque yellow stone in a barbaric ring on her finger caught the
flame and flared with a dull light. Her glance was enigmatic.

She wants to make the most of this dramatic suspense
she has built up, the doctor thought with amusement, and
how she enjoys her rôle of confidante to the Ladbrookes
and Minarys! Probably living it all vicariously, and trying to squeeze as much drama and excitement as possible
out of this situation. She is like a magpie too, darting
after every bit of stray information. There is a wealth
of intimate knowledge stored up in her, if only I knew
how to get at it.

Cissie blew out a column of smoke. "No, don't look so
hopeful, Doctor. I'm not going to reveal any skeleton in
the conjugal closet. But Eve was a person of strong
character, and in this matter she'll want to make her own
decision. . . . Do you think it's going to be much fun for
her to find out about Barbie and little Debbie? She is
going to suffer dreadfully, Doctor."

Bitterness sifted over Cissie's jaunty expression. "Why
do you want to drag her back to a life of pain and un-
happiness? It seems to me we're considering, not Eve's
happiness, but our own, in wanting her back at any cost.
If this had happened ten years ago, it would have been

wonderful . . . But now, it will smash up all three lives
—Eve's, Barbara's and Phil's. I don't see any answer for
them."

The doctor observed her reflectively. Her face reveals
passion and generosity, he thought. She undoubtedly lives
her life in all its aspects with the same grand gesture
with which she dresses—she would throw away that life,
or her fortune, for a friend. What she needs is a whole
brood of children to absorb the intense devotion of which
she is capable.

Cissie, looking like a brooding mastodon, continued
her unwontedly serious mood. "When Eve was taken
away, it tore the mainspring out of my life. We were
always very close, linked together from the beginning.
Two little babies, born the same year up there at Hillways. And both our mothers died before we were old
enough to remember them. My father died, too, when I
was eight, and since Judge Ladbrooke was my guardian
I was treated like one of the family, although I lived next
door with Aunt Polly."

Delighted at the flow of reminiscence regarding Eve's
childhood, McKeith listened, hoping to pick up something significant. But Cissie swung back to the present.
"When Eve was taken up here, it was one of the hardest
things I ever had to face, and believe me, I will do everything I can to help you, in spite of my misgivings. But,
frankly, Doctor, I don't see what I can tell you."

"I think that you—all of you who were close to Eve—"
he replied, "were so blinded by your love and loyalty
that you failed to perceive her behavior was abnormal.
That often happens, you know. It's very difficult for a
husband to face the fact that a beloved wife is a pathological case. He interprets her instability in any terms
except those of mental disease. He insists that she is just
sensitive, high-strung, feels things more deeply than other
people." The doctor sighed. "If relatives would only

recognize the symptoms of mental disorder in time, my job would be much easier."

"Eve *was* high-strung," Cissie admitted thoughtfully. "She lived in a different world, on a higher plane. For instance, most girls are fond of their fathers, but they rather take them for granted. And later when they marry, the bloom wears off shortly, and they realize husbands have their faults, but that no marriage is perfect, and they jog along happily enough, satisfied that life is like that, and that they're getting as much out of it as most. But Eve . . ."

She paused as if she were taking time out to sort through her memories, to separate the grain from the chaff. Or was she trying to decide how much she could safely reveal, how much she must conceal?

"You mean that Eve was a perfectionist, and her father and husband didn't fulfil her emotional demands?" McKeith asked.

"Oh, but they did!" she said. "Judge Ladbrooke simply worshiped Eve. Although his wife died when he was fairly young, he never looked at another woman. Eve took her mother's place in his life. Eve and her father adored each other. . . . And it was the same with Eve and Phil. She never thought of their relationship as the garden variety, husband-wife, sort of thing. To her it was something very special, something that happens only once in a thousand years. Like Heloise and Abelard. That's what makes it so cruel now. For her to learn about Barbie . . ."

"Did Phil feel the same way about it that Eve did?" McKeith asked, quickly veering Cissie back to retrospection.

"Oh, yes. They all centered their lives on her, Phil, and Judge Ladbrooke and Scott. Sometimes I felt it was almost too much for her, loving and being loved so intensely. The sword was too sharp for the scabbard. And then, too, she worked so hard to better conditions. It was an ideal, a mission, and she would use herself up until she was completely exhausted. Then she would get terribly depressed by the ugliness of life. Not her own life, but the hopelessness and misery of others. At these times she would sort of withdraw into herself. . . . You think all this indicates Eve was mentally unsound, don't you?" she asked, correctly interpreting the doctor's expression.

"It indicates emotional immaturity and an inability to face reality," he answered gravely. "She was living in a dream-world, a romantic, idealized, never-never land. It is important for me to know the cause of this flight from reality. Was she suffering from a frustration in her relationships, or a sense of guilt?"

"You doctors see only one part of life," Cissie interrupted vehemently. "You try to analyze the mind, but the soul escapes you altogether. Because the average human being isn't capable of sustaining an ideal relationship, you think anyone with a superior nature must be insane. . . . Eve didn't escape from reality, she made her dream real. Like all poetic souls she created beauty, gave it reality. If that is insanity, then Beethoven, and Da Vinci and Shakespeare were all insane. . . . Eve's relationships *were* ideal, and her life was happy. I was with her right up to the very day she broke down, and I didn't see the slightest indication that she had any frustrations, that anything was wrong with her personal life."

McKeith took up the folder containing Evelyn's record and turned to the notes he had made when first called in on the case. "You know, that last day—the day she broke down—becomes increasingly significant. I know you don't agree, but I'm convinced that Eve's personality was abnormal, and had been for some time. However, like a weak swimmer, she was able to keep afloat as long as the water was calm. Then a sudden storm caught her and she went under quickly. I think something happened that day she went to see Dr Gray. Something new and unexpected that precipitated her collapse."

"Well, you know I'm your star witness, Doctor. I drove her into town that day in my car."

McKeith wondered if there was defiance in her tone, or if he had only imagined it. "When you called for her, was she overly excited?"

"I think blithe is the word for her mood that day," Cissie answered, after a reminiscent pause. "She was happy to be out and interested in everything we saw— that the bridal wreath was budding in the Newmans' yard and that Mrs. Hardesty's black iris had finally bloomed after three years of trying—that sort of thing. If you had been with us, Dr. McKeith, I'm sure you could have read nothing ominous into her innocent chatter."

Again her manner baffled him. Was she slightly on the defensive, or answering readily in a spirit of cooperation?

He said, "You went up to Gray's office with her, I remember, and Gray found her in good shape. After that were you with her until you started back?"

"Yes—except when she went up to Phil's office. She wanted to look in on him for a minute and I couldn't find a parking place, so I dropped her and circled the block. She was waiting when I came around and said that no one was in the office."

"Did she seem . . ." McKeith began, but Cissie cut him off.

"The answer is No! Eve acted exactly as usual when she climbed into the car. She said that in spite of the buds on her magnolia tree, she hadn't realized spring was really here until she saw the new hats going up and down the street, and that now she knew why spring was called the silly season. But that she had caught the fever, too, and was going on an orgy of shopping and soon."

Can she possibly remember so well a casual conversa-

tion of ten years ago? the psychiatrist wondered, as Cissie's words flowed spontaneously on.

"No more ingénue clothes for her," she said. "The
men in her family wanted to keep her in ruffles and rib-
bons like an ante-bellum girl. They had a perfect passion
for pink and pale blue. But now that she was a mother
and a matron, she was going to buy herself the most suave
and sophisticated black suit she could find, and a chartreuse blouse to go with it. She deplored the fact that
ostrich plumes weren't worn any more, for nothing else
was quite so woman-of-the-world. She longed for a large
black hat, dripping with plumy feathers that would make
her feel like Madame Bovary."

The memory of that last jaunt with Eve was almost
too much for Cissie. Her eyes moistened and the tenderness in her voice wavered toward poignancy. But she
pulled herself up short.

"If that girl was hiding a secret disturbance, she was
the world's best actress. She prattled on about clothes
and we had fun together all the way home. When I let
her out at her doorstep, she noticed the French doors in
her father's study were open and decided to run in and
tell him what Dr. Gray had said. She waved to me and
started up the hill to her father's house. I drove on in
the opposite direction to my home." She hesitated, came
to a full stop with instinctive dramatic timing, and then
said, impressively, "And I did not see Eve again for over
ten years, until that day last June when we came here for
the first experiment with metrazol."

The doctor fingered his notes and frowned. "She went
up to her father's house, but apparently no one up there
saw her at all. And then Julia met her as she came into
her own home, barely able to walk. It is simply incredible." He closed Eve's folder and pushed it aside. "It
won't wash. It couldn't have just happened. There was
something under the surface that we have to find.

"Cissie," he dropped naturally into intimate use of her name, "could Eve have been more disturbed over Crane's death and the mess Phillip was in at the office than you realized?"

"Eve was much too sensible a person to lose her mind because her husband's assistant was killed or her husband was criticized in the press. As you just said, Doctor, it won't wash."

They sat in the silence of mutual bafflement for a moment and then the doctor probed cautiously. "Cissie, wasn't it around this time that you got your divorce? You know everything that happened in the vicinity of my patient may be part of the pattern."

She sat up a little straighter, and though she replied with dignity, there was an imperious note in her voice, a warning to trespass no further. "I had been separated from my husband for some little time—almost a year, before Eve's illness. We separated because of mutual incompatibility. I can't believe it affected Eve in any way."

There was skepticism and speculation in the doctor's gaze, but Cissie returned his look imperturbably. Finally, he asked softly, "Why are you concealing the truth from me, Cissie? There was another woman involved, wasn't there?"

The stolidity of her face absorbed his question without emotion. She rose quietly, and picking up her cape, drew it about her shoulders. Her voice was final. "I do not see, Dr. McKeith, how this impertinent gossip about my private life has any relevancy to your diagnosis. I am sorry that I have been of so little assistance to you, but I warned you at the start that I knew nothing that would help."

"Wait a minute, Cissie." He laid a restraining hand on her arm. "A woman's whole life is at stake. I thought you loved Eve,—would do anything to help her." When

his plea was rejected by the impassivity of her face, he
changed his tactics. "Wouldn't you prefer to tell me the
whole story yourself? I can find out from others, you
know . ."

She whirled on him, instantly. "That is where you are
wrong. No one knows anything about it No one can
possibly tell you . ." Bewilderment struck her midway
of her thought. "How did you possibly learn? . . . There
isn't anyone who . Oh, I begin to see. . . . Barbara! . . .
Did you get this from Barbie? But why should she tell
you . . ?"

Cissie turned back to her chair and flung off her cape.
"I suppose I will have to tell you about it, or you will go
around stirring up speculation among all my friends,
none of whom knows anything."

She sat down in exasperation. "Very well!" She pelted
him with a quick staccato. "In the first place there wasn't
any 'other woman,'—that is, in the conventional sense.
There isn't really anything to tell. The whole episode
was just a product, you might say, of Freddie's personality. It is a good thing you are a psychiatrist. My story
wouldn't make sense to anyone else."

"In my time, I've made sense of a good many apparently senseless things, Cissie," he remarked encouragingly.

She pulled a black enamel case from her bag and, snapping on the attached lighter, nervously lit a cigarette.
She smoked for a few minutes, while she thought out what
she wanted to say. Her voice, when she began, was as detached as though she were reading paragraphs from the
biography of an unknown.

"Freddie was a very unfortunate little boy. His mother
was a widow and he was her one interest in life. When
he was away from her, the curtain went down, the play
stopped, and she sat there empty handed waiting for him
to return and ring up the curtain again. I guess you have

run across cases like that. Child-eating mothers, I believe they are called."

McKeith nodded. "There is a lot of cannibalism in
modern love—especially mother love. We get the end results up here, all too frequently."

"Freddie had all the gregarious instincts of a healthy
little boy, but she never gave him a chance to play with
other children. He couldn't break away. She held him
by a sense of duty, gratitude for all she had done for him,
that sort of thing. Naturally he grew up to be a queer,
odd person,—we called him an egg.

"He was in our class at high school. We had a gay
crowd, but Freddie was never one of us. All during those
years he was miserably unhappy. He wanted to be like
us, but he didn't know how. He was outside, looking in."

"But you understood him, Cissie? You helped him
find himself?" McKeith eased her over a rough spot.

"It was just by a fluke that I got to know him. In our
last semester, our history teacher assigned projects to us
in groups of two, and I was teamed with Freddie. We
had to go down to the library to get materials, and work
up our paper after hours. That was how I became his
friend, his first and only friend.

"But I was more than that." Cissie's voice filtered with
difficulty through a closure in her throat. "To him I was
an absolutely fascinating and glamorous creature. I
moved easily and freely in that world from which he was
excluded. I had friends and my own house and servants
—I knew my way about. I was everything that he wanted
to be, and he thought I was wonderful. We were married
the next year."

Cissie stubbed out her cigarette, and swallowed hard.
"Have you ever seen those Japanese toys, little tight
matchsticks of paper that you drop in a glass of water?
They unfold and open out until the whole glass is filled
with a brilliant flower or tree. It was like that with

Freddie. His personality opened up after our marriage."

McKeith was bothered by something familiar in Cissie's gesture and expression. He had seen that long nose, those small ecru eyes illumined with emotion, elsewhere, in other guise. But he couldn't place it now.

The flatness had imperceptibly gone out of her voice, now filled with a terrible tenderness. "Freddie became one of the most popular members of our group. You see the things that had made up the social round for us for a good many years, were all wonderful discoveries to him. A swimming party, a dance at the club, were exciting adventures, and his fresh enjoyment of everything was infectious. This same naïve delight of his helped him at the office, too. The men liked him and he had several rapid promotions."

Cissie paused and moistened her dry lips with her tongue. She had reached the difficult part of her story, and was stuck there. Suddenly she rose, and walking over to the window, leaned against it, her eyes on the dismal autumn landscape. With her back turned to the doctor, she said, with forced irony, "Enter, the 'other woman.' Shall we be thoroughly melodramatic and call her Madame X? . . . I'm not telling you her name, and that is final."

"Agreed!" The doctor concurred, playing up to her mood. "Enter, then, Madame X."

"She was what men call 'a delightful woman.' She was married, but her coquetry was so constant and natural it was practically automatic. When she was with anything masculine, old or young, fat or thin, she couldn't so much as say Good Morning, without making him realize that he was a dashing gent and she was a desirable woman.

"Oh, she wasn't a cheap flirt." Although Cissie strained to keep her voice facetiously ironical, the underlying acid all but etched her words into the windowpane. "She flirted in the most delicate and ladylike manner. She had learned in the cradle that it was woman's chief duty to be charming, so she charmed as though fulfilling a social obligation. And the men loved it, her pretty, romantic approach. They understood that she was a pleasure— like listening to a Chopin waltz, or drinking a glass of Tokay—a passing beauty of the moment, not an invitation."

"I know the type." McKeith's voice was bleak. "All a teasing enjoyment of their own power of allure, with nothing of substance to offer. Such women are will-o'-the-wisps to men who love them."

Cissie, absorbed in painful memory, failed to perceive the bitterness seeping from him, from the hard core of an old hurt. With her head still averted she went on unheeding.

"But Freddie! . . . Poor Freddie had no immunity. No one had ever flirted with him before. He was a sitting target. . . . It was all terribly innocent of course. Just sitting out a dance at the club, chatting in a corner at a cocktail party . . . nothing for anyone else to notice. But she smilingly initiated him to the delights of provocative, feminine beauty. She showed him what life was all about, what a woman could offer to a man—and then he had to come home to me. It took the heart right out of our marriage. . . . Oh, Freddie was loyal! If it had been my wish he would be living with me today—going through husbandly gestures. But I pitied him too much for that."

Cissie turned back toward McKeith, her eyes as desolate as the garden at which she had been staring. "I went off alone on a Caribbean cruise. Perhaps I hoped that when I returned . . . ! But as Ethel Barrymore once remarked,—'You can't turn yesterday's cold mutton into today's spring lamb chops.'" Her grotesquely ugly face was a mask of tragedy, incorporating all the agony of those who suffer powerfully. "When I came home, I found Freddie had asked for, and received, a transfer to the New York office. . . . We were good friends,—nothing more, so after a while we were divorced."

"And Madame X . . . ?"

"Madame X never had an inkling the casual exercise of her charms had had anything to do with it," Cissie asserted positively, not allowing him to put the question. "No one else guessed the truth either. They just thought Freddie and I had been an ill-matched pair."

"But Eve was so close to you. She must have seen how you were hurt."

"I told her I'd discovered I wasn't the type for marriage," Cissie said proudly. "I didn't want pity . . . and I didn't need sympathy." She tried to laugh at herself. "I'm a pretty rugged piece of goods—built for durability —if not for love."

She held the doctor's scrutiny with steady eyes for a moment, and then with a shrug of her shoulder, she tossed off her somberness. "I don't know what earthly good it has been to you to listen to my little tragi-comedy—or did you think I'd be better off with some of the scar tissue scraped off my heart? . . . Well, your therapeutics didn't work. I feel like hell."

McKeith was on his feet in an instant, his face filled with concern.

"My dear Cissie . . . !"

"Oh, I'll make out," she cut him short. "I was just taking a dig at you psychiatrists with your emotional cathartics." Her smile was sterling. "I'm a rubber ball, you know. The harder you hit me, the higher I bounce. No harm done."

She picked up her cape and threw it about her wide shoulders. As her chin sought its dauntless angle, a vague recollection of McKeith's crystallized. Throughout the interview he had been tormented by something familiar, yet unplaceable in her features and mood. It came to him now, as she took her departure. The mourn-

ful, long-nosed visage of Chaliapin, in his superb por-
trayal of Don Quixote.

Don Quixote, alight with the emotion and vision of
chivalry, going out to charge at windmills in an unsym-
pathetic age. This woman, with her awkward vulnerable-
ness, carried the same underlying melancholy beneath her
gallantry. She, too, was filled with the necessity for
heroic acts in a world heedless of her gifts.

10.

His appointments over for the day, McKeith decided
that the aftereffects of the flu justified an unaccustomed
afternoon pick-me-up. Returning with glass in hand
from his white-tiled surgery, he was surprised to notice
how dark his office looked. It was only 4:30, but the low-
ering weather had broken into a dreary rain which sucked
the light from the sky. He crossed the shadowy room to
the couch and sat with his head resting against the back,
his feet stretched toward the embers in the fireplace.

His spirits sagged from more than the fatigue of recent
illness and the weariness of overwork. He was oppressed
by a pervasive sadness.

McKeith had had many beautiful women for patients
during his years of practice, and had developed a great
tolerance for their waywardness. He understood that
beauty was a facet of the personality and, like other

human attributes, it languished if it were not used. These lovely women who came to him in their trouble had been driven by an impelling law of nature. They were victims of social forces that ran counter to instinctive needs.

But this thing that he suspected! Cissie and her one poor love! He could be jumping at conclusions, though. . . Still, Eve must have been involved in some sort of mess, for a woman doesn't develop dementia over trifles. . . . And silence over details crucial to her recovery would be a terrible revenge. It was inconceivable that there wasn't someone who knew something of what had happened to her,—someone who must hate her intensely.

The wood that had crackled so cheerfully in the hearth was now a pile of ashes, except for one dull ember that blinked at him like a malignant eye from the dead mass. He sighed and swallowed the rest of his whisky. Setting his glass carelessly on the floor, he crossed over to his desk, switched on the light and turned off the dictaphone.

He had just seated himself, when the door was pushed silently ajar and Dr. Castleman stuck his dark head around the opening. Seeing that McKeith was not engaged, he came into the room in a short-sleeved white doctor's tunic, like an alert wire-haired terrier.

"Finished with the bunch of them, Mac?" He walked across and throwing one leg over the corner of the desk, pulled himself to an easy perch. "Get anything?"

"Not much!" For a moment McKeith found himself resenting the youth and resilience that had come into the room. But time would soon even the score. In a few more years, Marc would feel as fagged as he did at the end of the afternoon.

He smiled at his young colleague and tilted back in his swivel chair. "I picked up a few leads. They're pretty vague though. I didn't get anything specific enough to help me tomorrow. Eve's family idealize her to the extent that even now they can't realize her behavior was abnormal . . . or else they are joined in a conspiracy of silence. And they're sticking to it even though they know it will block her recovery."

"It certainly is a darn queer situation," Castleman said, frowning. "Obviously her condition developed so gradually her deterioration wasn't perceptible to her family, until she went into a tailspin. What could have set her off that way all of a sudden?"

"That's what I've been trying to find out," McKeith answered. "I've pinned it down to the day she went into town, the first and only time she was out of the house after the baby's birth. Cissie drove her in and she was apparently all right down in Gray's office. At least her pulse and blood pressure were normal. No signs of excitement then. It narrows down to three points where something might have happened. She stopped at her husband's office. She might have stumbled in on something there that upset her. Either Phil or Barbara could have talked with her. There's no way of checking."

"Or they could have both been in the office when Eve came in," Castleman suggested. "And if she discovered something that shocked her into collapse, they could say they hadn't seen her at all,—since she wasn't able to speak for herself, by the time you began to ask questions."

"But according to Cissie, Eve was undisturbed when she came out. She told Cissie no one was in the office," McKeith replied. "Of course Eve might have been covering up, trying to conceal something from Cissie. Or Cissie may be backing up Phil's and Barbara's story, for some reason not clear to me."

"Or Cissie may have invented the whole episode. Goodness knows why!" Marc said. "She's a completely uninhibited, unpredictable female."

"Also according to Cissie, Eve was all right when she reached home and decided to go over to her father's house," McKeith went on. "However, no one at the Ladbrookes admitted to seeing her that afternoon. Her father said he wasn't in his study at that time,—and both Scott and Madeleine said they were away from home. . . . Of course, it's probably struck you, that we have only Cissie's word for most of this."

Castleman laughed, ruefully. "We've narrowed it down until it's wide open. Any of them could have precipitated her disturbance that afternoon—Phil, Barbara, Cissie or the Ladbrookes. I wish we could psychoanalyze them instead of the patient."

"As a matter of fact, I uncovered a lot of queer twists and quirks in these people this afternoon," McKeith remarked. "The only normal ones seem to be Phillip and Barbara Minary—and they are in an abnormal situation."

"And the screwiest one of the lot is the Humber—or Madeleine—or Scott," Marc grinned. "Has Scott discussed this business of a divorce with you? What's Minary going to do about it, do you know?"

"He hasn't mentioned the subject to me, but from Barbara's attitude, I gather he hasn't told anyone what he intends to do. There is no reason why he should commit himself now, when Eve may not recover sufficiently to leave here after all. He's taking the wisest course in waiting. . . . However, I think he hasn't decided yet. He acts like a man holding on to himself tight, just meeting each moment as it comes. He's in the devil of a situation."

"Too bad he isn't a Mormon." Marc pulled a pack of cigarettes from his pants pocket. With a manipulation of the fingers of one hand, he shot out a cigarette and caught it deftly in mid-air. "Still, it shouldn't be so hard for him to make up his mind. Like choosing between filet mignon or corned beef and cabbage." .

"You forget that some men prefer corned beef," McKeith remarked dryly.

"You're young yet, Marc. You still judge a woman by her face value."

He tilted farther back in his chair, clasping his hands behind his neck. "I suppose no people in history have bred more beautiful women than the American. And we're hipped on feminine beauty. Look at our advertising, our photo magazines, the movies! We make a major industry of cosmetics and beauty devices,—and our women *are* seductive. But they're nothing except artful contrivances for arousing masculine passion. They don't know how to satisfy."

Castleman paused with his cigarette brought halfway to his mouth, surprised at the other's vehemence. Oblivious of Marc for the moment, McKeith went on bitterly, "None of them knows how to give herself to a man. The complexities of their personalities, their oversensitive emotions, their idealizations and intellectualisms come between them and the essential function of woman. They're all overcivilized. . . . These modern women!"

Abruptly he dropped his pet theme, and looked at Marc with shrewd eyes. "Now, I've noticed Barbara when she is with her husband. There is a real bond there. Not obvious to everyone, but the tie between those two is real. Barbara Minary has something modern women have lost. There's nothing complex about her. She has a simple nature. . . . Yes, that's it. She is a primitive person. She is still close to the earth. There is refreshment and renewal in her."

Remembering Mrs. McKeith, Marc gave the older man a covert glance of quick sympathy. Pulling out a kitchen match, he drew it loudly across the sole of his shoe and brought it up to his cigarette. When he had it going, he took it from his mouth to remark, "Madeleine Ladbrooke is one of your overcivilized women. She has everything a pin-up girl has got, and there is nothing wrong with my masculine reflexes. But when I'm with her, my eye takes it all in and approves, and my pulse doesn't notice a thing,—just goes along at a comfortable dogtrot. She certainly inhibits."

"It's because she is absolutely empty inside. She has had everything bred out of her." McKeith was smiling again. "I doubt she is ever disturbed by even the minor emotions. Can you imagine her irritated or flustered? It's probably a good thing, though, that she's just a paper doll. I imagine a red-blooded woman would find it rather trying to have Scott Ladbrooke for a husband."

"Scott has plenty of emotion. He generates enough for two."

"Yes, but it goes in just one direction, toward Evelyn. He sat beside his wife in my office this afternoon and told me he loved his sister more than anything in the world."

"He certainly is a devoted brother. I'm surprised you didn't get something significant from him this afternoon. He probably understands Eve better than anyone and he'd move heaven and earth to have her well again. Of course, he's worked himself into a state over this business of a divorce. He's blind to anything else. I guess he has a one-track mind."

"I'm not so sure that explains Scott's attitude," McKeith replied, slowly. "You know, I've been wondering if all that isn't just a smoke screen. I wonder if he really wants Eve back! He has made a regular fetish of her—those daily visits for ten years and all. It was abnormal. When you suggested metrazol, he took it up enthusiastically— but he acts like a man with a compulsion neurosis."

"Yes, he does. I see what you're driving at." Castleman's professional enthusiasm gave him the look of a hound on the scent. "Like Freud's case of the man who wanted his wife dead, but wouldn't admit it even to himself, and went bankrupt paying for extravagant treatments for her hopeless disease,—as a sop to his conscience. . . . You think Scott was emotionally dependent, . . . and wants to break loose?"

"Could be," McKeith answered thoughtfully. "It might

be a case of ambivalence. The dividing line between hate and love is mighty thin. He could love Eve so much he hates her. . . ."

"And there might be a guilt feeling behind his compulsion, if he felt responsible for her madness. He would be driven to do everything for her,—except tell us the things that would bring about a cure." Marc's eager mind was racing down the trail.

"And, on the other hand," McKeith smiled, "he may be just a devoted brother with a one-track mind. We can't tell without an analytic study of him. We don't know enough about his emotional patterns. Certainly, Madeleine is just an accessory to his life, not part of the main design. I'm curious how he ever came to marry her. . . . However, I'm forgetting something about Madeleine. I did discover an emotion playing about in her today. She very definitely does not like Eve. She is concealing it carefully. I couldn't get even a hint as to what was back of her attitude,—but her aversion, almost abhorrence, makes me feel we're going to uncover something pretty—bad. . . . However, it may be exaggerated feeling, just aroused Boston Puritanism."

"Why on earth should Madeleine's puritanical instincts get het up over Eve Minary?" Marc was flabbergasted.

"Well, it's quite a story. Cissie had a tale to tell, or rather I wrung one out of her, this afternoon, and Barbara gave me a few leads, too. It's all in there." McKeith waved toward the cabinet that concealed the dictaphone recorder. "As soon as Miss Evans gets it typed up, I wish you would go over it and we can swap impressions."

Marc gave a low whistle of surprise at the other doctor's implications. "Looks like you've got on to something?"

"Well, I'm not sure. It's all pretty vague—just some hints. But Eve may have been something of a Circe. I got a new slant on her personality. If it's true, it opens up a whole new approach to the problem. There's also some indication that a father-fixation may be at the root of Eve's trouble. In fact, Marc, if you can find time, you might run through these last records tonight. I would like to discuss the whole thing with you before tomorrow. I really got very little from this afternoon's interviews and I'm going to have to go at things blind in the morning. I've got to get her talking. . . . If she just closes up and draws back into herself, we're sunk."

"Of course I'll go over the records tonight, Mac. It's been a privilege to work on this with you."

"My chief hope is the fact that Eve feels very close to me," the older psychiatrist continued. "I'll be with her when she goes under this afternoon, and the first person she sees when she comes out of it in the morning. I'll try to get transference. If I can make her feel she can trust me absolutely, that there is nothing she can't tell me, I'll be able to pull her out of it. If it doesn't work . . ." He shrugged his shoulders.

"I think it *will* work." Castleman's sincerity was spread over his keen face. "Especially in a case like this—and with a woman. I think Eve will talk to you in the morning—at least enough to let you know where you are. By this time tomorrow you'll have the answer to a lot of things." He glanced at his watch. "It's nearly five,—I'd better be getting upstairs."

"You go on," McKeith told him. "I'll bring the patient up."

11.

McKeith, parting with Castleman in the lobby, turned into the south wing. The little redhead was still on duty. Preoccupied, the doctor asked curtly, "Has Schmeiser prepared Mrs. Minary for her five-o'clock treatment?"

"Why, no, I don't think she has come down yet, Doctor."

"Well send her in right away. It's nearly five now," he told her with irritable impatience, and walked on down the corridor.

The door to Evelyn's suite stood open. One floor lamp was lit against the early dusk and Eve was sitting in the pool of light with her head resting against the back of the brown upholstered easy-chair, her hands relaxed in her lap. Unless her attention was aroused, she would sit that way for hours, in a dreamy absent state. She was wearing her pinkish-beige dress with the broad suede belt of a deeper rose. A cluster of large chrysanthemums mingled yellow with rosy bronze in a vase on the table beside her.

When McKeith approached she looked up, and her whole face brightened with the radiant, uninhibited smile of childhood. "Dr. Mac."

"Hello, Eve." He came into the room, and picking up one of her soft little hands, felt for the pulse. Satisfied at the steady throb, he released her wrist and said, "How grand you look today! That's a very pretty dress. It's new, isn't it?"

She nodded, smiling with naïve pleasure.

"It must be a present," he continued. "Who brought it to you?"

Her eyes clouded with perplexity. After a struggle to remember, she looked appealingly to him for help.

"Did you have many visitors today?" he prompted.

"Yes, Cissie was here . . . and, oh, lots of others. All my friends came to see me this afternoon."

"But what about this morning? Who always comes to see you every day?"

". . . Scott . . . and Phillip." Slowly she dredged up the names. Out of sight was out of mind for her.

"And did one of them bring you a present? This pretty new dress?"

"Yes,—yes." She looked excited. This was quite a game. "Scott did. Scott brought it." She was triumphant.

"Well, that's fine. And it is very nice to have him bring you pretty clothes. But how would you like to go in town yourself and buy a lot of new things?"

"Oh, yes. Let's do that. Right away." She clasped her hands together in a childish gesture, her eyes dancing with eagerness. "When? Can we go now?"

"You are not quite well yet, you know. We'll go just as soon as you are better. After one more treatment. We're going upstairs now, and put you to sleep. When you wake up tomorrow you'll be well again. You'll soon be able to go home." He spoke coaxingly.

But Eve shrank back in her chair, her face puckering into a grimace of anguished protest. The pain and shock of metrazol was one memory that stayed with her. "No . . . no! I don't want to get well. I don't want to go upstairs. I won't go, I won't go!" She broke into the sobs of gathering hysteria.

The doctor seized both of her hands in his. "Eve . . . listen to me, darling. Look at me, Eve. You trust me, don't you, dear?" He waited until she looked up at him, her eyes filled with tears. "I'll make you well again. I'll be with you every minute. I won't leave you. I'll take care of you and when you wake up tomorrow you'll tell me everything that's wrong. I am your friend. I'll make it come right for you. You believe me, don't you, Eve?"

She nodded reluctantly, struggling between her fear of pain and the magnetism of the doctor.

"Now, just a minute, I'm going to give you something to make you feel better." McKeith stepped into the bathroom and half-filled a glass with water. He took a small vial from his pocket, and extracting a brown tablet, dropped it in and stirred it until it had dissolved.

He came back to Eve. "Here, darling, drink this."

She accepted the glass docilely, but after the first sip she made a wry grimace and thrust it away.

"Come on, Eve. Drink it down. That's a good girl." She looked at the doctor a moment in rebellion, but at the steady command she saw in his eyes, she wavered and then drank it down obediently.

"That's just fine. That's my girl." He took the empty glass back to the bathroom, rinsed it out and left it inverted on the washstand. "You feel better already, don't you?" he asked. "And now we'll take a little ride, a little trip upstairs. Here's Miss Schmeiser to get you dressed for the buggy-ride. I'll wait for you right outside." With a little reassuring pat on her shoulder he left the room, closing the door behind him.

Lighting a cigarette, he stood waiting in the hall. The overhead lights spaced down the length of the corridor were reflected dismally from the shining floor. It was that in-between time, when the afternoon is over and the night has not yet begun. There was always a restlessness in the hospital at this hour. The day shift were preparing to go off duty, hurrying with last-minute tasks as they cast surreptitious glances at the clock. It was the last mile of the day, when nerves surrendered to weariness.

A bad time to have to go through a thing like this metrazol treatment. But it was the best time for the patient. After the injection she would go off into a deep sleep of exhaustion and wake late in the morning ready for therapy.

All the same it was a strain on the doctors to go through the ordeal at the tag end of the day,—that is on a middle-aged doctor, McKeith thought gloomily. The last light of the afternoon still clung to the hall, blurring the radiance of the electric bulbs in their frosted shades. He hated this twilit period. Perhaps because it was explicit of his own sad and restless mood. It gathered into itself and reflected back his frustration and wistfulness. His life was in phase with the day. Youth was gone, but night had not fully arrived,—and some of the glow of afternoon still lingered in his blood.

He dropped his half-smoked cigarette on the floor and stepped on it, grinding it out with quick violence. But a moment later, in keyed-up restlessness, he pulled out another cigarette. Before he could light it, Eve's door opened, and he turned toward it nervously.

Eve's pretty clothes had been exchanged for that white livery, so unfortunately like a shroud, in which hospitals wrap up victims before an operation. McKeith placed his arm encouragingly around her and helped her into the waiting wheel chair. "Now, here we go."

Eve's face was white and set and her eyes were frightened. "Make it snappy, now," McKeith told the nurse, and she fairly raced the chair through the south wing, across the lobby and into the elevator. On the upper floor they hurried out again and into the treatment room.

Castleman and two orderlies were waiting in readiness. Evelyn was lifted quickly onto the bed. She struggled frantically as they strapped her down, turning panic-stricken eyes to McKeith in mute appeal. He took his place by her side and picked up her hand.

The barrel of the syringe Miss Schmeiser handed over

was much larger than the one they had first used. Castleman had had to step up the dosage with each treatment.

He made the injection, and Eve's body sprang instantly into a raised bow. Only her heels and head touched the bed, as those dreadful cries broke out.

McKeith closed his eyes, and bent over her wrist. "Thank God this is the last one," he thought to himself.

Suddenly he tensed, all of himself concentrated for the moment in his fingertips. Then he glanced quickly at Eve. She lay limp, with blue lips, drawing shallow gasps of breath through her open mouth. He looked over at Castleman, his eyes telegraphing a message. Castleman reached instantly into the dressing tray and picked up adrenalin and a small hypo.

McKeith fired a rapid staccato at the nurse. "See if Peterson is still here! Get him at once! Wait,—have them send up oxygen and hot blankets. . . . And we'll need another nurse. Hurry now!"

Miss Schmeiser rushed out of the room on flying feet and down the corridor to the telephone at the floor desk.

In a moment over the loud-speaker system came the call. "Dr. Peterson. . . . Dr. Peterson. . . . Dr. Peterson wanted in Room 435. . . . Dr. Peterson. . . . Room 435."

A quickening of tempo, an urgency, ran like quicksilver through the hospital. Nurses glanced up with startled faces, and then whispered together in excited groups. The building stirred with life as its emergency machinery was set in motion.

Down in the basement an orderly trundled an oxygen tank out of the laboratory and pushed it hurriedly toward the elevator. Two nurses pulled blankets from the hot-box, piled them on a portable table, and ran it rapidly to Room 435. The director of nurses started breathlessly for the fourth floor. A stream of hurrying, life-saving helpers converged on the room where Eve lay.

Down in the lobby, the receptionist heard the message of the loud-speaker and running outdoors, caught Dr. Peterson as he was starting up his car. He was a heart specialist from the city and had been in to see an unfortunate schizophrenic who combined thrombosis with his psychotic condition.

By the time Peterson, in hat and overcoat, reached Room 435, there had been a slight lessening of tension. The two doctors and their aides were still working doggedly on, but the moment for hope had passed.

Peterson examined the patient carefully and shook his head. Castleman and McKeith were alternating with artificial respiration. They kept at it as the moments crawled slowly on.

After awhile, the chief nurse slipped quietly away, certain that her services would not be needed. A half-hour later, Peterson shrugged his shoulders, picked up his bag and stepped out in the hall for a cigarette while he waited. Eventually Castleman joined him.

McKeith was the last to admit defeat. Finally he straightened up, and looked down at Eve, his face ravaged. Then, gently he picked up her hands and laid them one over the other on her breast.

Castleman came back quietly into the room. McKeith didn't look up. Marc glanced at him and saw that he was taking it hard. He felt shaken up himself. It had been so entirely unexpected. His hands were trembling slightly.

He moved over beside the older man. They stood in silence looking down with mingled emotion at the face of the woman on the bed.

They had worked over her for so many months. By degrees, at such a cost of suffering, they had pulled her slowly up from the depths of non-being into which she had plunged years before. They had urged and stimulated that awakening mind,—forcing it back to a life it was reluctant to resume. They had probed into her past,—

seeking from her memory and from her friends the answer to the enigma of her personality. They had thought they were almost there.

But Eve had eluded them, and they could pursue her no further. She had withdrawn into the final retreat, taking her secrets with her.

PART THREE

MARC CASTLEMAN
October 27 - November 4, 1943

12.

IT HAD BEEN raining hard that afternoon when Evelyn Minary died, but by nine o'clock the downpour had tapered off to a drizzle. It was a raw and cheerless night. No lights showed from the front of the Ladbrooke home. Its dark façade was the face of a house in mourning. As he approached it, Marc Castleman's misgiving deepened.

Scott had shown unexpected control that afternoon when he came down to the hospital after Eve's death. Probably numbed by shock. But he might be in a state of collapse now, Marc realized,—and his mission was awkward enough at the best.

He went up the steps and pushed the bell button. He could hear no answering ring from within, but in a moment a subdued light came on behind the door. It was opened by an old negro in a white coat. He was trembling slightly as though seen by wavering candlelight, and his voice had a matching quaver. "Good evening, suh!"

"Good evening. I am Dr. Castleman from Oaklawn. Is Mr. Ladbrooke still up?"

"Yes, suh. Mr. Scott, he is in back. Please to come in, suh."

Marc stepped inside, and found that he was in a large center hall, only partially lit by a small lamp. On either side of him dark arches yawned into unlighted rooms. Ahead he could make out the shadow of a stairway. From far down the hall the ghost of a light came through an open door. The atmosphere hung heavy with the feeling of recent death.

The darky spoke in a hushed tone. "I'll take your coat, please, suh."

Breaking suddenly into the quiet of the house, the voice that came from the end room, although husky and low-pitched, was startlingly distinct.

"Madeleine. . . . you are all I have. . . . now that she is gone."

There was a little silence, a rustle of taffeta, and an answering woman's voice crowded with emotion. Marc caught an exultant note underlying its passionate tenderness.

He turned in embarrassment to the servant. "Will you let Mr. Ladbrooke know I'm here?"

"Yes, suh. Yes, suh." The old man wavered down the hall and disappeared into the room at the end. Marc heard a low murmur of voices and then the darky returned. "Mr. Scott would like for you to come on back, suh."

The fire in the study gave more light than the one shaded lamp. Its glow fell on Scott, and in the dimness, Marc could scarcely see Madeleine in her long black house coat. Her face and hands were pale blurs of white against the dark, but her glittering eyes were like reflections of the coals in the fireplace.

Scott rose and offered his hand. "It was good of you to come and see me, Dr. Castleman. I appreciate your kindness."

"I want you to know that you have our sympathy, Mr. Ladbrooke. We regret deeply what happened this after noon. It was totally unexpected. If we'd had any idea, we would have warned you. But we thought, at this stage, she was out of danger."

"You did everything you could, Castleman. We knew the risk we were running before we started. And I'm not sorry we tried. If she couldn't get well, it's better this way. However, coming when it did, it has been a shock. Her recovery was so near—we almost had her back. . . . But it couldn't be helped. It is just one of those things."

"It is a thing I don't understand though, Mr. Ladbrooke. In other fatal cases, the patients died because they couldn't tolerate metrazol, and they died at the first injection. But Eve's system reacted beautifully all these months. There was no reason at all for her sudden inability to assimilate the drug."

"Don't worry over it, doctor. You mustn't blame yourself. . . . It just wasn't in the cards for Eve to come through."

"But it's possible her death could have been avoided. Metrazol is still in the experimental stage. We have run into something new here, an unknown factor. . . . Of course, Eve received injections longer than any other recorded case. One of her vital organs may have undergone a slow atrophy in reaction to repeated doses of metrazol, or the glands could have been affected in a way that didn't show up on our tests. A poisonous by-product may have built up in her bloodstream. . . . An autopsy would give us the answer to a lot of things, Mr. Ladbrooke."

"An autopsy!" Scott's head jerked up, and he stared incredulously at Castleman. "An autopsy on Eve! My God! . . . No, I don't want that, doctor. What difference does it make now, how she died? A post-mortem won't bring her back."

"It won't bring her back, Ladbrooke, but it may save other lives." The young doctor leaned close in eager pleading. "Some doctors are still afraid to use metrazol. Others will go ahead . . . and some of their patients will die, as Eve has just died, because we don't know enough, yet, about the effect of repeated doses. The only way we can make any advance is through the study of cases like Eve's. . . . Don't you think that Eve herself would have wanted. . . ."

"No," Scott interrupted with finality. "I won't let you cut up . . . Eve's little body . . . just to satisfy your medical curiosity. I'm sorry, but I can't give permission for that. . . . And you wouldn't learn anything, anyway. Her heart just couldn't stand the strain. That is all there was to it." His face was adamant.

Marc stood up with a sigh. "I'm sorry you're taking this attitude, Ladbrooke. I'd hoped you would see it differently."

He walked over to the door. "I sympathize with you in your loss, but I think it only fair to tell you I'm not going to let the matter rest here. . . . Good evening."

Scott did not reply. He sat with his elbows on his knees, his head thrust into his hands, a figure of grief. "Good evening, Mrs. Ladbrooke." Marc left the room and went back down the hall. He found his overcoat on a chair beside the door, and was putting it on when he heard a silken rustle, and turned to find Mrs. Ladbrooke at his side.

"Do you really have to go on with this, Dr. Castleman?" She moved closer and placed one hand on his sleeve. He looked at her in surprise. McKeith's paper doll had come to life. She raised pleading eyes to his. "You don't know what you are doing. Please let it drop. We have been through so much . . . and it is all over now. Don't drag us through anything more. It means a great deal to me." She caught hold of his lapel with her other hand, in a beseeching gesture.

Marc was enveloped in an essence of feminine loveliness. She looked up at him, imploring with radiant dark eyes, her red lips parted, both hands clinging to him.

For a moment he leaned toward her, almost took her in his arms. But he drew back, and embarrassed at how she stirred him, he spoke brusquely. "It's my professional duty. I'm sorry. But I can't let it drop."

Outside again, he sat in his car, considerably shaken. He could still feel her seductive nearness and her perfume was in his nostrils.

He could have laughed as he thought of his conversation with McKeith that afternoon. There was certainly nothing wrong with his masculine reflexes now, and by God! there was nothing lacking in Madeleine either.

But what was it all about? . . . Anyway you looked at it, Madeleine was abnormal, he thought uneasily. There was something weird about that episode with her . . . her strange metamorphosis . . . as though Eve's death had brought her vibrantly to life. . . . Of course there were cases—atavism—the Austrians linked the sex impulse and the death instinct. He hadn't met it before in his own experience, but he'd heard of modern ghouls,—abnormal people, enervated, overbred,—like Madeleine—who were stimulated only in the presence of death. . . . A vampire?

Even Marc's professional alertness dimmed. Shades of Jung, he thought. I've been reading too many of the Viennese. They're a morbid crew themselves, like their dying country. We don't put much stock in that sort of thing over here. But then he recalled Landescru—and Loeb and Leopold, here in America. Such dark undercurrents did exist in the unconscious. Was that what McKeith had been sensing—the unnatural emotion he was talking about? he wondered grimly as he released the brake.

The car started to move slowly forward, and he let it coast down the curving drive to the Minarys' house. Light showed in the front windows, and a maid answered his knock promptly.

When he stepped into the hall he saw that Barbara and Phillip were in the living room. After months of uncertainty and strain, the end, regardless of how it came, had brought an inevitable let-down. Relieved of tension, they were sitting idle and silent.

The room itself was in keeping with the mood it held. Faded and outworn, its nostalgic charm appealed to Marc. Tiny electric candles with yellow silk shades shed a gentle light from many sconces. The shadows on the walls were silver and mother-of-pearl, like the stuff of memory. Here and there a gold thread gleamed dully from ivory brocade or glinted in the faint pattern of yellowed damask.

It was an interior lifted from the pages of an eighteenth-century French novel.

Two small sofas with delicately curved backs faced each other from either side of the fireplace. The Minarys were sitting together on one of the love seats. Phillip's tired face and melancholy eyes gave him a striking resemblance to young Abraham Lincoln.

He looked up in surprise, and pulled himself to his feet when Marc entered the room. "Why . . . Dr. Castleman! Come in, doctor."

"Good evening, I'm sorry to intrude at a time like this, but I must talk with you for a moment. First, though, I want to express my sympathy. Dr. McKeith and I both feel very badly over Eve's death."

"Thank you, doctor. Won't you have a chair?"

Marc sat down beside the fire. He looked across a little glass and gilt table at the weary couple opposite him, and decided to ask, without preamble, for an autopsy.

Phil's rugged features were never expressive, and tonight he seemed utterly used up, but Castleman's request roused in him a look of pained surprise.

However he did not protest, listening like one beyond further effort or interest until the doctor finished his explanation. Then he said, uncertainly, "Why, I didn't know you were considering anything like that, doctor. . . . I don't know what to say. . . . I don't like the idea. . . . If it is really necessary, though . . ." He glanced at his wife.

She read the question in his eyes and considered. "I wonder how Scott would feel about it?"

"Yes, we'll have to consult Scott," her husband answered. "I'd like to talk this over with Mr. Ladbrooke before coming to any decision, doctor."

"You were Eve's legal guardian, though, weren't you?" Castleman asked. "Is your permission all that is necessary for us to go ahead?"

"I was appointed guardian—and after the divorce, we let it stay that way. However," he continued slowly, "Scott would now be considered next of kin. But the point is irrelevant. I wouldn't act against Scott's wishes. I'll see how he feels about this, and let you know."

"I have already talked with him, and he is unreasonably opposed to the idea. But I hope you won't be influenced by his emotional attitude, Mr. Minary. If you allow this post-mortem, the results may mean new life for numberless cases now shut away with hopeless dementias."

Minary frowned and let out a long sigh. "My brother-in-law was unusually close to his sister. He takes a view that may seem sentimental to you, but I know he would feel a thing like this deeply. It would make a great difference to his peace of mind." After a moment he looked up with a shrewd glance. "What about McKeith? Does he think this post-mortem is necessary?"

Marc made a rueful grimace. "He doesn't see it quite

as I do, I admit. Of course, he thinks it would be a good thing to have an autopsy,—but, I guess he expected opposition. He doesn't want me to press you."

"Well, Dr. Castleman, I think I incline to his view. If Scott doesn't give his consent, I won't go over his head. And since you say he has made up his mind, I guess that settles it."

Marc continued to sit, staring into the fire. Finally he said, "I don't think you quite understand the situation. I was the doctor conducting the treatment . . . and I don't intend to sign the death certificate until I am satisfied as to the cause of death."

Phillip Minary absorbed the declaration with a slight tightening of his face. He deliberated for a moment and then asked quietly, "Aren't you overstepping bounds a little, Castleman? It is true that a doctor can demand an autopsy, if he suspects his patient didn't die from natural causes. But in this case, you have nothing like that. You merely want to satisfy certain questions in your own mind, regarding the use of metrazol. I don't think the court would consider you had sufficient grounds for your demand."

"I feel so strongly about this, Minary, that I'm willing to raise the question of medical murder,—if you will. Maybe I gave her a lethal dose of metrazol. If I killed her, I want to know it. I don't want to make that mistake twice, and I'm going to ask for a court order in the morning and find out why she died."

When Minary did not reply, Marc went on tentatively, "Of course, you could make it much easier for me,—and for yourself if you would give consent now. I can go right ahead, tonight, with the autopsy. If I do this, there need be no change in your plans for the funeral, and no publicity. If I have to get a court order, it will probably get into the papers."

"You are pointing a pistol right at me, aren't you, doc-

tor? With your finger on the trigger! I guess you know
this family has had enough publicity." He spoke wearily,
as though beyond rancor. "I hope you feel justified. . . .
Well, I'll go over and talk to Scott. I'll let you know what
we decide."

Castleman got to his feet. "Thank you. I'm going back
to the hospital. You can reach me there any time, tonight."

Driving out to Oaklawn, Marc wondered whether he
had acted like a resolute young research man, or a damn
fool. He felt like the latter. It had decided to rain again,
and impudent drops of water dashed mockingly against
the windshield.

It would help a lot if McKeith would back him up, he
thought. Of course, the Ladbrooke family had influence,
and Oaklawn was supported in part by municipal funds.
But even so. . . .

Mac acted almost as if he personally disliked the idea
of an autopsy. He had taken Eve's death hard. It wasn't
professional. Still he always let himself go all-out on a
special case.

Castleman was beginning to realize that if he went on
with this p.-m. now, it would probably mean a break with
McKeith, and the older man's friendship meant a lot to
him. . . . Of course, his commission was coming through
any day now, but after the war he would have liked to
come back. And as for finding a position, elsewhere,—
"Personality difficulties" didn't read well on a letter of
reference.

But if he held to his course, he might discover something that would change the entire method of treating
dementia. . . . He knew he was going on regardless of
consequences. He was just made that way. He couldn't
help it that he had the research type of mind. When he
got his teeth into a problem, he couldn't let go until he'd
found an answer.

When he reached his room at the hospital, he found a note telling him that McKeith wanted to see him. "Well, here it comes," he thought. Bareheaded to the rain, he hurried across the lawn in a reckless mood.

McKeith came to the door himself and led the way back to his study. "I've just had a phone call from Minary. It seems you handled him pretty roughly this evening, Marc." He looked at his young colleague with tolerant amusement.

"I'm sorry he feels that way. I tried to be tactful about it, but I pointed out I wasn't going to sign the death certificate until I was satisfied why she died." Marc was on the defensive, not only against the older man, but against the doubt within himself.

McKeith sighed. "When you are a little older, Marc, you'll realize that you can't ride rough-shod over other people's feelings,—even in the name of science. You know, emotion has a certain validity, too. And science is not infallible. . . . I doubt you'd get anything decisive from a p.-m. I don't understand why you're so set on it."

Castleman hesitated before replying, and McKeith said, "You have a brilliant mind, Marc. But you've got a ruthless streak in you that needs watching. We're handling people,—not test tubes, in our profession."

He leaned over and poked at the fire as he continued. "Minary left a message for you. He told me to tell you that neither he nor Scott wants this autopsy to take place. But that, if you are determined to go ahead, they'll give their consent rather than have you ask for a court order."

"Well, that makes it easy sailing, then," Marc answered with enormous relief.

McKeith replaced the poker and faced about in his chair. "I wish you would reconsider, Marc. If you go ahead you may give Scott a psychological wound that won't heal easily. He may end up here himself, if you push him too far."

"Maybe so. But it seems to me that one man's sentimental qualms shouldn't be allowed to stand in the way of something that may prove of considerable benefit to others."

McKeith stood up, and when Marc rose, too, he laid his hand on the younger man's shoulder.

"Marc, this isn't the army. I can't give you orders. But I am the head of this hospital and you are on my staff. I have years of experience behind me, and you are just starting out. I have both your welfare and that of the hospital in mind, when I ask you to let this thing drop."

"I am sorry, sir,—I am very sorry. But. . . ."

McKeith removed his hand and turned away. "Very well, Dr. Castleman. I would appreciate it, if you would let me know the results of the autopsy in the morning."

The formality of his tone served notice that their comradeship was over.

13.

IT WAS SEVEN o'clock wartime, and the sun had made but a feeble impression in the morning sky, when Marc, red-eyed and disheveled, knocked on the door. The McKeiths' Irish maid looked at him with disapproval. "The doctor isn't down yet. I just heard him drawing water for his bath."

"I have some news for him that can't wait any longer. Tell him I'm here, Rose."

McKeith heard them from above as they talked in the hall, and came down in his dressing-gown. "What is the matter? Come on into the study."

As Marc followed down the hall, he burst out excitedly, "I finished that autopsy on Eve last night. I ran the tests for alkaloids and found a suffusion of nicotine in her stomach. It had spread on into the kidneys, too."

"Nicotine?" McKeith whirled around to face Marc. "You must be mistaken!"

"No, sir, it's no mistake. I couldn't believe it myself, at first. I woke Jackson up, and he came up and helped me run the tests a second time. It was nicotine all right,— and plenty of it. That's what killed her."

McKeith hurried into his study and sat down in consternation. "My God, Castleman! How did she get nicotine in her? You've never prescribed anything like that, have you?"

"Certainly not. And she didn't get it by accident either. At least not through the hospital. Jackson checked up, and he doesn't have nicotine, or any of its compounds in the pharmacy."

McKeith looked somewhat relieved. "Then it must have come from outside. . . . Somebody brought it in to her in something."

"Yes, someone brought it to her all right. But I don't think she has had any candy or fruit, lately. . . . I don't see how she came to take it, though, anyway. It tastes like the devil."

"Oh, it would be easy enough, in her state," McKeith's tone was weary. "We've taught her to do as she was told. I gave her a bromide myself, just before the treatment. She didn't like it, but I told her to swallow it down, and she did. . . . Anyone else could have gotten her to take nicotine the same way. She had a lot of visitors that day. And they were in there alone with her. . . . How long does it take for nicotine to act?"

"I just looked it up in Pearson. There have been a few cases of nicotine poisoning recorded, and the time lapse between absorbing the poison and onset of the symptoms varies considerably. Depends on the dose and the patient's reaction. However, she must have gotten it some time that day, and if she had nicotine in her system, the injection of metrazol would bring things to a head, quickly. . . . Phillip Minary and Scott each came in during the morning to see her."

"And all those people I interviewed in the afternoon looked in on her," McKeith added. "Let's see . . . the two Ladbrookes were here . . . Halsey came by for Scott . . . and then there was Barbara Minary and Mrs. Humber. . . . We'll have to talk to all of them."

Marc was still standing. He leaned against the mantel with his hands in his pockets facing McKeith, and answered thoughtfully, "Nicotine is sold as an insecticide spray. It comes in a highly concentrated form. And of course you can make a suffusion from ordinary smoking tobacco. . . . But I don't see how anyone could have given it to her by mistake, Mac."

"No,—I don't believe for a moment she got it by accident. . . . This thing is incredible, Marc! One of those people . . . ?"

McKeith pulled himself together in sudden decision. "There is only one thing for us to do now." He reached over and picked up his desk phone which connected with the hospital switchboard.

"Sarah, I want police headquarters. Get me the chief of homicide."

In a fairly short time a police car drove quietly up to McKeith's door and three men in plain clothes got out. Marc had braced himself for a parade of cars, screaming sirens, and an avalanche of red-faced, back-slapping politico-police.

He knew that McKeith, explaining the circumstances over the phone briefly, had reminded the head of homicide of the nature of the hospital, and suggested they try not to excite his patients. And of course this murder was over twelve hours old, and the body had been removed and dissected. There was no need for police photographers, fingerprint men and squads of detectives. But even so, Marc had not expected the arrival of the law to be so inconspicuous.

He had, he realized, been thinking rather naïvely in stereotypes. For Chief-of-Police Fletcher, who had been informed of the call, and considered the case important enough to warrant his coming himself, was neither hale nor hearty. He had a skin like unbleached muslin, wore glasses and walked with the sedentary stoop of an accountant. And while his manner was cordial, it was not indiscriminate. He made Marc feel that he was friendly because he liked what he saw in the two doctors. Introducing himself, Schwartz, the Chief of Detectives, and the police stenographer who accompanied them, he remarked, "I understand you've had a little trouble out here, doctor."

"Yes, come on back and I'll tell you about it." McKeith led the way to his study. The stenographer opened his notebook and sat down at the desk. Fletcher, Schwartz and the two psychiatrists found seats about the empty fireplace, and McKeith gave a concise account of the circumstances of Eve's admittance to Oaklawn, her subsequent treatment and her death.

While he was talking, Scott Ladbrooke and Phillip Minary arrived. After calling the police, McKeith had decided to notify them of developments. Mrs. McKeith, who had risen and dressed far earlier than her accustomed hour, took them into the living room, where Fletcher asked that they wait until he was ready for them.

When McKeith finished his account, the police chief asked a few questions and then summed up quickly and decisively. "We'll have our laboratory check your findings, Dr. Castleman. I'm sure that they are correct, however, and as you've eliminated the possibility of her having gotten the poison by accident, through the hospital, it makes it look like murder. Unless her relatives gave it to her by mistake—and that seems unlikely on the face of it. Of course, almost anyone here at Oaklawn could have killed her if they had wanted to. We'll have to look into that angle as a matter of routine. But I think it will narrow down to one of her own people. Let's see, now, there were how many . . .? Six? . . . visitors that day. Well, there it is.

"We'll want to go over her room, see if there are any traces of nicotine in there, and question the attendants who were in that wing yesterday. We'll try not to upset your schedules or disturb your patients any more than we can help, Dr. McKeith. I'll want to talk to both of you again, of course. We'll be around here a good bit probably for the next few days. I'll go in and see Ladbrooke and Minary now. . . . I don't need to keep you from your work any longer this morning."

Castleman went back to his rounds at the hospital, feeling emotionally dressed up with no place to go. But the thing was out of his hands now. For several days, off and on, he noticed men in plain clothes standing about in the south wing, or shutting themselves up in Evelyn's suite. One by one the nurses and orderlies on duty in that section were called down to McKeith's office where they were questioned by the detectives. The other doctors on the staff were interviewed, and the hospital dining room buzzed with speculation the rest of the week.

Fletcher and Schwartz had another long session with McKeith and Castleman. The two psychiatrists did not give them the confidential typescripts of the dictaphone recordings, but they discussed freely the nature of Eve's illness, the questions it had raised, and her relationships with her family. The policemen gave close attention, on the surface, to the psychiatrists' testimony. But they were noncommittal, and, Marc thought, unimpressed by the doctors' discussions. They asked them both to testify at the inquest, which had been postponed for ten days.

After that interview, the police seemed to have concluded the initial phase of their investigation. At least no more police cars were parked in the drive and Oaklawn settled back to an undisturbed routine. Marc supposed that Schwartz was questioning Eve's family, but he had no occasion to see any of them. He had lost all connection with the case.

But he read through Eve's record again and studied closely the transcriptions of the interviews just before her death. Her case had interested him from the first and during the months of treatment he had speculated more and more about the personality of his patient and the circumstances that had driven her into her desperate condition. Then, when he was on the very point of discovery, her death had snatched the threads from his hands, raising another question even more imperative.

The unsolved puzzle of Eve's life and death teased and gnawed at him constantly. It was there in his mind when he got up in the morning, it was present at the table when he ate his meals, it accompanied him on his hospital rounds and it followed him to bed at night. It came between him and his work, it gave him no peace, and as time went on it became even more persistent. It was a week after Eve's death, during his morning visit to Potts, that he suddenly came to a decision.

Potts was saying, "I've never had another like it. Just the one dream the whole night! I don't understand what it means. There was this roc,—I believe they are extinct— but in this dream I knew it was a roc. Although it was big, the egg it was hatching was enormous. The bird was black. It perched there on this great white egg like one of these little women's hats cocked over one brow. . . . And it looked at me with an expression. . . . I don't know how to describe that look, Dr. Castleman . . ."

Marc stood up abruptly. "Edwin, I'm sure this dream is significant, and we must consider it carefully. I want to see you again, a little later, but I have to leave you now."

"But, doctor! . . . It can't wait. I . . . !"

Leaving Potts expostulating in dismay, Marc hurried over to the nearest desk phone, called police headquarters, and made an appointment with Fletcher for eleven. He tried to compress his morning rounds into the next hour, but running into Dr. Smythe-Jones on the third floor, he told him he had to leave the hospital for a while, and Smythe-Jones agreed to handle the overflow.

By quarter of eleven he had on his overcoat, and hat in hand, stopped by Miss Evans's office to ask her to let Mac know he would be away for a couple of hours. Then he hurried to the garage and drove off in his cream-colored convertible, like a truant schoolboy on his way to the old swimming hole.

14.

WHEN HE reached headquarters Castleman hadn't decided on his opening gambit. But he need not have worried. Fletcher gave him a cordial reception. Greeting him like a colleague, he drew him into his office and pulled up a chair for him by the desk. "Have a cigar?"

When Marc declined, the chief selected one for himself and tilted back in his swivel chair with an air of a man who had unlimited time to devote to the conversation at hand. "I don't believe I told you, doctor, what a smart piece of work you did on that autopsy."

He cut off the end of his cigar. "I understand you ran into quite a bit of opposition on it from everyone, including McKeith." He looked at Marc shrewdly over the flame of his match. "What made you so determined to go on with it? Did you suspect her death wasn't natural?"

"Well, no, I can't say I did. At least, not consciously. . . . But perhaps subconsciously . . ." Marc considered, thoughtfully. "It was a queer case from the beginning. We couldn't get any lead to the underlying factors in her condition. We suspected there was some mystery her family was covering up, and then, just when we had her ready to talk, she was killed. . . . Don't you think that's significant? It strikes me there might be a connection between the motive for her murder and that earlier situation, whatever it was that led up to her insanity."

"I wouldn't be surprised but what you're right," Fletcher remarked. "All that may tie right in with the angle we're working on."

Marc broke in eagerly. "You've found out something definite then?"

"Yes, the case is shaping up for us. But first, you tell me what you've got in mind. Go ahead with what you were starting to say."

"I'm afraid I haven't anything specific for you." Marc hesitated and began tentatively, "As I said, we were trying to find the source of the patient's dementia, and even before her death, we had begun to wonder if there wasn't some connection between her mental disturbance and the murder of this boy Crane."

Fletcher had obviously been expecting something else from Marc, and seemed disappointed at the turn things had taken. "I remember the Crane case. I was on homicide at the time. But I don't see how his death could have had much effect on Mrs. Minary. What makes you think . . . ?"

"His murder occurred just a short time before the onset of her psychosis, and there didn't seem to be anything else of a disturbing nature in her background," Marc answered, warming up to his theory. "And since she has been killed, I feel the evidence linking her with Crane is stronger because it takes a powerful motive to murder. Whoever poisoned Eve wasn't driven by a light impulse. I doubt the desire to avoid scandal,—or to be free of emotional dependency,—or even a ten-year-old jealousy, would account for such drastic action. But the instinct of self-preservation would. . . . I think Eve Minary knew who killed Crane, that the knowledge drove her out of her mind ten years ago, and that when we were on the point of bringing her back, the murderer had to kill her to insure her silence."

Fletcher took his cigar from his mouth and looked at Marc in blank amazement. "Why, Sam Tilton killed Crane. Do you mean you think Tilton came back and poisoned Evelyn Minary? How would he get to her?"

"It's never been proved that Tilton killed Crane," Marc answered, contentiously. "That is just an assumption. We haven't heard Tilton's side of the story. . . . We know he was worried about Minary's investigation, and that he'd been raking in money for a long time. As it was all undercover, he'd salted it away in hidden bank accounts. He was all set to clear out if he had to. On Crane's testimony he had the wind up badly. Suppose he decided to go, that night, while the going was good?"

Fletcher was listening intently with a poker face. Marc lit a cigarette and extinguished the match with a nervous flick of the wrist. "Suppose Tilton ran away from a charge of misfeasance, but woke up a few mornings later to find he was under indictment for murder, and that there was strong circumstantial evidence against him. Do you think a man of his caliber would come back to face the music?"

"Probably not," Fletcher conceded, "but there was enough evidence against Tilton to indict him, and not a shred of suspicion against anyone else."

"Nevertheless, I think it quite possible that Crane was murdered by someone else, for an entirely different reason,—a personal reason," Marc contended. "You didn't go into Crane's private affairs, because Minary sent you chasing after Tilton. I think Crane's activities against the grafters was handed to you as a red herring. . . . I don't know why Crane was killed. But I think he was shot by one of the six people who had access to Eve the day of her death."

Fletcher puffed on his cigar with narrowed eyes. "What do you have that ties Eve Minary in with Crane's murder? Did she tell you something?"

"No, we didn't get anything from Eve, but we turned up several things, not very definite perhaps, . . ." Marc hesitated. He was thinking of those blue-edged letters of Crane's that had mysteriously disappeared from Minary's files.

That information was given in confidence, but if it had a bearing, the police were entitled to it. Still, some elementary caution held him back.

"Then why are you dragging Crane into this murder?" Fletcher prodded impatiently. "I don't see what you're getting at."

Marc decided to skip mention of the letters for the time being. "It seems to me there is a thread running through all this, connecting Eve and Crane. Consider the timing. Crane is murdered. Within a month Eve, for no apparent reason, develops a dementia. Then, when she is on the point of recovery, she herself is killed. Crane was murdered and Eve was murdered. She is linked by the very fact of her murder."

Marc discovered that Fletcher was smiling broadly. "I expect you read detective stories, doctor, and I doubt your experience has made you familiar with crime rates. We average between forty and fifty murders a year here. Sometimes we get more than one murder in a single week. Not long ago we had two killings on the same night. . . . In a detective story, it would turn out that those two murders were linked. But as a matter of fact, there was no connection at all. Now," he looked at Marc with tolerant amusement, "I see how you've been figuring. Because Eve was acquainted with Crane and he got killed, and ten years later she was poisoned, you think there ought to be a connection. But if you'd been more familiar with crime statistics you'd have realized that was nothing at all to build on, just that Eve knew Crane and was herself killed later."

Marc felt his cheeks turn hot, and suspected that he was blushing furiously. Such a thing hadn't happened to him since high school days, and he felt rather like a pupil again, called down by the teacher. To hide his discomfiture, he picked up an ashtray from the desk and slowly stubbed out his cigarette.

"However, I think you may have something when you say Mrs. Minary's mental trouble was connected with her murder." Fletcher went on with genial condescension. "That ties in with the case we are working up. We would be glad of any help you can give us, doctor."

Marc, forgetting his embarrassment over his naïve reasoning, asked with quick interest, "What angle are you working on?"

"We approached this murder a little differently from you." Fletcher puffed at his cigar, regarding Marc complacently through the smoke. "We looked for three things, in this order,—opportunity,—connection with the murder weapon,—and motive. If we rule out the hospital personnel, we get six people with equal opportunity. A suffusion of nicotine can be made at home, or bought so easily that there's not much point in working on that part of it. But when we come to motive—there's only one of those six persons with a motive, and Barbara Minary has one that stands out like a headlight."

"Barbara Minary," Marc ejaculated, trying to focus his thoughts at this new angle.

"Barbara Minary had everything to lose if Eve recovered her sanity," Fletcher pointed out. "Scott Ladbrooke tells me that Minary was going to divorce her and take Eve back. Barbara had been a secretary, but she was sitting pretty as Phil's wife. Lots of money, fine home, a leading social position and all that. And she was due to lose it all if Eve returned. Now she has nothing to worry about," he concluded significantly, resting his case.

"It sounds reasonable," Marc answered doubtfully. "You've got a motive for her, I admit, but how are you going to build a case that will stand up in court? You'll need more than a possible motive and an opportunity shared by five other people."

Fletcher was smug. "We'll get evidence enough, once we start things rolling. If we indict Barbara, and Minary is any kind of a man, he'll come forward and say she hadn't any motive. That he never intended to divorce her. And that will put him right behind the eight ball."

Marc was completely at sea. Fletcher laughed at his baffled expression. "This is where your question about the first wife's insanity comes in. How do you like this picture? Minary is married to Eve, one of these bloodless intellectual types, probably as neurotic as hell. He is working down at his office all hours of the night with a healthy, warm-blooded secretary, who gives him what he doesn't get at home. Eve finds out about it and goes clean off her rocker. As soon as he decently can, Minary divorces her and marries Barbara."

I think you're off the track there," Marc disagreed. "Minary waited a long time . . . seven years. And Scott says he married again to give his son a home, a commonsense marriage."

"I got a different story from the maid out there, that Julia. Have you met her?" Fletcher asked, enjoying a secret joke. "From the way she speaks you'd think it was indecent for a man to kiss his wife. But anyway, I gathered it's pretty hot stuff between Phil and Barbara, and that Ladbrooke doesn't know which way the wind is blowing. . . . Suppose that Minary is pretty crazy about his present wife, and doesn't want to divorce her and take back the loony one?"

"But good God, Minary didn't have to kill Eve to keep from taking her back," Marc protested. "He was divorced from her, and that divorce would stand. Even Scott admitted that. Cunningham was going to contest it just as a threat . . ."

"Do you mean Scott was going to contest the divorce? That he'd hired Cunningham?" Fletcher leaned forward eagerly. "Well, that certainly fits in. I'm glad you told me that, Castleman."

"Scott knew he didn't have a leg to stand on. It was just a gesture to prod Minary along." Marc tried to minimize his inadvertent disclosure. "That divorce was valid and Minary was legally married to Barbara. If he wanted to stay that way, all he had to do was sit tight. He hadn't any motive for *murdering* Eve, even if he didn't want her back."

"Just the oldest and strongest motive in the world." Fletcher's grin was triumphant. "Money! When Phil Minary married Evelyn Ladbrooke, he didn't have a red cent. Her father left her nearly a million dollars and Minary has been administering her estate. Now, under an old will of hers he gets it all. Unless Scott contests it."

Fletcher tilted back in his chair. "I've been going into it with Jeffrey Halsey. He's the executor of Judge Ladbrooke's estate. He says that if Scott contested Eve's will, it would lead to quite a legal tangle. Eve made out that will when she married Phil. Afterwards she loses her mind, the Judge dies, and she inherits her half of the Ladbrooke money. Then her husband divorces her and marries again. She isn't competent to make a new will, and when she dies, the man who is no longer married to her, gets her fortune under that old will."

Marc nervously lit a cigarette, his narrow face charged with interest at top voltage. Fletcher, savoring the legal knowledge he had recently acquired, mulled over the case with a judicial air.

"Halsey says Scott is not going to contest. That it's all right with him for Phil to get the money. Of course Jonathan will get his third under the law but as things are now, Phil gets the most of it, with no questions asked."

Marc was silent, considering all these new facts that had been hurled at him so precipitately. Fletcher rocked gently back and forth on his swivel chair. "Of course the Judge never intended to leave all that money to an insane woman. He was too sound a man for that. He told Halsey he was going to change his will and put Eve's share into a trust fund for his grandson. He intended to leave something to Minary outright, about twenty or thirty thousand. That's what he was planning, but he died suddenly before he had a chance to do it."

"You mean Judge Ladbrooke died right after Eve lost her mind?"

Marc was startled. A tingle of excitement raced through his nerve centers.

"Within a pretty short time,—a week or so. He was

badly broken up over her condition." Fletcher's eyes were quizzical, and showed a gathering amusement. "Didn't you know about his death?"

"I knew he had died since Eve was at Oaklawn, but I didn't know his death came right on the heels of her commitment. I've only been here a couple of years . . . and Eve's case was an old one. . . . You say the Judge died suddenly? . . . What caused it?"

"Death from apoplexy or heart attack is usually sudden." Fletcher smiled in deprecation at Marc. "There was no funny business about his death. Had the best doctors in town attending. It was a natural thing to happen at his age,—he was in the late fifties and had just had a bad shock." He dismissed the question and returned to his thesis.

"But to come back to Phil Minary. You see the spot he was in? If he stuck to Barbara, he kissed the Ladbrooke money good-by. And not only that, he was certain sure to run into trouble with Scott. If he let Eve down, Scott would have kicked him out of Ladbrooke and Halsey quick as a flash. Minary made an awful mess of things when he was in the D. A.'s office, and with his reputation, he could never build up a practice here on his own."

"Scott was certain, though, that Phil *was* going to divorce Barbara,—and—" Marc, still floundering, tried to arrange his ideas but Fletcher cut in.

"Maybe he knew he didn't have a chance to get Eve back. If he'd been carrying on with Barbara ten years before, and Eve knew it, she probably wouldn't want him back. You doctors would have gotten her talking, and the cat would have been out of the bag. You can picture for yourself how Scott would feel about that."

"I get your point all right," Marc conceded. "But you base everything on the premise that Phil had been unfaithful to Eve, and didn't want her back now. I don't have that impression. And I don't see how you're going to get the ball rolling, as you put it. I still don't believe you have enough to ask for an indictment of Barbara,—just a motive and an opportunity that was pretty general."

"Oh, the D. A. will ask for an indictment all right! We're not worried about that." Fletcher's expression said he was mentally licking his chops and rubbing his hands together in satisfaction.

Marc looked at him in perplexity for a moment—and then light broke! He had been taken in by a studious appearance and a mild, intelligent manner. But he saw now that he had been dealing with a streamlined version of an old article.

Fletcher was just a cog in a political machine, that same machine Minary had tried to buck ten years before. They had tried to smash him once, but he was making a comeback. He was the arch enemy, and he was in their hands again. They were going to finish him off for good, and teach a lesson to the community that it wouldn't forget in a hurry. If anyone ever again aspired to hold a special investigation in this city, he would stop and think about what had happened to Phil Minary.

Marc gripped the arms of his chair and his eyes blazed. Fletcher didn't give a tinker's dam as to who had killed Eve. Her murder had provided a weapon to get at her former husband. With a conniving district attorney, the gang was going to haul Phil into court on trumped-up evidence. They knew they couldn't get a conviction, but they would force a break between him and Scott, take away his means of livelihood and run him out of town with his reputation irrevocably ruined.

Marc's guard was down and his surging anger and contempt reflected plainly in his eyes. Fletcher's face stiffened. "I see you don't agree with my analysis of the case. I'm surprised. I should have expected that you'd want this thing cleared up quickly. Barbara and Phil Minary are the only possible suspects." His voice fairly purred. "If

we don't get a conviction, it's going to look bad for the
hospital. People are going to ask questions. They'll think
it was an accident up there after all, or worse. . . ."

"If you're trying to insinuate—" Marc jumped up
furious,—but Fletcher cut in smoothly, "Of course, your
skirts are clean, Dr. Castleman. You were the one who insisted on an autopsy. But McKeith didn't want one, did
he? He fought against it, I understand . . . and queer
things go on in mental hospitals. Doctors shut up alone
with their patients, for hours at a time, giving psychoanalysis. No nurses in there with them. . . . We haven't
looked into that side of the question yet, because we think
we know who's guilty. But, if our case falls through . . . !"

So that was it! The velvet glove was off and the iron
fist exposed. Two fists, to be exact. Marc had just stopped
a quick jab from the left and here was the body punch
from the right.—You keep out of this, or else . . . !—That
was what Fletcher meant.

Marc gripped the desk hard with both hands, as he
fought down the impulse to physical violence. He wanted
to mop up the floor with Fletcher literally and verbally.
But he kept a tight grip on himself until his disciplined
mind put his furious emotions in leash. He'd get some satisfaction out of telling Fletcher what he thought of him,
but he'd feel like a fool afterward. There was no point in
saying anything now, with the cards stacked against him.
But later on, when he'd gathered his facts, he'd come
back shooting. He dropped his hands and straightened up,
saying evenly, "I'm not worried about the reputation of
the hospital or any of its staff, Fletcher."

The chief came around the desk, smiling with his lips.
"I'm glad to have had this little talk with you, doctor.
Any time I can help you, just let me know."

Nobody is fooled, Marc thought. The challenge has
been made. The fight is on to the finish, although there's
been no overt move yet. And the force of civilized habit

was so strong in him that he answered, "I'm afraid I've used up a lot of your time, to no purpose, Fletcher. It was good of you to see me. . . . Good-by."

At least I didn't shake hands with him, Marc thought with satisfaction as he walked down the corridor of City Hall.

His watch told him that, by the time he got back to Oaklawn, he would have used up the two hours' grace he had allowed himself. But he didn't feel like going back to the hospital. He was boiling inside and appalled at the turn things had taken. Minary had been through such a devil of a lot, and they were getting ready to crucify him all over again. And in a way, he'd gotten Minary into it, by forcing that post-mortem.

Marc had made up his mind they weren't going to get away with it. But he had so very little, just those missing letters of Crane's, the mysterious Madame X . . . and the vague outline of a pattern. He was confused by all the new facts Fletcher had fed him. The money,—the wills,—the Judge's sudden death!

Marc realized that he needed to know a great deal more about everything. He'd just had a partial view, a keyhole glimpse of Eve's life through her case history.

Well, he decided after a moment of reflection, he could go to the same source Fletcher had used. Jeffrey Halsey, the executor of the Judge's estate, Scott's and Phil's law partner, was the the man to see now.

15.

W HEN THE elder Ladbrooke and Halsey opened their
offices in the Marvin Johnson, it was the newest and tallest
building in town. In the forty years since, a succession of
more modern skyscrapers had gone up, farther to the
north, but the firm had seen fit to remain where it was.
The high-ceilinged anteroom with long windows had a
bare look, in spite of a heavy center table and the expensive leather chairs that had worn well. Behind a low
railing in a corner, a stenographer in bifocals was pound-
ing away on her typewriter.

Marc wondered if that were where Barbara used to sit.
No, he remembered, she was a private secretary. Her
office would have been in back. But it was probably in a
room much like this that she had served tea to "the boys,"
in those early days. The Judge would come over from his
chambers for a chat, and perhaps Eve would drop in from
shopping, or a meeting at the League.

Marc walked over to the typist. "I'd like to see Mr.
Halsey. I don't have an appointment, but will you ask him
to give me a few moments? It's urgent. I'm Dr. Castleman from the Oaklawn Hospital and I've come in about
a matter connected with Mrs. Minary."

Amelia plugged a wire into the small switchboard at
her side. When she had repeated his message into her
phone she got up and led him into an inner office where he
found Halsey sitting at a desk, busy with some papers.
The lawyer looked up with an agreeable smile. "Sit down,
Dr. Castleman. I'll be free in a moment."

Halsey's office had the old-fashioned proportions of the anteroom, but book-lined walls, a heavy carpet, and curtains at the tall windows gave it more solidity. Halsey himself looked like the sort of man who brought bellboys running and put head waiters on the *qui vive*. Not, Marc thought, because he tried to create an impression. He had just been born that way, to expensive schools and clubs and importance. His appearance suggested tennis ,and squash courts, easy masculine companionship over a highball, and a clever, hard-driving mind. He would, Marc concluded, be a good man to have for a friend, and a formidablé adversary to meet in court.

When he clipped together the typed sheets he had been reading, thrust them into a drawer, and looked attentively at Castleman, Halsey made the doctor feel that the seconds of time slipping away were worth dollars and dollars. And that wasn't deliberate either, Marc decided. It was probably just the truth.

"I wanted to finish going over that brief while it was all in my mind," Halsey apologized. "Sorry to have kept you waiting."

"That's quite all right. It's good of you to let me break in on you this way. I want to discuss some aspects of Mrs. Minary's death with you." He hesitated. "There are three reasons why I am still interested in this case. In the first place, she was my patient, and I think that perhaps I have an insight into the situation that will help clarify things. Secondly, it was because of my insistence that the postmortem was held. I feel a sort of responsibility for the consequences, and I don't like the turn they've taken. I've just been talking to Fletcher. Do you know the line he's following?"

"Yes,—I do." Halsey was grave. "From the first we realized that the City Hall gang would gun for Phil. Fletcher is not very subtle you know, and we've heard of his plans. He's going to use Barbara as a clay pigeon to get Minary to commit himself. Then the D. A. will try to rush through an indictment on a shoe-string accusation."

"But surely, even in this town, they can't get away with anything like that. Won't they have to have some legal evidence? Can they just railroad a man into a murder charge because they don't like the color of his hair?" Marc protested.

Halsey smiled. "I think Fletcher forgets we have in-fluence in this town, too. The Ladbrooke family still has considerable weight around here. I think we can bring enough pressure on the D. A. to keep him from asking for an indictment,—unless Fletcher gets a lot more than he has now."

"Well, I'm certainly glad to hear that," Marc answered in relief. "And maybe if you take away his fall guy, Fletcher will really try to solve this murder, although I doubt he has the intelligence for it. For the sake of the hospital, I'd like to see this thing cleared up quickly."

"We would too," Halsey assured him promptly. "Do you have any ideas about it, doctor?"

"Well, I've wondered if Crane wasn't tied into the situation some way," Marc ventured.

"Crane?" Halsey inquired evenly. He showed no sur-prise. In fact his expression showed nothing at all,—not even interest. He lifted off the lid of a mahogany humi-dor. "Do you care for a cigar?"

"No, thanks."

"A cigarette, then?" He touched the base of the pol-ished onyx horse which ornamented his desk. In a moment the saddle of the statuette glowed red, and the two men lighted their cigarettes.

"How do you think Crane comes into this?" Halsey's blue eyes were intent now.

"It's rather involved," Marc began. "Let's begin with his murder. I've asked myself what motive Tilton had for killing him. After all, he thought Crane was his friend,

tipping him off about what the D. A.'s office was up to.
Even if he found out about Crane's connection with
Minary, why should he kill him? It was Phil who en-
dangered him. Tilton believed that Minary was ready to
bring him before the grand jury and he skipped town.
Why should he have killed Crane before leaving?"

"I've never thought much about it." Halsey eyed his
cigarette reflectively. "Of course Tilton had been drinking . . . and if Crane was trying to block his get-away,
he might have killed him in a sudden panic. . . . But what
has all this to do with Eve's death? Did she say something about Crane's murder?"

That was the second time that day he'd been asked that
question, Marc remembered.

"No, we didn't get anything at all from her. But there
was one circumstance following Crane's death. . . . I don't
know whether you've heard about it. Among Hal's personal effects, there was a bundle of letters, written on feminine stationery. He had them all tied up with a fancy
ribbon as though they were of a sentimental value to him.
Those letters disappeared from Minary's files." Marc
hesitated and then took the plunge. "I wonder if they were
written by Eve."

This got a reaction. Through his trained perceptions,
Marc was aware of an explosion of emotion in the other,
but only the tail end of it was reflected, momentarily, in
the lawyer's controlled face. Quickly he suppressed the
emotion, — Marc thought it was anger — and answered
calmly, "Your insinuation is preposterous. If you'd
known her, you couldn't possibly think that." He looked
at Marc curiously. "Even so, why on earth did you jump
to such a conclusion? Just because the letters disappeared? They could have been written by any woman in
the city,—or in the United States for that matter. Why did
you hit on Eve of all persons?"

"It seems to me the circumstances point directly to

her," Marc replied, unabashed. "Only two persons, Barbara and Phil Minary, had access to those letters. Since Barbara was the one who told about it, Phil must have abstracted them. If those letters had been written by some woman in town, and had no connection with the murder, he might have wanted to spare her unpleasant publicity. But he didn't need to get rid of them as he did. Nelson was D. A. then, and I understand he's quite the gentleman. They could have kept it from the papers and quietly returned the letters to the lady.

"But," Marc concluded trenchantly, "It didn't happen that way. Phil acted on his own, put himself in a questionable position, just at the time when he was fighting hard to continue in office. I don't think he would've jeopardized his chances further, unless those letters had been written by some one he had to protect at any cost. And that brings us straight to Eve."

"Very nicely put, doctor." Halsey smiled appreciatively. "That was neat reasoning. It would be a pleasure to hear you in court. . . . Of course you are handicapped by one thing, you didn't know Eve. I did, and I know you're wrong. It would be hard for me to imagine any sort of circumstances in which Eve could have gotten mixed into a clandestine love affair—and certainly not when she was first married to Phil. She was in love with him, you know. There has to be some other explanation for those letters."

He picked up a pencil and tapped it lightly on the desk as he thought it over. Suddenly he smiled with a suggestion of laughter in his eyes. "You know I wouldn't be surprised if the explanation is very simple. Those letters were probably just lost."

"I don't see how important evidence in a murder case could get lost out of locked files."

"You must remember that Phil was in a bad state then. Eve nearly died when Jonathan was born, and right on top of it came this murder of Crane. When Eve lost her mind, and Nelson asked Phil to resign, he was on the verge of a nervous breakdown. He had only a few days to clean out his files and turn over his records. It would have been easy for him to have mislaid something in the midst of all that confusion. Those letters could have gotten shoved into another pile of papers, or pushed off into the waste basket. . . . I think we'll find it was something like that, that happened."

Without words, Marc stared at the classic onyx horse on the desk. He was utterly deflated. His second line of reasoning had gone down the wind, too. And the explanation was so devastatingly simple. He decided he should have stuck to his own trade at Oaklawn instead of making a fool of himself before Fletcher and Halsey.

Halsey's smile deepened. "I'm not sure which way you're heading. If you had been right about those letters, you see what it would mean, don't you? You try to clear Phil in Eve's death and you pin Hal Crane's murder on him"

Marc managed a laugh, but he spoke stiffly. "I don't think you understand my position, Halsey. I don't want to see Minary framed for murder to satisfy an old political grudge. But I'm not holding a brief for Minary,— or anyone else. If Fletcher has the right man, on the wrong count, and I put him straight, that's all right with me. All I want is to get to the bottom of this thing."

"I know that, Dr. Castleman, and I appreciate your efforts." Halsey's serious legal mien returned. "If there's any way I can help you, I'll be glad to do it."

"There is something else, then, I'd like to ask you about." In spite of his sabotaged clues, Castleman wasn't quite ready to abandon ship. "I learned today that the Judge died when he was on the point of changing his will. Did it happen soon after Evelyn was sent to Oaklawn?"

"Yes. We always thought her insanity brought on his stroke. He died on a Saturday, and it was some time during the previous week that he'd learned what was wrong with her." Halsey glanced unobtrusively at the onyx clock, mate to the stationary lighter on his desk.

"Was he ill very long?"

"His death came suddenly. He'd taken it very hard about Evelyn, and he had a bad cold. His doctor kept him at home all week, but we had no idea his condition was serious, until he collapsed that afternoon. He died the same evening."

"I suppose he'd been taking medicine, a cough syrup or something like that?"

"He probably was, since Jerome was the doctor. He always prescribes a foul-tasting brew for me, no matter what's wrong." Halsey's geniality did not veil his impatience, but Marc was persistent.

"Did the Judge have convulsions before he died?"

The lawyer's glance was sharp. "I don't know. When I got out to the house, he was unconscious and remained that way until his death. Jerome and a nurse were there and several consultants were called in. If he had convulsions, the doctors didn't tell us. . . . What is the point of these questions, Dr. Castleman?"

"I've been reading up on nicotine poisoning recently," Marc remarked. "A big dose of fairly pure nicotine acts almost as quickly as prussic acid, but in most of the recorded cases the reaction didn't set in for several hours or longer. . . . At first, blood pressure goes up, the eyes are dilated, there's a trembling of the limbs and a feeling of weakness. Usually, but not always, there are mild tetanic convulsions at this stage. Then the blood pressure falls, the pupils contract, breathing is difficult and the victim falls into a coma which lasts until death. Artificial respiration and heart stimulants don't help, because nicotine acts directly on the brain, paralyzing the nerves. . . . In fact, Mr. Halsey, death from nicotine is very much like death from apoplexy."

Disapproval and exasperation came into Halsey's face, but he delayed his answer until he had carefully weighed Castleman's implication. Finally he said, looking coldly at the young doctor, "I don't doubt that you have the best motives in the world for interesting yourself in this case, Castleman. But you're not familiar with the people involved or most of the circumstances. You're making the wildest conjectures on a very slight basis. Do you realize the damage you can do?"

Without giving Marc a chance to reply, he continued forcefully, "Fletcher and his gang will stop at nothing to get at Phil. They haven't enough now to get very far, and as matters stand, we can handle them. But if they get hold of these—these unfounded speculations of yours,—all hell will break loose."

"Fletcher isn't going to get hold of anything through me, except facts," Marc replied, stung to heated defense. "A thorough consideration of all the factors in this case, here in your private office, can't hurt Phil . . . unless he is guilty. And if my speculations are unfounded, I don't see how they could affect the issue."

"I know you don't see. That's just the trouble." Halsey's exasperation increased. "They can't prove anything with those missing letters, but they can confuse the issue, and raise insinuating questions about Eve. There will be nothing concrete for us to refute. All we can do is offer testimony regarding the character of a dead woman."

"But, look here . . ." Marc began placatingly, but Halsey rode him down.

"And this matter of Judge Ladbrooke's death would be even worse. Phil was the only one who benefited from the Judge's dying before he made out a new will. Fletcher could go to town on that. . . . I suppose we could get an exhumation, if questions were raised in court. Would anything show up, now?"

"I don't know," Marc admitted. "Nicotine is an organic substance, and it's been over ten years. There might be traces,—and there might not. I couldn't say offhand."

"Well, there you are. Even if we exhumed, and found no poison, we couldn't prove a natural death. . . . Of course, Minary would never be convicted, but don't you see? 'Insinuations are extraordinarily hard to combat. Minary would be acquitted for lack of evidence, and yet we couldn't prove he was innocent. There would always be a question."

"There is a question now. Fletcher's already raised it. Even if you quash the indictment against Minary, there'll always be a cloud of suspicion over him. The only way to clear him is to get to the bottom of the whole thing."

Halsey's exasperation gave way to decision. His face closed up with finality. "Appropriate legal measures will be taken to safeguard Phil. You can do a tremendous amount of harm, Castleman, with that lurid imagination of yours. Your legitimate connection with this case terminated with Eve's death. I feel obliged, in the interest of the family, to ask you to let your inquiries drop."

"I don't doubt that you will take care of Phil's interests all right," Marc answered hotly. "But what about the murderer?"

"That is a job for the police."

Marc was on his feet. "When I came in here, I told you there were three reasons why I was concerning myself with this thing. You have heard two of them. The third is the most important. Unless Eve's murderer is apprehended, my hospital is going to suffer. And until I know why Eve Minary was killed, and who did it, my interest in this case will continue."

16.

"So, I've been kicked out of both camps," Marc reflected as the elevator carried him toward the first floor of the Marvin Johnson Building. "No one appreciates me except Potts."

He felt no little compunction as he thought of Potts and the roc with the weird expression in its eye. However, there was no going back to Oaklawn, now. His glove was in the ring and he'd taken on all comers.

But the missing letters and the connection between the two murders had been explained away so simply. He had nothing, now,—except an incipient headache and a gone feeling in his stomach. There was nothing mysterious about those. It was after one, and it had been a long time since the early breakfast served at Oaklawn.

There was a drugstore in the corner of the building and Marc went in and climbed on a stool before the counter. He ordered the blue plate, mechanically, but he wasn't really hungry. A reaction was setting in and he felt as though all the nerve ends in his body were wrapped around a peg screwed into the back of his neck.

The thing to do was to stop thinking about the Minary case for a while—put it completely out of mind—concentrate on something else, on the people around him.

Idly he observed the counter girl fixing up a tray. She had put two mounds of ice cream, pink and chocolate, between the split halves of a banana on a long glass dish. As he watched her incredulously, she poured a stream of chocolate syrup over one mound, and spooned marsh-

140

mallow sauce onto the other. When she had made an elaborate twisting of whipped cream up and down the length of her concoction, she strewed pecans generously over the surface, and added a garnish of maraschino cherries. She whisked her masterpiece down the length of the counter into the hands of a waitress who carried it out of sight. Fascinated, Marc speculated about its destination.

It would be a woman, he decided. A middle-aged woman whose bulging curves bespoke a reckless intake of calories. And she would be wearing a pink georgette blouse and a little hat with a beau-catcher veil. His creation delighted him. He was sure she was sitting there in the flesh on the other side of the double row of booths, gluttonously lapping up marshmallow, chocolate and nuts.

But life was always fooling you. A banana split was a woman's dish,—therefore it must have been ordered by a man. A conservative, prissy little man in a pince-nez, who was timidly indulging a secret taste for the voluptuous.

Woman in Pink Blouse or Man with Pince-Nez,—That would make a good title for a detective story. Well, he thought, as he saw the counter girl heading his way with a laden tray, it would remain one of life's little unsolved mysteries, like what had become of Aunt Sophie's cameo brooch?

By the time he was ready for his second cup of coffee, the crowd had thinned out and he took it into a near-by empty booth. Settling down with a cigarette, he picked up the parked Minary case. It looked better to him now.

Taken singly, each of his points could be explained in terms of crime rates, accident, or coincidence. But collectively, they could not all be laid to chance and shrugged away. Eve's murder following Crane's, the missing letters, Madame X, the Judge's death in conjunction with the new will and his daughter's insanity,—it all added up to something. But Marc was not sure what.

As he considered the characters in the little drama, they revolved before him like figures on a merry-go-round. And one of the riders a murderer! It was an obscure game of guess who. They circled before Marc in a macabre review. Scott, blind to reality in his fanatical devotion to his sister, a sealed rocket bound for the moon. The paper doll, turning her beautiful blank face toward him as she rode past. Halsey next, raking him with an appraising glance from his shrewd blue eyes.

Then the turning wheel brought Don Quixote into view with her grotesque face and passionate empty heart. Hard on her heels came Barbara, the earth woman, and after her the granite enigma that was her husband.

Around and around they whirled to a confusing tune. All revolving about an unrevealed figure at the center of the mechanism,—Eve, who had set them in motion by her madness and her death. The whole merry-go-round hinged on her, and Marc could not see her face.

He tried to piece her together from the glimpses he had caught through others. But either the pieces would not fit, or else some were missing. The key to it all lay in her personality, but what Marc could learn of her was vague and contradictory. He could reach her only through the memory of those who had known her long before, and each of them saw in her only what he had wanted to find, —a devoted sister, wife and daughter,—a zealous reformer, or a beautiful charmer with a secret life, who had seduced her best friend's husband and taken Crane for her lover.

Only this was certain, that Eve had been caught in a dark tangle that destroyed first, her reason, and finally her life. And her personality and her trouble were deeply hidden by the obscurity of ten long years. But someone had been entangled with her. Someone with whom Marc had talked, whom he could probe, someone in whom the past was still living.

If Eve had written those letters, her husband was not
the only one with a motive for murdering Crane. In fact,
Marc had thought first of all of Scott. But he saw now
that the field was even wider. For, if Eve had lured Freddie Humber, and loved Crane, she had probably had other
affairs, too. . . . Jeff Halsey could have been one of her
lovers! . . . But it all hinged on the character of Eve, and
how could he ever find the answer now?

There *was* one thing. Marc connected the writer of
Hal's letters with Freddie's siren, for he felt it must be the
same seductive woman in both instances,—and Cissie
Humber knew the identity of Madame X.

It was all right for Cissie to play around with her eva-
sions, and reticences, and Madame X's, before Eve was
killed. But there'd been a murder since and the time for
silence was over. He swallowed the last of his coffee and
walked back to the phone at the rear of the store.

He dialed Cissie's number, and in a moment a pert
voice told him he had Mrs. Humber's residence, but Mrs.
Humber was busy and would he leave a message, please.

"This is Dr. Castleman speaking. Will you ask Mrs.
Humber if I may run out and see her this afternoon?"

As the receding tap-tap of high heels came over the
wire, Marc leaned against the wall, facing the length of
the drugstore. He discovered that he could now see on the
other side of the row of booths, and there, in the one at
the end, a pimply faced youth, in a high-school blazer, sat
smoking a cigarette. And the long glass dish before him
unmistakably contained the remnants of what had once
been a banana split.

Marc laughed in pure enjoyment. Of course! It was as
simple as that. It would have been obvious to anyone but
a psychiatrist, that a banana split was a dish for the high
school crowd. But his oversubtle brain had to conjure
up women in pink blouses and mousy little men.

With quickening perception, he wondered if he were

doing the same thing with Eve's murder. Maybe he was running down devious motives, looking for tenuous relationships, while all the time the obvious answer was right before him. What was the most obvious thing about this case?

As the beginnings of a luminous idea floated toward him, Cissie's buoyant voice boomed into his ear. "I'm frightfully sorry, Dr. Castleman, but I'm just on the point of leaving, and I'm going to be tied up all evening. Will tomorrow afternoon do?"

"Oh . . . why yes, . . . tomorrow will have to do then, I guess."

"Do you want to have tea with me at four, or come for a cocktail at five?"

"Would two o'clock be too early? That would be the best hour for me to get away from the hospital."

"Two o'clock it is, then. . . . I suppose you're still sleuthing. Do you want me for a Watson or a body-guard?"

Marc laughed. "I'm afraid I'm not far enough along to use either, yet. What I need now is a little illumination. . . . I think you've been keeping your light under a bushel. . . . I hope you're going to shed some of it on my darkness. There are some things you alone can tell me. I'm counting on you,—and the stakes are high."

There was a pause, and when Cissie answered, her voice had changed timbre. "What is it you want to know?"

"I'd rather wait until I see you. I'll tell you about it, tomorrow."

"Oh," . . . The banter came back into her voice. "You know you're titillating my curiosity most unmercifully, Dr. Castleman. It's not fair of you to take advantage of my most susceptible point this way. . . . But then,—I've always known that you psychiatrists were heartless brutes. . . . Tomorrow, then, at two."

17.

WHEN MARC got back to the hospital he was immediately waylaid by the blonde receptionist at the front desk. "Dr. Castleman, Dr. Smythe-Jones wants to see you as soon as you come in. I think he's been having some trouble with one of your patients."

"All right, thanks." Oh, Lord,—Marc thought, as he hurried toward the second floor men's wing.— That'll probably be Potts.

It was Potts and he was in a state when Castleman reached the room. Smythe-Jones, who was there with him, drew Marc aside. "I haven't known just how to handle this case. Not familiar enough with the background. . . . It looks like he's going over into a manic phase. And I've had to give him so much time, I couldn't finish up your rounds for you."

"I'm sorry, S.-J., to have left you holding the bag today. I didn't know Potts was going to blow up this way. . . . Thanks! I'll take over now."

"And . . . Oh, yes . . . another of your patients has been asking for you. Isobel Shively."

Potts *had* worked himself up. The afternoon was almost gone before he was quiet enough for Marc to leave him and start in on his round of visits interrupted since the morning.

By the time he had finished his work in ward five, the staff dining room was closed. That meant a table d'hôte across the street at the Greek's. . . . But the loud-speaker caught him before he could get out of the building. "Dr.

145

Castleman . . . Dr. Castleman . . . Dr. Castleman wanted in Room 135," it droned insistently.

He found Miss Schmeiser with Isobel. The patient was in bed, and when Marc came in, she was gripping the mattress with both hands, her face contorted with pain. As soon as the paroxysm passed, she looked up at him triumphantly.

"I'm in labor, doctor. The first pain came this morning right after you were here. They're coming about three an hour now." She glanced at one of her recent purchases, a large alarm clock occupying a conspicuous position on the bedside table. She'd had it in readiness for several days now. "That means the first stage is almost over, doesn't it?"

Marc looked down at her in dismay. He couldn't let Shivelly have her baby now. She'd probably be at it all night. He had to get something to eat. He had to see McKeith. He wanted to get the Minary case straightened out in his mind. He'd caught the tail end of an idea, back there in the drugstore, and he didn't want it to get away from him, before he had a chance to pull it into full view and look it over.

He stooped down and pulled back Isobel's bed covering. With skillful, gentle fingers he probed her flat stomach, simulating to her satisfaction a thorough examination. There was an anxious question in her eyes when he finished. He pulled up a chair and sat down by the side of her bed. "You're not very far along yet, Isobel. I don't think things will really get under way until the morning. . . . You want this baby to come through all right, don't you?"

"Oh, yes, doctor. . . . Nothing must go wrong now!"

"Well, then, you've got to cooperate with me. You know at your age we must be careful. Now, I want you to get a good rest tonight. These are just preliminary pains you've been having. It often happens that way. I

think they're about over now. The best thing for you to
do is to have a long sleep, so you'll be ready for tomorrow. Do you think you can do that?"

"I'll try, doctor. I'll do my best."

"Well, I'll give you a hypodermic, now, and I think
you'll drop right off."

Isobel sank back on her pillows obediently. A drowsy
look came over her face even before Marc gave her the
sedative. He looked back at her in satisfaction as he left.
Her eyes were closed and she was breathing quietly.

Miss Schmeiser followed him into the hall. "I think
she'll be all right, now," he told her. "The mental suggestion and the intravenous of nembutal should take
care of her until morning. She can have another nembutal orally if she asks for it tonight. . . . If she starts up
again, though, I want you to call me at once."

When he finally got over to the Greek's, all the items
on the menu had been scratched out except scrambled
brains, pickled pigs' feet and fried tripe. As Marc didn't
relish eating entrails, or pickled meat, the proprietor
promised to fix up something special. He had a nice
little steak in his icebox.

When he had filled up on steak, French fries, coleslaw and a double helping of coffee for the second time
that day, Castleman started over to McKeith's. The
truant had to make an accounting. He had a feeling that
Mac wasn't going to like his getting mixed up in this case
again. The breach that had suddenly gapped between
them on the night of the autopsy, had closed automatically when Marc discovered the presence of nicotine.
They were back on the old basis again.

Or they seemed to be. You could never tell about those
things. There had been a break, and although it had
healed, Marc knew that every experience leaves its mark
in the subconscious. There was scar tissue in their relationship now.

Mrs. McKeith answered Marc's ring. The overhead
light behind her brought out the gleams in her hair and
outlined her slender silhouette. Marc suspected that
beauty shops had a lot to do with the golden glints, and
he knew that if she turned, her profile would be marred
by the dowager's hump at the back of her neck.

She was careful to keep full view toward him as she
stepped back, saying in the beautiful voice that was her
chief charm, "Good evening, Marc." But the light caught
her face at an unfortunate angle, emphasizing the creases
that ran from her nose to chin like micrometer calipers.

"Is Mac in?"

"Yes. He's back in the study. . . . I want to talk to you,
Marc. Come on in here."

"I'm sorry, Mrs. McKeith. I haven't time. I want to
see Mac right away." He knew she liked to be called
Dorothy, but he stubbornly persisted in giving her her
married name. You had to be careful with Dorothy. It
used to be that when she entered a room, all the men present naturally gravitated into her corner. But for a long
time the force of gravity had operated in reverse, and she
had learned to use external pressure. She had a habit of
sweeping up the young men in her vicinity and forcibly
carrying them off for intimate little tête-à-têtes.

"But I have to talk to you. It's abou Ian. I'm worried
about him, Marc. He's not getting over this flu as he
should. He hasn't been himself at all this week. I'll wait
until you're through with him, and then I'll tell you about
it."

"Well,—if it isn't too late." With the ruthlessness of
youth, Marc left her standing there and went on back to
the study.

McKeith was sitting close to the fire, and from the expression on his face, Marc guessed that his neuritis was
bothering him again. He looked up and asked irritably,
"Where the devil have you been all day, Castleman?

Smythe-Jones has been having his hands full with Potts. He called me in to help him, but I couldn't do much. I hadn't time to study his case history this afternoon."

"Yes, I know. I'm sorry about Potts. He had a dream that he couldn't analyze. He worried himself into a stew over it. Then finally he hit on an interpretation, and that was worse. He scared himself half to death. He's verging on a manic phase. But I think I can get him straightened out in the morning when he's calmed down. I have him in a cold pack now. I wish I was in one myself. I'm fagged out, but I feel too keyed up to sleep. If I didn't have such a heavy day ahead tomorrow, I'd take some amytal."

"What did Fletcher want to see you about?"

"Well, that's not quite the way it was. I wanted to see Fletcher. He's turned out be a louse, Mac. He's gunning for Minary because of that old business, the special investigation and all. He's trying to make trouble. I had a talk with Halsey, and he and Scott think they've got Fletcher's guns spiked. . . .

"But none of them seems to give a damn about who killed Evelyn."

"I don't see why you want to mess with it, Marc. That's their business. You've got work to do out here. Why don't you leave it alone?"

"It's bad for the hospital to have this thing go unsolved, McKeith. Unless it's proved that Eve was murdered by one of her own people, it's going to look like we were responsible for it."

McKeith answered in exasperation. "The reputation of the hospital was hurt as soon as it came out that she was murdered. She was up here and we let her get killed while she was in our hands. It doesn't matter much now, as far as our reputation goes, who killed her. It's something we'll just have to live down. . . . The best way to do that is to forget the whole thing and get on with our own work. . . I don't know what you hope to do about it any way. You're a psychiatrist, not a detective."

"Well, Fletcher isn't much of a detective either, as far as that goes. I'm as good a one as he is. At least I'm interested in clearing the thing up, and I have some leads that no one else cares to follow. . . . I've had a hunch, from the first, that Eve wrote those letters to Crane and that her murder is connected with his. I thought of Scott of course, but Halsey feels that the letters, if they were Eve's, point to Minary. He may have hit on something, you know."

Encouraged by a flicker of interest in McKeith's eyes, Marc went on eagerly, "Phil was supposed to have been out at the Women's Hospital with Eve when Crane was killed, but no one checked into his alibi. The police went hot-footing it after Tilton. . . . Now we know Crane was trying to get in touch with Minary that night. Suppose he went out to the hospital to see him? That gives us Phil and Crane together at a critical time. . . . But—" he frowned in perplexity, "but then, Minary would have had to have known previously about Eve and Crane. And if he had known all along, I don't see why he waited until that night at the hospital to do something about it."

He scowled into the fire, his brow wrinkled with the effort of concentration. Suddenly he burst out excitedly, "Eve had just come down from the operating room and Phil was with her. . . . That was over ten years ago. I wonder if they were using scopolamine then? Well, it doesn't matter, some patients talk their heads off just from ether. Maybe Eve got to talking while she was coming out, let Phil know all about her affair with Crane. . . . Why, the baby,—maybe that was Crane's . . . ! And then, just when Phil finds out everything, Crane comes walking in on him. . . .

"Anything could have happened!"

"But where is all this getting you, Marc?" McKeith

asked wearily. "Even if Crane was at the Women's Hospital that night, how can you go about proving it now?
No one out there is going to remember what happened
on a particular night ten years ago. Probably none of
the nurses even knew what Crane looked like. And the
letters were destroyed long ago. Phil was the only one
who had read them, and he isn't going to tell. . . . You
don't even know that Eve wrote the letters. That's just
a guess, and it's not consistent with what we've heard
about her. In fact, all the evidence is just the other
way . . ."

"We can't go by what her family tells us," Marc
pointed out. "Naturally, if she was on the loose, her
relatives aren't going to advertise it. And maybe they
didn't know about Crane—or the other side of her nature.
She was pretty young, her real personality was just emerging. I imagine Scott was jealously possessive of her before her marriage. Never gave her a chance to play
around. Then when she married and had some freedom
she'd find her attraction for men a pretty exciting
thing. . ."

"But Eve was in love with her husband. Her marriage
was altogether happy," McKeith interposed. His distaste
for Marc's comments was plain on his face, and under
that some other stronger emotion fended off the suggestion.

"But even so," Marc contended, "she probably got a
kick out of trying out her charms on the other men around
her, like Freddie Humber. And before she knew it she
got in too deep with Crane. Maybe she was more susceptible than she realized,—and with her husband all tied
up with this investigation of his . . . !"

"But it all depends on Eve's personality," McKeith
said. "And you never knew her."

"I think I'm going to get something positive on that,"
Marc answered. "I have an appointment with Cissie

Humber for tomorrow I'll go see Cissie. If nothing comes of it, then I'll drop the whole thing and knuckle down to harness. Will that satisfy you, Mac?"

McKeith smiled, that likable, understanding smile of his. "That's what you say now, Marc, that you'll drop it tomorrow But when tomorrow comes, you'll be chasing hot on another trail you'll have picked up. . . . You'll keep at it, knocking your head against a stone wall, until you're convinced that stone is stone, and a wall is a wall."

"Or until I find the murderer."

McKeith sighed and looked into the fire. Tonight his face was drawn and old-looking for a man of fifty. "And when you find out the truth you may be sorry. . . ." He continued to gaze reflectively at the fire with the sadness in his expression that Marc had noticed there frequently of late.

The younger man's eagerness chilled. He felt himself slipping into the other's melancholy mood. McKeith rubbed his fingers over his forehead as though he were trying to press out an ache there.

"Have you ever stopped to think, Marc, how you would like to go through the rest of your life knowing you had sent a fellow-human being to the electric chair? . . . Perhaps someone you find yourself liking very much. . . . You don't know what sort of a mess Eve was in—or how she may have involved someone else. She may have been killed in desperation."

"Well, I can always keep what I learn to myself, if I sympathize with the murderer."

"Maybe you can't. Once you start something, it gains momentum, it gets out of your hands. These questions you are asking . . . you don't know what they'll lead to."

"Well, I'll see Cissie tomorrow and then I'll give up—unless I get something absolutely sure fire from her. . . . That's a promise, Mac." Marc pulled himself out of his chair.

McKeith sat looking up at him. "Take care of yourself, Marc. . . . Don't forget you're hunting tiger!"

"Oh, I'll be all right." He turned back. "You look after *yourself*. Sinus troubling you still? We're getting some sun again now. That ought to help clear it up. . . . See you tomorrow."

Marc, hurrying through the hall, heard footsteps on the floor above. As he let himself out, Dorothy McKeith called to him, "Are you finished, Marc? Wait a minute, I'm coming down!"

He closed the door quickly behind him and started off diagonally across the grounds. The sky was overcast and at first he could see nothing but enveloping black. He walked carefully, trying to remember the location of the big trees. When his eyes had become adjusted to the dark, he still couldn't see much, but he felt the need of fresh air, and strolled further from the hospital.

He made his way slowly over to the north boundary and took out his cigarettes. There was a sharp wind blowing and he leaned against the wall, cupping his hands around his match as he got a light. Just before the match went out, it flared up for a second, and out of the corner of his eyes he caught a movement in a clump of bushes ahead.

My God, but I'm getting nervy when I start jumping at shadows,—he thought. Uneasily he rested his back against the wall and faced out into the darkness as he smoked. He had suddenly become acutely aware of the lonely black expanse separating him from the hospital. It was just a week ago, that the murderer had struck in that darkened building on the far side of the wide lawns.

McKeith had suggested an aspect that hadn't occurred to him. He had been thinking of the case as an intriguing problem which he would solve by deductive reasoning. Fletcher and Halsey's opposition had turned it into a game of wits. But now, in the loneliness of the night, he realized he had taken on someone who played for keeps. It wasn't an academic problem or a game of chess to his hidden adversary. It was a matter of life or death. And it had been death for Crane and Eve, . . . and Eve's father too?

There was a sudden creaking of dark branches and rustling of invisible leaves blown before the gust. Castleman felt chilled through and not by the night wind alone. He had leaped without looking and now he found himself equipped with only a beebee gun, tracking down a man-eating tiger. He couldn't even guess at the identity of the killer, and here he was blindly threading his way through a dark maze toward a vicious, deadly beast.

His sense of personal danger heightened as he tried to peer through the obscurity surrounding him, wondering if the tiger was prowling in the black.

He dropped the butt of his cigarette on the ground, and was turning to stamp it out, when he felt the movement toward him. He threw up his arm and ducked as a heavy blow glanced off the side of his head, throwing him onto his knees. Instantaneously he heard a loud, uninhibited yell coming from his own throat, and farther off, piercing screams in a woman's voice. High heels running over pavement came nearer and heavier footsteps rushed away from him.

In a moment the beam of Dorothy's flashlight found him, and she let out a louder shriek. When he tried to scramble to his feet, she bent over him. "Oh, Marc, what happened? Are you hurt? What is the matter?"

The whole side of his face was numb,—but he could move his jaw,—so it wasn't broken. And he didn't feel any loose teeth in his mouth.

"Did you fall? The way you were yelling, you nearly scared me to death."

He was on his feet now, but he swayed dizzily, and Dorothy propped her shoulder under his. "Can you make it up to the house?"

"Yes, let's go." She guided him over to the walk, and although he could get along all right now, she persisted in her gesture of supporting him.

McKeith met them halfway up the walk. He had on an overcoat, but was without a hat. In the light of Dorothy's torch, Marc saw the wind ruffling his hair, and thought about those inflamed sinuses.

"What's going on out here? What's the matter, Marc?"

"Someone tried to knock me out a few moments ago. It felt like the butt end of a cannon. Probably a sandbag."

Dorothy let out another of her squeals. "Somebody attacked you, here on the grounds? . . . One of the patients must be loose! Oh, let's hurry in. It isn't safe out here."

"Come on in, Marc, and let me look you over." McKeith led the way back to the house. He took Marc into the downstairs lavatory, telling his wife to call the hospital and ask Miss Kraft to check on the patients.

When he had washed his face and examined his head, McKeith told Marc that he seemed to have gotten off lightly. "There's a bad contusion on the cheekbone,— but nothing's broken. Of course there might be a crack in one of those bones. We'll have to X-ray tomorrow— but there's not enough swelling to indicate anything like that. Come on in the other room and I'll give you some whisky."

Dorothy was waiting for them in the living room. She had called Miss Kraft, who said she thought all the patients were in their beds. She was making a check and would let them know.

Marc accepted his Scotch gratefully. His face felt heavy, but it didn't hurt yet, and he could talk pretty well. "I don't think it was a patient. You know we don't have a man on the gate after six any more. Anyone could have come in here tonight."

"But Marc, why should someone from outside come in here and attack you?" Dorothy asked in perplexity. "Who would know the grounds, and what you were doing? If it isn't a patient, it must be someone on the staff." She looked coy. "Have you been poaching on some one's pet preserve? Some of those new nurses are honeys . . ."

At Dorothy's words an insidious thought snaked through Marc's mind. He kept his eyes on his whisky for a moment and then asked casually. "Did the wind blow your hat off, Mac? You shouldn't have been out tonight bareheaded with your sinuses."

"I didn't stop to get my hat with Dorothy screaming out there like she was being murdered. It's a wonder she didn't rouse the whole hospital, but I guess her voice didn't carry that far." He turned to her, abruptly. "What were you doing out there, anyway, prowling around this time of night?"

She flushed and looked at him defiantly. "I was try-ing to follow Marc. I saw him start off, going the op-posite way from the hospital, and I went after him. . . . I wanted to talk to him about you, Ian. You know you aren't well, but you won't do anything for yourself. The flu sometimes affects the heart. . . . I've been worried sick, and I wanted Marc to check up on you."

"I'm enough of a doctor to tell if I've got heart trouble or not," McKeith answered impatiently, then he spoke more gently to her. "There's nothing wrong with my heart, Dorothy. I'm run down from the flu, and neuritis and sinus are both pretty painful. I guess I haven't been very easy to live with, lately. . . . Wish I could get down to Florida for a few weeks of sun. But there's no chance for that now that half our staff's in the army. When they take you too, Marc, I ought to close up shop. And they'll probably put you to work checking latrines like they're doing with Green."

Marc laughed and drained his glass. "I'll be running along now."

"You'll do nothing of the sort. You're staying here tonight, where I can look after you. That head of yours is going to start hurting like the devil in about an hour. . . . That's probably Kraft now," he broke off as the phone rang in the study.

He hurried to answer it. When he came back his face showed relief. "Well, it wasn't a patient. They're all accounted for. . . . We have to decide now what action we want to take. There was a marauder on the grounds tonight. It looks like you were followed and singled out for attack—or did you surprise him at something, Marc?"

"No. He,—or she,—was lying in wait for me. I was the bait. And it's all over now. The tiger is probably miles away. I don't think there were designs against the hospital. You needn't worry about it."

"Do you want me to report this attack to the police?"

"To Fletcher? Good God, no!"

18

DESPITE McKeith, Potts, Shivelly and a bashed head, Marc turned into the drive at Hillways at three o'clock the next afternoon. The trees that provided such a thick screen in summer had dropped their foliage, revealing the three houses ahead. Marc had been in two of them the night Eve died. He looked curiously at the other, which rather resembled Cissie's own rough-hewn exterior. A huge stone castle where she lived alone in the obsolete splendor built to house a dynasty.

A cute little trick in organdy cap and apron, belonged to the pert telephone voice. She admitted the doctor and left him in a book-lined room with deeply recessed windows, a Gothic fireplace, and proportions appropriate only to knights in armor. The portable bar beside the sparkling fire was the only touch of modernity, and of Cissie.

Cissie herself came in, in a moment, dressed in a scarlet sweater and corduroy pants. Her red face had a windwhipped look. "Hello, Dr. Castleman. You're a rare sight to find on these premises,—a delectable young man like you here in the middle of the afternoon."

She turned dramatically to the rows of solemn books along the far wall. "No, I didn't lasso him and carry him off across my saddle. Nor was he lured hither by promise of dinner with vintage wine. I ask you to believe he came of his own free will."

She faced Marc with a teasing smile. "You were lured here, all the same though, weren't you? and not by the light of my beaux yeux. I understand you're after another sort of light, one usually kept under a bushel. Want me to turn lodestar?"

"I certainly do, Mrs. Humber. This thing has taken a serious turn . . "

"Wait!" Cissie interrupted. "If ever I saw a man in need of a drink, you're it." She walked over to the bar. "What'll it be? Scotch or rye?"

"Rye, please . . . and no water."

She went on talking as she brought bottle and glass together. "If you don't mind my saying so, you're looking more and more like something recently dug up from an ancient Egyptian tomb. You can't afford that, you know. A nice young doctor just starting in practice! It's a bad advertisement. Consider the effect on your patients for you to come into a room all wan and wavering, fairly reeking of the grave."

"Mrs. Humber, my appearance is based on sound psychology. Shoemaker's children you know. . . . Thank you!" He accepted her proffered drink, and sat down in a fireside chair across from her. "Now patients would be instantly suspicious of a fresh-eyed, rosy-cheeked doctor. They'd suspect too much unsought leisure. People want their medical man to look harassed and worn down from dashing to and fro, rushing from patient to patient.

"That's my trouble." He sighed lugubriously. "My practice is too heavy. I had to simply tear myself away to get here today. I was an hour late at that because I came to you straight from delivering a baby. Difficult case, too!"

Cissie paused with her glass halfway to her mouth. "Why, I didn't know you went in for obstetrics, doctor. Do so many women go crazy on learning they're about to become mothers, that you've built up a special practice with them?"

Castleman grinned at her tantalizingly without answer, and she asked, half serious, "Do you really have a maternity wing at Oaklawn? . . . What goes on out there anyway? Do you mean to tell me you have insane couples living in wedded bliss? . . . Haven't you heard about eugenics?"

"Put your mind at ease," he reassured her. "There's nothing wrong with our eugenics. It was a fine, big, thirteen-pound baby boy I pulled out this morning. The mother's doing nicely, too. . . . She is a virgin lady of sixty-odd. God took pity on her and in answer to her prayers he opened her withered womb, same like he did

with Samuel's ma, only in this case, there was no Old
Testament patriarch at hand."

"Oh, I get it," Cissie laughed. "A case of mental con-
ception! But tell me, which one kicked you in the face?
. . . the mother or the baby? There was nothing mental
about that kick. I cast my vote for a mule's hind leg."

"So you've noticed my shiner." Marc set down his
empty glass and looked at her closely. "Mrs. Humber,
yesterday you suggested a bodyguard for me. What
prompted that?"

"Oh, I'm a smart girl, I am. I didn't need to look into
my crystal ball to figure that one. . . . McKeith and Castleman had been prying around in Eve's past, trying to cure
her. But Eve is dead and Castleman still wants to ask
Cissie questions. *Voilà!* The doctor's turned detective,
and amateur detectives who go nosing around murder
always get bopped on the head. So you got bopped!
Right?"

"Too right!" he admitted ruefully.

"Too good! Did you really get bopped?" Cissie
leaned forward delightedly, her little eyes avid with
curiosity.

"Who? When? What happened to you?"

"Just apply the classic formula and you've got it.
Darkness! The witching hour of midnight! The witless
detective, mysterious assailant with sandbag, unseen at-
tacker escaping in resulting confusion;—that's it!"

"Where?"

"The grounds of Oaklawn, during my nightly stroll."

"Inside Oaklawn? . . . But that means someone at the
hospital! You keep yourselves all locked in at night, don't
you?"

"No, we don't. That front gate is to keep people in—
not out. During the day when we have patients on the
lawn, we keep a man there to see that none of them
wanders off. But at night, when they're tucked in their

beds, there's no one at the gate. Anyone could get in. Someone did, and not just to warn me off. That would have been a fatal bop if Dorothy McKeith hadn't been following me. I'd have been finished off for good."

"But why? Have you discovered who . . . ?"

Marc watched her carefully. "Maybe in nosing around this murder, I'm getting too close to some one. I hope that's it. But I can't be sure. That attack could spring from something else. While Eve was our patient she was in a mental fog. She told us nothing at all about herself or her life before she came to us. But maybe the murderer isn't sure of that. . . . If he isn't, McKeith and I are both in danger until this murder is solved."

Cissie picked up Marc's glass and took it to the bar. "This calls for another drink. More of the same?" She gave him a critical glance. "Your appearance is improving slightly. But you look far from healthy. Here, take this and sit back and unlax." She filled her own glass and sat carelessly on the arm of her lounge chair.

"Mrs. Humber . . ."

"Let's drop this 'Mrs. Humber' business, shall we? It's too cumbersome. I don't like cumbersome things. I've had to live with one all my life."

Perched on the chair arm, she swung her big foot insouciantly as she sipped her drink. "You know there are some people who are born to be called by their first names from cradle to grave. Don't ask me why. It has nothing to do with their intelligence or their avoirdupois. . . . Now I, myself, am one of the first name legion. To every man, woman and child in this town I am Cissie. Every time you say 'Mrs. Humber', I look around to see who has come into the room. So you see, Marc, . . . that's your given name, isn't it?"

"Yes it is. And henceforth I'm Marc to you. It makes it quite cozy. But, we've horsed around long enough Cissie. You've unlaxed me beautifully. The time ' now come to talk about something besides cabbages and kings."

He looked at her sharply. He had to pin her down some way. She had been fluttering around skittishly like some awkward creature with big fragile wings, shying away at each suggestion of coming to grips with him. He couldn't decide whether all this putting him off was done for a purpose,—or if it were just Cissie.

"All right," she replied easily. "I'm congenitally light-minded, but I'll try to concentrate on whatever it is that is consuming you from within."

"It doesn't seem to bother you that McKeith and I are going about in danger of our lives. But there is another aspect to this thing. Do you know that Fletcher is getting ready to indict your friend Barbara for Eve's murder?"

All frivolity left Cissie instantly. She turned to him a face filled with concern.

"No . . . ! No, they mustn't do that! It's ridiculous . . . and abominable!"

"Of course they're just using her to get at Phil . . . because he tried to buck them ten years ago. They intend to finish him off this time."

"Oh, it isn't fair . . . not Phil! After all he's been through!" Her voice was fiercely protective. "They can't do that."

"Oh, but they can. He's the one who inherits from Eve. To protect Barbara he'll say that he wasn't going to divorce her . . . and maybe he wasn't. Then Fletcher's going to suggest that Phil was carrying on with Barbara before Eve got sick."

"But that's not true at all. Phil was crazy about Eve. Fletcher can't find any evidence to indicate anything else."

"Maybe he can't. But he doesn't have to have evidence. Once the D. A. gets to cross-examining, he can make some nasty implications just by the kind of questions he asks. The Judge may rule them out, but the damage will have been done. Suspicion will be planted, and Phil can never live it down. Not only that! It seems Julia is bursting to go on the stand and describe Barbara's and Phil's billing and cooing in their little love nest. Married billing and cooing, of course, but it'll put a doubt in Scott's mind about Phil's intentions toward Eve. See? . . . Now the only way to keep Fletcher from dragging all this in court, is to find out quickly who did murder Eve. Can I count on you?"

"For anything!" Cissie looked ready to charge with the light brigade straight into the cannon's mouth.

"Good." Marc took a swallow of his drink, and relaxed a little. "There are a lot of angles to this thing, Cissie. I'm on the trail of something, and one thing ties in with another, in a way you may not understand. You're not going to like the question I'm going to ask, but I have a good reason for it. I'm not just prying around promiscuously. . . . I want a straight answer. It's important! . . . This woman who came between you and your husband,—was it Eve?"

"Eve!" Cissie's galvanized start knocked over her glass. It fell to the floor without breaking, spilling ice and liquid onto the heavy carpet. She sprang to her feet and stared at him. "Dr. Castleman, you are stark, staring, raving mad! You're crazier than any patient in your institution. . . .

"No, it wasn't Eve. Of course it wasn't Eve!"

She stooped over, picked up her glass, set it on the bar and went back to her chair. She sat there without speaking as moments passed. Marc, watching her, sensed her inward struggle, and kept silent for fear of saying the wrong thing.

Finally she looked over at him with despair in her eyes which slowly gave way to a look of defeat. She lay back.

drained, and said, as if yielding the last treasure, "No, it wasn't Eve. . . . It was Madeleine Ladbrooke."

19.

"MADELEINE LADBROOKE!" It was Marc's turn to be electrified. He didn't knock over his glass, but he felt as if a second sandbag had come down on him hard. "Madeleine!" he repeated unbelievingly. Not that paper doll! That vapid, conventional fashion plate, that sexless . . . ! Suddenly he remembered her as she had been the night Eve died, there in the front hall at the Ladbrookes'. He recalled the tug on his senses as she stood close to him pleading!

"I know it's hard to believe." Cissie lay in her chair, her eyes half closed, speaking with a voice of one who no longer cares about anything. "But Madeleine was once a very different sort of person. She has changed, tremendously changed, from the girl she was when Scott first brought her here. . . . You'd never think it now, but Madeleine used to look a lot like Eve. She was the same sort of dark, fragile, sensitive young thing. People were always taking them for sisters. That was the heart of the whole thing."

She got up, poured herself another drink and took it back to her chair, while Marc waited for the story he knew was coming. Cissie took a long swallow and gazed reminiscently at the stone frieze over the mantel. "One of my earliest childhood memories is of Scott coming across the lawn holding Eve by the hand, careful that she didn't stumble, watching her proudly, protectively. His little sister, who was cuter than any toy he'd ever had. who was his to take care of, to look out for! When she grew older, she became his constant companion. Scott's mother died when he was very young. Eve was the only feminine influence in his early life,—and she remained the predominating one always."

"Yes, McKeith and I had gathered that Scott was emotionally dependent on Eve," Marc said. "How about other girls—didn't he have any interest in them?"

"Scott went through school here and to the local university, but I can't remember his ever having had a sweetheart. Girls were always after him and occasionally he had a date with this one or that one, but never the same girl twice, and never when he could be with Eve instead. . . . That was it. you see. He preferred Eve's companionship to anyone else's."

Cissie's long Don Quixote face. was oddly illumined as she delved into things past. "When he went off to Harvard Law, it was the first time he'd been separated from Eve, and that was when he met Madeleine. I think he began to go around with her because she reminded him of his sister. But of course, she couldn't know that."

"So Madeleine was just a surrogate for Eve," Marc said, when she paused. "What happened when he came back here to live, did his dependency on Eve reassert itself?"

"Yes." Spurred by her attentive audience Cissie went on at a gallop. "Eve went to Cambridge to visit Scott one Easter and met Phil, and they both went head over heels. With Phil and Eve absorbed in each other, Scott felt left out in the cold. Eve's wedding was in June, and Scott married Madeleine that fall. They moved in with Judge

Ladbrooke next door to Eve and Phil, and Scott fell right
back into the old pattern of life, with Eve for leading
lady again.

"It was hard lines for Madeleine. She was passionately
in love with Scott and had expected to find herself the
petted and adored little bride. Instead, all she got were
the crumbs from Eve's table."

"But," Marc broke in, "why did Eve go on monopoliz-
ing Scott? Couldn't she see that it wasn't fair to Madeleine? That she would wreck her brother's marriage?"

"Eve didn't want to monopolize Scott." Cissie defended
her dead friend hotly. "She couldn't help it if he was
aware of no one else when she was around. In fact, I
think she found it rather trying at times. . . . I don't know
why Madeleine stuck it out, . . . a Victorian novelist would
say she was bound to her pillory by a chain of passion.
Then, too, she was from one of those Boston families that
have never had a divorce in their history." Cissie had
been slowing down. Now she came to a full stop.

"Madeleine wasn't built for neglect," Marc prodded.
"She began to play around a little I suppose,—to soothe
her vanity—and maybe to make Scott jealous?"

"Madeleine didn't take it sitting down," Cissie agreed.
She went on with reluctance, her own suppressed emotion
troubling her, welling up in the overtones of her voice.
"She gathered a regular little court of gallants about her.
Maybe she hoped to make Scott jealous, but he never
seemed to notice. Of course she wasn't unfaithful or anything like that. She just indulged in a series of little
drawing-room flirtations." Cissie hesitated. "Freddie
Humber was one in the series. I suppose McKeith has
told you about that? Madame X?"

When Marc nodded, she went on, haltingly, fighting
down an old pain. "Well, that's all there was to it. . . .
She dazzled Freddie, without the least idea of what she
was doing. . . . Madeleine would be utterly amazed if

she knew she'd been the cause of our break-up. . . . She just smashed up my marriage, sort of casually, in passing. . . . That's the story. Not much of a secret skeleton, is it?" She gave a weary. deprecatory shrug.

"That isn't all the story, Cissie. She got in a little deeper with Crane, didn't she?"

"How on earth . . . ? What do you know about that?" Cissie was jolted from her preoccupation with her aching heart.

"There were some letters."

"What letters?" Cissie sat up with returning animation. Her little eyes gleamed like a magpie's caught by the bait of a glittering button. "Do you mean Madeleine wrote some letters to Crane and you've found them?"

"Something like that. I'll tell you about it when I've heard your side of the story."

"Well," Cissie continued with renewed interest, "when Freddie and I broke up. I went off on a cruise. I was gone for several months and when I came back everyone was involved in this reform campaign. Eve tried to get me interested and took me around to their meetings and sessions. This young reporter, Hal Crane, was there. He swallowed Madeleine's bait,—hook, line and sinker. But he wasn't another Freddie Humber! Hal had been around.

"At first their little interplay was all open and aboveboard. Just sophisticated give and take, the sort of thing that goes on in the smart set, you know. That's all it was in the beginning."

"And then?" Marc asked persistently.

"But then it went underground! They suddenly became elaborately casual with each other and avoided being seen alone together. But now and then there would be a quick look between them that told the whole story."

"How did Scott react to that?" Marc asked eagerly.

"He didn't notice a thing." Cissie assured him, "and

all the others were blind as bats, too. They were so absorbed in this political business, they couldn't see what was right before their eyes. . . . Not that Madeleine and Crane weren't careful. Maybe I wouldn't have noticed either, if I hadn't been watching her closely. You see, I was allergic to Madeleine,—after what she had done to me.

"I was surprised though at Madeleine's going in for something like that." Cissie pondered a problem that had apparently bothered her a long time. "She wasn't fundamentally that kind of person, and all the time she was having her affair with Hal, I know she was really crazy about Scott. . . . Of course, she was restless, and unhappy, and passionate . . ." Marc laughed abruptly, and she looked at him in surprise. "What's the matter?"

"The joke's on me," he was ruefully amused. "You see I was telling Mac all about this last night. I had the background sketched in, correct in every detail. Only I got hold of the wrong woman for subject. I painted a convincing picture all right,—the neglected wife having herself a little fling, with innocent intention, and bang! She's overboard before she knows what's happening to her."

"I guess it must have been something like that," Cissie agreed, thoughtfully. "But it wasn't long until Crane was killed, and Madeleine just froze up completely! I never *have* understood why she took his death the way she did. I'm sure Scott was the grand passion of her life. Why should she go into perpetual mourning for Crane? She turned into a different person after his death. She has gone around ever since like a woman in an iron mask."

"I can tell you one thing that happened," Marc said. "She'd written some letters and they were probably pretty indiscreet. Phil found them when he subpoenaed Crane's things after the murder. He probably returned them to her, or told her he'd destroyed them."

"So that was it!" Cissie exclaimed in eager enlighten-
ment. "I see it all now. . . . Wouldn't it have made juicy
headlines—?" She improvised with obvious relish,

" 'BEAUTIFUL YOUNG SOCIALITE
MYSTERY WOMAN IN CRANE KILLING

The police revealed today that young Mrs. Scott
Ladbrooke, the former Madeleine Embry, Boston debutante of 1928, is involved in Crane
murder . . .' "

"I suppose if that had come out, it would have been the
end of everything with Scott?" Marc asked,—and at the
confirmation in Cissie's eyes, added, "And that family
back in Boston! She must have gone through hell until
she got those letters back."

"But that was bad, too," Cissie said. "It must have
been an awful humiliation for her. . . . And all these
years since, seeing Phil almost every day, and knowing
that he knew. She probably felt he was watching her all
the time, and if she so much as smiled at a man, he
would begin to suspect . . . !"

"No wonder she has changed!" Genuine compassion
surged into Cissie's voice. "You know she wasn't over
eighteen when she married Scott. . . . There was a time,
Marc, when I hated her guts! . . . But she has had as bad
a time,—maybe a worse time, than I've had.

"When Eve was sent to Oaklawn, I thought it might
make a difference, but Scott seemed more obsessed than
before. He'd go out to the hospital to see her every day,
and he'd talk to us for hours about her, her condition,
the care she was getting and all. He's mourned and worried for years. We'd all be together trying to have fun,
and he'd sit there silent as though he were thinking how

can you enjoy yourselves with Eve up there shut away
from everything?

"But this past week he seems to have accepted things.
Death is pretty final, isn't it? . . . Maybe now, Madeleine
will have a chance!" Cissie had been trying to keep her
manner casual, but some emotion was bubbling through
her control.

"You've been keeping an awful lot of things bottled
up inside of you, Cissie," Marc said, softly. "What's
been the matter?"

Cissie sank back into her chair, looking like she'd just
come through a wringer. "I know you wonder why I've
made such a mystery of all this,—refusing to tell Mc-
Keith who Madame X was, and all. I'm not sure myself
why it was so hard for me to talk about it."

"It had become an obsession with you, Cissie, to repress
all this," Marc began gently. "You refused to remember,
pushed it into your subconscious because . . ."

Suddenly words spilled from her vehemently. "When
Madeleine took Freddie from me, I hated her. God, how
I hated her! I wanted to wring her neck with my own
hands. I wanted to gouge her eyes out, pour boiling lead
into her, put her through every known torture! . . . I
wanted Eve to know and Scott to know what she had done
to me!

"There must have been a thousand times I was on
the point of telling them the whole thing.

"But I knew, if I wanted to keep any dignity in my love
for Freddie . . . if I wanted him to remember anything of
what he had once felt for me,—I had to keep still.

"But I had to fight myself every minute. There wasn't
a day that I didn't want to stand up in front of everybody
and scream out the truth about her. I wanted to see her
kicked out of Scott's house in disgrace, I wanted . . .!"
Cissie had begun to pound her fists on the arms of her
chair in violent expression of her unleashed feelings.

She stopped, suddenly self-conscious, clasped her hands tensely in her lap, and said in a tight voice, "But I fought it down. I pushed back the words. I got so I didn't even dare think about it for fear of what I would do. That went on for months and years. 'Madeleine and Freddie,' 'Madeleine and Freddie,'—that association was taboo. I wouldn't touch on it in even my most secret thoughts,— and gradually I learned to put it behind me. I could keep on going, only if I never let myself look back.

"And then, when McKeith began to ask me about it, I found that I simply couldn't answer him. I really couldn't, physically. My tongue just locked when I tried to mention her name." She looked over at Marc helplessly.

He had been listening to her with intent understanding. "I know how it was, Cissie. You walled that thing up inside of yourself. You laid on layer after layer of inhibition. You organized your whole life around the keeping of that secret. It was the keystone of your personality. You couldn't pull it out without tearing yourself to pieces. . . . But it's out, now, and you're going to feel a lot better. You're going to be free of it for the first time in ten years."

She tried to smile at him, and then suddenly the tears cascaded down her cheeks in torrents and she buried her face in her handkerchief. While she cried herself out, Marc watched her with a satisfied, professional gleam in his eyes.

Finally she looked up. "I don't know why I'm making such a fool of myself. I haven't cried since the night I left Freddie. I howled then for hours. But never since,— not once in ten years,—not even when they took Eve to Oaklawn. I felt like death inside but I didn't cry. And then I sit down for a little fireside chat with you, and cry like a baby for no reason at all."

"Babies have rather sound nervous systems," the psychiatrist answered. "If we could all cry like babies, and laugh like babies, we probably wouldn't need to build places like Oaklawn. I was glad to see those tears coming out, Cissie. They've washed away a lot. Feeling better now?"

Cissie put away her handkerchief and her smile had more body to it. "I don't know why I overflowed that way, but I'm good for another ten years of dry weather."

"I expect you are, but don't force it. A little rain, now and again, is rather refreshing you know." Marc drank the last of his whisky, and shifted his position a little. His head felt pretty heavy today.

"I'm already deeply obligated to you, Cissie, for the things you have told me, and the stimulating hospitality you've given the relic of the Pharaohs. . . . But may I ask one more favor of you? . . . You've knocked the props from under me, and I need to put myself together again. May I borrow this library of yours for a little quiet thinking?"

Cissie rose with a smile. "I shall be delighted to have you use my room to think in, Marc. Without the distraction of my presence. That is, if class is dismissed. No more questions?"

"One," he grinned at her. "If Scott had found out about Madeleine and Crane, what would he have done?"

"Turned away from her with fastidious distaste, brushed her right out of his life," she answered promptly. She turned toward the door. "I'm getting my garden all tidied up for winter. . . . I'll be out in back if you want me."

"All right. I may go over and talk to Mrs. Minary after a bit. Do you know if she's home?"

"Yes, I think she is. This is Julia's day off, and Barbara never leaves Debbie alone with just Christine in the house. . . . Well, I'll hie me to my hoe. . . . Help yourself to whisky as the occasion arises."

20.

L EFT TO HIMSELF, Marc thought over Cissie's parting words and was surprised to discover with what promptness the aforementioned occasion had arrived. He poured a jigger of whisky into his glass, and hearkening to the voice of discretion, added several squirts of soda and two half-melted cubes fished from the silver ice bucket. Settling back in his chair, he rested his bopped head carefully against the cushions. It felt decidedly queer, but it wasn't hurting actively, thanks to the anacin he had been swallowing at intervals all day.

Well, he reflected ruefully, this was where he was supposed to quit. He'd promised McKeith he'd drop out if he didn't get something sure-fire from Cissie, and she'd taken away all his clues in one fell swoop. He was worse off now than when he'd started.

Or was he? The case had been all messed up with red herrings in the beginning. Now that the underbrush was cleared away, the essentials should stand revealed in bare outline. It was bare all right. As bleak and bare as the coast of New England to the Pilgrim fathers. He couldn't find a toe hold anywhere. The facts that were left to him rose up, straight and unscalable—leading—where? He considered the skeleton outline of events.

One—Evelyn had gone insane. There was no doubt
about that!

Two—She had become involved in a situation so intolerable to her that madness was the only way out. But none of her associates would admit

173

they'd noticed anything out of the way about her, until the very end. There was plenty screwy about that!

Three—Hal Crane, Eve's high school friend, and assistant to her husband, had been killed just previous to her insanity. But he wasn't personally involved with her. Cissie had settled that!

Four—Judge Ladbrooke died, or was killed, immediately following the diagnosis of his daughter's illness and before he could alter his will. Plenty of food for thought in that!

Five—Eve was poisoned when she was on the point of recovery. Unfortunately, there was no doubt about that!

There was something very obvious about that sequence of facts. Back in the drugstore yesterday, there was a moment when things had taken on a new perspective. But before his idea could crystallize, it had faded out again. Potts' roc, Shivelly's baby, his talk with McKeith, the bop on his head, and Cissie's revelations had driven that illuminating new thought out of his mind. He concentrated on it, but it was no use. It was gone.

He came back to Evelyn Minary and Hal Crane, those two lives flowing along in the parallel courses that had ended in murder. Somewhere those two streams had touched,—and not casually. He had to find that connection,—there was a link missing in the chain of events.

He thought over all the testimony he had heard,—from Eve's husband, brother, sister-in-law, friends,—and father. That, now, was a piece missing from the jigsaw. They had only the one brief statement of Judge Ladbrooke's, made ten years before when McKeith had told him the nature of Eve's malady. If he could speak now. . . . Judge Ladbrooke!

Judge Ladbrooke! Marc sat up straight. There *was* something obvious . . . right before their eyes all the time, mentioned a hundred times, but so taken for granted that no one stopped to consider what it meant. That was the missing link between Eve's life and Hal's! . . . And it led straight to something even more obvious! Something that had stood out from the first. But he had refused to see it. He had deliberately shut his eyes to it. He had turned away from it to go chasing after subtle, imaginary clues. And if he put together these two obvious conclusions . . . ? Yes, they did,—they fitted into each other, they clicked right into place.

Marc leaned forward in excitement as though the pieces of a puzzle were actually spread on a table before him. He picked up, first this one, and then that one, and as he put them into place, the picture gradually took shape. He had to make one guess. But it was all so consistent, everything fitted in. There were no loose ends. He knew he was on the right track now.

21.

WHEN CASTLEMAN let himself quietly out of Cissie's front door an hour later, he knew what had happened the night that Crane was killed. He knew what it was that had driven Eve mad, why Judge Ladbrooke died when he did, and why Eve could not be permitted to tell what she knew. He knew the how and the why. He understood the motive. But it was a motive that could apply to any of the people who had been with Eve the day she died. Yet he felt certain that there was only one who was involved in the tangle that had led to murder.

Marc's convertible, a snappy little cream-colored job with red-leather upholstering, was standing in the drive before Cissie's house. He had taken a lot of chaffing over it in the staff dining room. The other men insisted it was a symbol of Freudian repression, but Castleman took pleasure in it and kept the top down throughout the winter. He drove it now across the five hundred feet of graveled driveway leading to the house next door.

When Barbara opened the door, she showed no surprise at finding Marc on her doorstep. "Good afternoon, Dr. Castleman. Come on in." The strain and tiredness Marc had seen in her face during the past months were gone. She looked fresh and happy, almost pretty in a homespun way.

"Hello, Mrs. Minary. I've been over next door, and I thought I'd look in on you for a moment," Marc answered, stepping into the hall.

The adjoining living room was in full view, and he looked into it unbelievingly. Surely a difference in light could not make such a change. Had he been dreaming that other night? He remembered that room so definitely —the silvery, mother-of-pearl walls, the brocades, the little sofas and the glass and gilt table. The walls now looked a clear lemon yellow in the late afternoon sun, and there were two dark-red wing-back chairs flanking the fireplace.

Barbara, noticing his bewilderment, followed his glance. She flushed and said with an embarrassed little laugh, "So you notice the change. We decided to do the room over last summer. I bought the new furniture, and ordered the slip covers and curtains made up in June. Then . . . we decided to wait for awhile. But, last week I thought I might as well go ahead, since everything was ready. . . . How do you like it?"

"I like it very much." Marc moved over to the archway and looked in appreciatively. There was a big, comfortable-looking couch at the end, done up in a tailored slip cover, narrow red and white stripes on a green background. The green had a lot of yellow in it, the shade women called chartreuse. The same colors were scattered through the flowered window curtains, and repeated in various ways about the room.

It all looked a little too carefully thought out, perhaps. Like one of Pages' show windows or a picture from *Better Homes and Gardens*, but it was cheerful and happy looking. The fat little baby sprawled in the play pen before the fire, and Barbara's knitting, left on the seat of one of the red chairs, gave it a redeeming note of domesticity.

The house was built into the hillside with the living room raised slightly above the hall. When he stepped up into the other room, Marc's eyes came level with the picture over the mantel and he stopped transfixed. Eve, the patient with the childish doll's face, had once been like that! Lively intelligence, capacity for emotion, and eagerness for life,—the artist had managed to compress the personality of the whole living woman into that square of canvas. . . . That was all that was left of her now, that artist's vision and a fading memory. Looking into that sensitive face, Marc, remembering the doubts he had harbored, offered silent apology to the dead.

Barbara appeared to take no notice of his preoccupation with the picture. She walked over to her chair and picked up her knitting. "I understand that you are still interesting yourself in the case, Dr. Castleman. That you are trying to clear up Mrs. Minary's death."

"Yes, I am."

Barbara's busy hands were engaged with her yarn and

needles, fashioning what appeared to be a baby's coat. As she sat there, looking strong and capable, with her infant at her feet, she seemed to Marc a symbol of primitive womanhood—earthy, practical, active, with endless reserves of endurance and devotion. In marked contrast to the woman over the fireplace! He glanced at the portrait again. Eve had been intellectual and fragile, a finished product of civilization. Over-civilized, perhaps! Lacking stamina to withstand the brutality of life.

It wasn't right, psychologically, for the same man to have chosen in turn each of those women who were such opposites. For nearly always, a man is attracted throughout his life by the same feminine type. A widower, on remarrying, selects a woman like his former wife. And his choice is usually made in the first place because of a resemblance to his own mother.

Phil Minary's nature must be very complex, Marc decided, if he had found emotional fulfillment successively with each of those two women who were so unlike. He thought again of Phil's dilemma, and wondered what course he would have followed if Eve had come back.

"I'm glad you're trying to do something about it," Barbara continued imperturbably. "Because, you know, I am the chief suspect now."

Marc glanced at her in surprise. I wonder if she'd be so calm, he thought, if she knew the danger her husband's in.

Barbara went on serenely. "Of course, it's really Phil they're after. . . . But I don't think they're going to get very far. Scott and Jeff Halsey are working on it. They say Fletcher has no case against Phil, really. . . . But it would be a relief to have it all cleared up."

Marc gave up. In spite of the hundreds of psychology books he'd read, he'd never understand women. The police were planning to put her husband on trial for murder, and she decided to do over her living room, she looked fresher and happier than she had for months,—and she sat there calmly knitting away while she discussed Phil's jeopardy. . . . But, then, Marc concluded, maybe after the strain she had been through for months, something like this seemed only a minor worry. She had dreaded the possibility of having to give up her husband to another woman. And that was over. She had him, now. He was undisputedly hers again, and she could take a little thing like a murder trial in her stride.

"Have you a theory about it, doctor? Have you found out something definite?" she asked, surveying him with steady eyes over her rhythmically moving needles.

"I'm working on a hunch and I need some details to give me the whole picture. Just exactly what was Phil doing with this investigation of his?"

Barbara laughed. "That's a question that requires some answering. Phil worked at it for months, you know. Chiefly, he was looking into all the contracts the city had made for several years back, trying to uncover evidence of graft. . . . Let me see." Her needles stopped and she dropped her work onto her lap. "I can think of one example that is right down your alley." She picked up her knitting again. "Are you familiar with our city hospital?"

Marc made a grimace of distaste. "Not personally, but McKeith's on their board and I've heard about how things go down there. They never have been adequately equipped and what they have is falling to pieces."

"Yes, that's the way it was ten years ago. And yet the hospital has always gotten a large annual appropriation. Phil looked into a little matter of mattresses. The hospital had recently bought a thousand mattresses, at fifteen dollars apiece. Now, Dr. Castleman, I can go down to Pages' and buy a pretty decent innerspring mattress for fifteen dollars. But those that turned up at the city hospital, purchased wholesale, with discount for cash, were worse specimens than the three-dollar ones on sale down on Market Street, and Phil wanted to know why."

"What did he dig up on it?" Castleman's eyes were narrowed in concentration.

"We found the order had been okayed by various officials, among them one Sam Tilton. These gentlemen passed the buck back and forth, each claiming he'd initialed the order on the recommendation of one of the others. The canceled check given in payment was on file, and the hospital had the mattresses. That was all that showed on the surface,—just that the city had made a singularly bad bargain."

Marc's laugh was sour. "The old story again. The politicos giving the taxpayers the run-around. I suppose most of that fifteen thousand dollars was handed back as a secret rebate to somebody at City Hall, and distributed all along the line. The pigs wallowed in clover, while patients sprouted bed sores."

"Exactly. But you see what Phil was up against? The rebate was returned as cash money, and it's hard to trace a dollar bill when it changes hands privately."

A sudden protesting cry from the play-pen brought their attention to the baby. Debbie had been lying on her stomach playing with a long-eared white cotton bunny. The bunny now lay on the carpet outside, just beyond reach of the chubby hand thrust between the wooden bars and Debbie was enraged. Barbara leaned over quickly, tossed the toy into the pen, and looked up with an amused, tender little smile.

"It's a cute baby," Marc ventured with the uncertainty of a bachelor. "I admired it along with the room when I came in. How old is it?"

"*She.* Debbie will have her first birthday next month. We think she's pretty cute too." She began her knitting again. "That fifteen thousand dollars was small potatoes, of course. But when you consider the size of the city budget, and realize that the gang had been taking a rake-off on every cent of it for years,—you can see why politics is such a lucrative profession hereabouts."

Marc pulled out his cigarettes and lit one. "I'd figured out it must be something like that. Phil found it pretty tough going,—and then Hal Crane worked out a short cut, and was killed just when he had Tilton at the breaking point. . . . Let's go back to the night he was murdered. He came into your office about eight o'clock, didn't he?"

Barbara answered in that deliberate, conscientious way of hers. "He rushed in, in great excitement and asked where Phil was. I told him he was at the hospital and Eve was awfully low. Crane said that Tilton was ready to break. They'd been drinking together since about four o'clock, and Tilton had given out more than he realized."

"Did he tell you anything of what Tilton said?" Marc broke in eagerly.

"No,—just that he'd boasted at first of the interests protecting him. 'But that won't help. There were no witnesses,' Crane said, 'We've got to bring him in and question him now, in the D. A.'s office!' I couldn't contact Phil, and Hal decided to go back and stick with Tilton at Mike's. . . . That was the last I saw of him."

"Didn't he say he was going to get in touch with Nelson?" Marc asked with keenness.

"He thought of that at first. But he realized it wouldn't do any good. Nelson didn't know anything about Hal. He wouldn't take action without checking with Phil, first, and that nurse wouldn't even call Phil to the phone."

"Well, it all fits," Marc said in satisfaction. "I don't know just how I'm going to prove anything, but I'm pretty sure I know what happened to Crane."

There was a break in the smooth rhythm of her needles

and Barbara looked at him quickly. But she glanced down again before he could determine if there was more than surprised interest in her eyes.

From the window at his side, Marc had a view across the lawn toward Cissie's house. A group of boys had been playing ball, racing back and forth between the two houses. The sun was going down now, and their forms were becoming indistinct in the dusk. Cissie came out with a plate in her hands.

The boys gathered about her eagerly and she handed around something,—cookies or doughnuts, Marc guessed, beginning to feel hungry himself.

Barbara reached over and switched on the lamp beside her and the figures outside vanished from the suddenly darkened window.

"I take it that you feel Crane's death is connected with Evelyn's?" Barbara's remark was a question.

"Yes, I've felt from the first that there was a connection there. But I've just discovered what it was."

The light fell across Barbara's face at an angle that emphasized the width of her cheeks and threw oblique shadows over her eyes. Her primitive look became more pronounced. Marc realized that he had never really seen her before, not as she was revealed to him now. Against the blood-red background of her chair, her dark face with its prominent cheek-bones made him think of an Aztec princess. . . . It was odd, he thought, that such an association had sprung from his subconscious, an association with the Aztecs, noted for their cruelty and barbarism.

"But I don't see how Crane's activities or death could have anything to do with Evelyn. In what way do you think they're connected?" Barbara seemed genuinely confused.

"Evelyn and Crane had this in common,—they were killed by the same person, and for the same reason. The

murderer. . . . I think of that murderer as a tiger. Mc-
Keith suggested it. He told me last night to remember
that I was hunting tiger."

Barbara gave him a long, undecipherable look. "I
think you should be very careful, Dr. Castleman. That
tiger is dangerous. Evelyn's death . . . and now you tell
me Crane, too!"

"I'm not forgetting it's tiger I'm trailing. . . . I'll take
care of myself, all right." He asserted it boldly, but he
remembered uneasily that he was unarmed, and that he
still didn't know which of them it was. Right now the
tiger might be on the prowl, waiting for him outside the
darkened window,—or was it closer still?

He shifted uncomfortably in his chair. "I want to ask
you about something else, Mrs. Minary. Are you familiar
with the circumstances of Judge Ladbrooke's death?"

"Yes, I am." She said it matter-of-factly. "I was alone
with him when he was stricken."

"*You* were!" The exclamation sprung from him invol-
untarily. Barbara alone with Crane the night of his death!
Barbara alone with Judge Ladbrooke!

Barbara's eyes met his across the lamp light, and a
sudden prescience flickered in them. Something hovered
in the air for a moment. His own thought, perhaps, palp-
able. Then Barbara looked down at those ominously click-
ing needles and continued quietly.

"Judge Ladbrooke died on a Saturday. I usually took
the half-day off, and I decided to come out and see Jonathan. Phil had moved over to Judge Ladbrooke's. He was
leaving shortly for a long stay in the East and I wanted
to see the baby before they left."

"Did Phil move in with the Ladbrookes when Eve
left?"

"Yes,—he'd closed up his own house. I didn't stay with
Jonathan very long, and when I came downstairs I met
the Judge coming in the front door. He looked terrible,

really ill. He'd been at home with a cold all week. He staggered and leaned against the wall, but he said he was all right and asked if I'd mind taking some dictation.

"Of course I agreed and we went back to the study. I found paper and pencil but he just sat there like he was trying to make up his mind about something. Then all of a sudden he slumped over. I jumped up, but he pulled himself together quickly and told me to sit down and write. He began to speak rapidly but it was just a jumble. He kept frantically motioning me to write and I pretended to take it down. Then he had a sort of convulsion and fell over. I ran for McKinley, the houseman, and we got him onto a couch . . ."

"Weren't any of the family at home? Where were Phil and the others?" Marc interrupted.

"Phil was still at the office, cleaning out his files. Scott and Madeleine were out, I don't know where. But Phil got in touch with them, and they all came in together, just after the doctor arrived. McKinley had called him at once. . . . When I saw they didn't need me any more, I went on home. The Judge died that night without regaining consciousness."

"And what became of the dictation you had taken? Did you tell anyone about that?" Marc was fairly pouncing on her words.

"I hadn't written anything down and I didn't say anything about it. It was all meaningless."

"But the message he tried to give you, didn't you get any of that? Not even a word?"

"I could understand some of the words but they didn't make sense. He mentioned Eve's name several times. It sounded like he was saying 'Eve's room.' He said 'Phil' once, quite distinctly, and I thought I caught something about Crane, but . . . oh, Debbie!" she exclaimed, as the baby suddenly let out an insistent howl.

Debbie had become increasingly restive, but absorbed

in their conversation, they had ignored her whimpering.
Now she lay on her back with apoplectic face, kicking
furiously and screaming at the top of her lungs.

Barbara rushed to the pen and picked up her baby,
muffling its cries against her shoulder. "Poor little Debbie. Is it hungry? Did mother forget all about its supper? Does it want its bottle?"

She turned to Marc. "Will you excuse me a moment?
It's time for Debbie's supper, and Christine has forgotten,
or overslept again. I'll take the baby up to the nursery."
She smiled over her shoulder as she went out into the
hall. "I'll leave her with Christine and come right back."

Marc was too nervous to sit down. He lit a cigarette
and walked restlessly about the room. It was exasperating
to be so close to discovery, and then have it snatched
away. If only Barbara remembered a little more. That last
message of the Judge's had been important. It fitted in
exactly with the reconstruction Marc had made.

The fire spluttered and a log broke in two, one piece
rolling out onto the hearth. Marc crossed over, pushed
away the screen and put the smoldering wood back into
the grate. He sat down and lit another cigarette.

She was taking the devil of a long time about it, he
thought. Probably up there fooling around, playing with
that baby while she kept him waiting down here. A rather
cavalier way to treat him. As if his time weren't important! He should have been back at the hospital an hour
ago. He glanced at the clock on the mantel. Five-thirty.
Of course moments dragged when you were anxiously
waiting, but it did seem as though she'd been gone at least
half an hour.

When the little timepiece ticked its way around to
quarter of six, the doctor got up in exasperation and
went out into the hall. The stairs and the upper floor
were in darkness. "Mrs. Minary! . . . Mrs. Minary!" He
called up into the darkness. There was no answer.

She had gone back along the hall, he remembered. There must be some stairs in the rear. He went through the door at the end of the hall and found he was in a transverse corridor. Only the faintest light came through, reflected through the front hall from the lamp in the living room. He could make out another door opposite him, and opened that. It was pitch black inside, but he felt around the door frame and found a switch. The light came on to reveal the tiled interior of a bathroom.

With a muffled oath he withdrew, leaving the light on and the door open. He could see now that the cross hall had doors at either end,—probably leading outside. There were more doors along both walls. He tried the one next to the lavatory. It opened into a butler's pantry. He went on through into the brightly lighted kitchen. The gleaming white surfaces of stove, refrigerator and cabinets reflected brilliantly but the room was empty. Nonplussed, he was hesitating when he heard a door open into the passage he had just left. Hastening back, he met Phillip Minary coming in from outside.

"Why . . . good evening!" Minary greeted him, obviously surprised at the unexpected sight of the doctor emerging from his kitchen.

"Good evening," Marc answered, hastening to explain. "I was looking for your wife. She left me some time ago in the living room to take the baby to the nursery. She asked me to wait, but I find I can't remain any longer and I wanted to see her before leaving."

"Just a minute," Phillip said, removing his hat and coat and hanging them in a hall closet. "She must be up in the nursery." He led the way back to the kitchen, and opening a door, revealed a boxed-in flight of stairs.

"Barbara!" he called up the steps. Receiving no answer he called Christine. They heard steps moving over the kitchen, a door opened above and Christine's voice floated down, "Yes, sir?"

"Is Mrs. Minary up there with you?"

"No, sir. She brought Debbie up and then went downstairs about a half-hour ago."

Minary turned to Marc with a smile, "I guess she is in front, wondering where you have got to. Come on, let's go in there."

The fire crackled on the hearth in the living room, the lamp by the red armchair cast its glow of light, Evelyn's portrait, half-shadowed, gazed down at them, but there was no sign of Barbara.

Perplexed, Minary murmured, "She must be in her room. I'll go get her." He ran up the front stairs, snapping on the light in the upper hall. As he came back down in a moment, a door slammed loudly in the back passage and a tousled youngster of ten came through the hall.

"Hello, dad. Where's mother? Isn't she going to cook dinner tonight? Gosh, I'm hungry!"

"No, your mother isn't here. She must have stepped out for a moment. Run over to Aunt Cissie's and see if she's there. Tell her Dr. Castleman wants to see her before leaving."

"She isn't over there. I've been playing ping-pong with Aunt Cissie. I just came back."

"Well, see if she is at Aunt Mad's. Hurry up."

He turned to Castleman. "She must be over there. I can't understand why she left you like this. Something must have come up. But she'll be back in a moment. Come in and sit down. Will you have a drink with me?"

"No, thanks."

Marc stood restlessly in the center of the floor until Jonathan returned with the news that Aunt Mad hadn't seen his mother at all that day.

Minary was baffled. "I'm sorry about this, Castleman. I can't understand why she went off this way."

"See if her hat and coat are gone!" Marc was terse.

After one quick look at the doctor's face, Minary went out without replying. He took the stairs two at a time, and after an interval, returned as precipitately as he'd gone His face was filled with alarm.

"She didn't take her coat. They're both there, her fur coat and her cloth one. Her purse is on the dresser, with her money and keys in it Her car was in the garage when I came in. . . . I don't know what to think, Castleman."

"I think there's not a moment to lose, Minary. . . . This is a matter for the police! Remember what happened to Evelyn!"

22.

THE ARRIVAL of the law was not inconspicuous this time. Marc could hear the siren screaming as the police cars came down the boulevard. It grew louder when they turned into Hill Road and was not shut off until the cavalcade came to a stop with screeching tires in front of the house.

Minary met Fletcher at the door, ready in his desperation to appeal to his old enemies for help. But the chief was bellicose. He pushed into the living room and surveyed them all with suspicion.

Phil had let the little clan at Hillways know that Barbara was missing, and Cissie, who had changed into a red velvet dinner gown, had come over immediately.

Shortly after, Madeleine had arrived with Scott, who had just returned from the city.

Fletcher looked them all over, as they sat anxiously confronting him. He settled finally on Marc. "So, you were here alone with Mrs. Minary, having a little tea party, when she vanished into thin air, right before your eyes! Very neat!—I don't suppose it occurred to you that in tipping her off you played right into our hands. Our case was pretty thin,—but now you've handed it to us in tissue paper. She didn't run away for her health. . . . And," he assured them all, confidently, "we'll get her all right. This town is sewed up tight. We'll have her before morning."

"Good God, Fletcher!" Minary broke in. "My wife didn't run away. She had nothing to run from and you know it. Where could she go? . . . without her hat and coat or money. How did she leave here . . . ? Her car's in the garage."

"Oh, yes—her coat and her money! It's a nice plant, but you aren't fooling me any, Minary. You're in this up to your neck. What were you doing between five and six, this evening?"

"I came home straight from the office, and when I got here Barbara was gone."

"What time did you leave?"

"It was after five,—I don't know exactly. But—" Fletcher snatched the words from his mouth. "Anybody in the office when you left?"

"No . . . I was the last one out."

"Where is the phone here? How many extensions have you got?"

"The phone is in the back hall. It's the only one."

"Very pretty, Minary. Your wife leaves Castleman sitting here in the front. She phones you from the back and slips out to meet you. You had plenty of time, from five to six, to take her wherever you've got her and get back here to Castleman when you did. That is, if he's not in it, too! You're probably all in it." He glared at them indiscriminately.

"Mrs. Humber, can you account for yourself from five to six?"

"I was at home the whole time. I worked in the garden, bathed and dressed for dinner, and played with Jonathan in the game room until six. I didn't see Barbara at any time today,—except through the window this afternoon. The lights were on in here and I saw her talking to Dr. Castleman."

"I suppose your servants are ready to corroborate all this?"

"They don't keep a stop watch on me, Fletcher. The cook was in the kitchen when I went there for some cookies. After that I was alone upstairs. My house is a big one and it would be easy for me to slip out or for someone to come in unobserved. You are welcome to draw any conclusions you like,—privately. If you wish to make any accusations, you can discuss them with my lawyer."

Fletcher turned impatiently to the Ladbrookes. "All right, what about you?"

Madeleine was condescending. "I was in my room writing letters most of the afternoon. None of the servants had occasion to disturb me. My room is on the other side from this house, and I wasn't in a position to see anyone coming or leaving here."

Scott frigidly accounted for himself, without waiting to be asked. "I was in court this afternoon. Then I went over to the law library for a while. After that I ran several errands, stopped at the bar at the Jackson for a drink and reached home a little after six. Maybe you can check on my movements and maybe you can't. I don't know whether the bartender or the clerks who waited on me in the drugstore and at the men's shop know me by sight or not."

"All right," Fletcher barked in the top sergeant manner he'd taken on today. "I've got your stories. . . . But this is one time you're not going to pull a fast one. You haven't given her as much of a head start as you did Tilton . . . that is if she was here when you said she was. Where's that maid who said she saw her in the nursery at five?"

He went off to interview Christine and to phone the District Attorney. He was back in a few moments. "Come on,—get your coats on. The D. A. wants to talk to all of you . . . down at headquarters."

"We're ready to go with you,—to do anything!" Phillip answered. "Only for God's sake start looking for my wife! I want the F. B. I. called in—this is kidnaping—or worse."

Scott interposed, "Considering the unwarranted attitude you're taking, Fletcher, I think I'd better have a lawyer,—Jeff Halsey, meet us at headquarters."

"Go ahead, phone him," Fletcher agreed with large magnanimity.

"Phone a couple of lawyers. You're going to need them all, before you're out of this jam."

"And I'll have Lucy come over and stay with Christine while we're gone." It was Cissie speaking. "Barbara wouldn't want Debbie left alone in the house with no one here but Christine."

"Christine isn't going to be alone here, Mrs. Humber. Don't you worry about that," Fletcher assured her with theatrical sarcasm. "There's going to be one of my men here, and in your house, too. If Mrs. Minary tries to get in touch with any of you, we'll know about it."

Marc drove his own car downtown, with a freckle-faced plain-clothes man in the front seat and Cissie wedged in between. It was a tight fit. When they reached the court-house, they found Halsey had already arrived.

The District Attorney, an unpleasant specimen named

Bowsler, was waiting for them. He decided to question them individually, taking Phil first, and ordering the rest of them held *incommunicado* in separate rooms.

Marc was given a small room off the second-floor hall, furnished with one straight chair, an oak table and some filing cabinets. He was tired and hungry and exasperated. McKeith was going to be pleased over this situation. Oh, yes!

He glanced at his watch. It was after eight. He supposed he should phone the hospital, but he didn't relish the prospect,—letting McKeith know he was being held at headquarters as a material witness, or as a suspect in abetting the escape of a fugitive from justice,—he wasn't sure which He decided to postpone that call until his position was clarified. But there was something else he was not going to put off.

He opened the door and looked out in the hall. Several of Fletcher's men were sitting out there. "Hey," he called to them, "what's Fletcher trying to do? Starve me into submission? I haven't eaten since noon today."

"You can have something sent in from the drugstore across the street, if you want," one of them answered.

"Petty, run over and get something for the doc to eat."

The youngest of the trio departed and Marc went back to his quarters. In about ten minutes Petty came back and set a tray on the table. "It was fifty cents," he announced.

"Thanks." Marc paid him and investigated what lay under the napkin. It was a paper plate containing a steak sandwich, French fries and coleslaw. A carton of hot coffee stood beside it. Well, I can say this for my recent diet, he thought, it has no element of surprise. . . . Perhaps it's just as well. Petty might have picked out a tuna salad sandwich.

When he had finished off his dinner, Marc lit a cigarette and walked restlessly over to the window. It had begun to rain again. It had been a dreary fall. Never twenty-four hours at a stretch without water.

Ever since that moment at the Minarys' when he realized Barbara had stepped out without hat or coat and disappeared, his head, filled with leaping thoughts, had been like a pot of jumping beans. One moment he had a vision of Barbara, a fleeing tiger, running from an overtaking justice, and the next he feared she was an innocent victim in deadly danger.

He walked back to the table and poured out the remaining dregs of coffee from the carton. If Barbara were the tiger, why should she run away? Because he had told her he had figured the thing out? . . . But he had also admitted that he had no proof. There was no necessity for immediate escape, under circumstances that would instantly start up a police pursuit. Surely, if she were contemplating flight, she would have waited until he had left, at least. Certainly nothing that he had said to her could have precipitated such a sudden flight.

Why, then, Marc wondered, had she been afraid to come back from the nursery and face him? They had been talking about Judge Ladbrooke's last words. She hadn't seemed to attach much importance to them. Acted as if she hadn't thought about them since he died. . . . Perhaps those jumbled words of the Judge's hadn't seemed significant to her until that afternoon when he began to question her.

Marc's eyes narrowed. Then maybe she saw them in a new light, maybe she remembered the rest of what he had said . . . and putting two and two together, was afraid to come back and finish that conversation, for fear she would betray something she wanted to hide. That implied she was protecting someone else.

Those last words of the Judge's then must have significance. He was undoubtedly trying to leave a dying message. This fitted in with the reconstruction Marc had made earlier that afternoon, when he had thought things out in Cissie's study. He was convinced at that time that Evelyn's father had known who murdered Crane, and that he had kept still until after his daughter went insane. After that, his knowledge weighed heavily upon him, but he hadn't been ready to speak even then,—until, alone in his house on that Saturday afternoon, he had felt the hand of death on him. What had he done then? Did he write out a statement?

He was coming in from outside when Barbara met him. Where had he been? Marc jumped up in excitement. "Evelyn's room," the Judge had said, had reiterated it frantically for Barbara to write down. Of course, the Judge had just returned from the house next door. He had left something, his dying statement probably, in Evelyn's room. Because he was afraid to leave it in his own house, because the tiger would find it there.

Marc sat down again dejectedly. That was over ten years ago, and no one had found that statement. It wasn't conceivable that that room had not been used in the interim. The tiger had gotten to it first, or it had been thrown away with Evelyn's things. However, there was a thin chance that the note was still in existence, stored away some place with the dead woman's belongings. Why hadn't he stopped to think things out before stampeding Minary into calling Fletcher? He had been right there at the house that afternoon. He should have hunted for that paper, and if he had found it he would have solved the whole mystery,—except what had become of Barbara.

But this much was clear now. Since the Judge had been trying to give his message to Barbara, it was evident that he trusted her. She wasn't mixed up in Crane's killing, then, nor connected with anyone who was. She was innocent, and the tiger had got to her before she could reveal the rest of the Judge's message.

Marc remembered again that sensation of danger he had had in the living room, as he sat there beside the window, wondering if the tiger were on the prowl outside in the dusk. But the tiger had been in the house, in the darkened hall, just off the archway, listening to the two of them in the lighted room.

Marc remembered he had told Cissie he was going to talk to Barbara. He could picture her, driven by her insatiable curiosity, slipping through that door at the end of the rear passage. It wasn't locked. Jonathan had run in without knocking.

But it didn't have to be Cissie. It could have been any one of those people. He had blazed a wide trail yesterday. He had told Halsey that he connected Crane's murder with Eve's, and that he was suspicious of Judge Ladbrooke's death. Undoubtedly Halsey would have told Scott and Phil and they would have passed it on to the women. They all knew! And the tiger, worried and apprehensive of its next move, would have been watching him. He had certainly advertised his presence at Barbara's with that unmistakable car of his parked right in front. They all must have seen it many times on their visits to the hospital. It was usually standing in the circle at Oaklawn.

Madeleine could have looked out a window, and noticed it in front of the Minarys' that afternoon. Or Phil or Scott, coming home, could have seen it distinctly from the road. Either of them could have left his car on the street and slipped up to the house on foot. Halsey might have been on his way to call, or could have seen it from the road as he was passing by. Maybe he, too, lived in the neighborhood. It could be any of them who had slipped into the back door, while Christine slept upstairs.

The tiger, creeping into the hall, and crouching there, just outside the living-room arch, listening, had heard for the first time the account of Judge Ladbrooke's last conscious moments. The tiger had known all along that the Judge knew the secret,—but hoped the knowledge had died with him. And then, panic-stricken, it heard Barbara's disclosure.

But Debbie had begun to cry at the crucial moment, and Barbara had gone to the nursery.

The tiger, hiding in the dining room, until she passed, had followed her, and lain in wait at the foot of the back stairs. At any cost she had to be prevented from finishing her story. So when she descended, there was a quick blow from behind,—or a coat thrown over her head.

What then? Did the tiger feel it was necessary to dispose of Barbara permanently? Marc chilled with trepidation. Maybe, though, she merely had to be kept out of the way,—prevented from completing the Judge's message, until that incriminating evidence that had been in Evelyn's room was destroyed. But the tiger, for the time being, was cut off from the upper region of the house. Christine was awake now in the room at the head of the back steps and Marc, waiting for Barbara to come down, had a full view of the front stairs.

But Barbara, dead or alive, had to be removed from the kitchen. It would have been risky to carry her far,— clear down to a car parked in the street. Her unconscious body would have been heavy and it would have taken quite awhile. Phil and Scott were due home, Jonathan and his gang might run through the grounds at any time, and Madeleine or one of the servants might look out of a window at any moment. It was pretty dark by that time, but a figure carrying a body would have attracted attention. Marc hadn't heard a car drive up to the house until Phil came in.

It looked as though the tiger couldn't have carried her off from Hillways. Barbara was hidden in one of the houses up there, or concealed on the grounds. Marc glanced at the cold rain slashing at the windows. There was a chance she was still alive . . . and that the Judge's statement was still there at Hillways. But if the tiger got there first . . . !

He sprang up and threw open the door into the hall. The same trio were sitting, half asleep, in chairs tilted against the wall. They looked up at him with bored preparation for expected protests as he asked, "Those people who came down with me,—have any of them left here yet?"

"Sure," Petty told him. "They all left five minutes ago. Bowsler is through with them. I think he's about ready for you, now."

"I must see him right away. Tell him I have a statement to make. It can't wait!"

"Okay!" Petty sauntered over to a door at the end of the hall, and in a moment beckoned to Marc. "Come on, doc, he'll see you now."

Bowsler was sitting behind his desk. Fletcher, who had drawn up a chair beside him, looked at Marc with amused complacency. "Well, well, so you've decided to come clean, doctor."

"I did come clean, earlier this evening. I told you all I knew then. But I've had time to figure things out since. Listen, Fletcher," Castleman leaned across the desk and spoke with desperate urgency, "one of those people you just released murdered Eve and attacked Barbara this afternoon. She's up there at Hillways now, and if she isn't already dead, she's in mortal danger. Get some men up there, search those three houses from attic to cellar, and the grounds, too, before it's too late."

Fletcher exchanged a smile with Bowsler and regarded Castleman with skeptical eyes. "That would be just dandy, wouldn't it? While we're all dashing up there, looking over the coop after the chicken has flown, you'd be hotfooting it to Barbara. Where've you got her, Castleman?"

"If that's what you think, put a tail on me and let me

lead you right to her. My God, Fletcher, why should I help Barbara make a get-away? I scarcely know the woman. I hold a responsible position out at Oaklawn. Why should I jeopardize my professional career to keep her from being arrested?"

"For a man occupied solely with his professional career, you've been taking a singular interest in this case for some time, Dr. Castleman. It rather looks to me as though you were involved personally, you know." Bowsler's voice and eyes were acid.

Fletcher added his bit, jocosely. "That woman has certainly got something. I don't know what it is. It doesn't show on the surface, but she has what it took to break up Eve Minary's marriage, and she apparently has you going all out for her, Castleman."

"Am I under arrest? I want to know what I'm being held for. I want to see a lawyer. I want to get out of here. If you won't look for Barbara, I'm going to do it myself,—and don't forget the situation you'll be in tomorrow when her body is found, and I say I told you where she was and you wouldn't go yourselves and wouldn't let me help her either."

"We're not detaining you, Castleman." Bowsler still looked unimpressed. "You can go and hunt to your heart's content. But we'll accept your suggestion. Petty goes where you go, until we find Barbara. Any objection?—all right. Stick to him, Petty. Don't let him put anything over on you."

"And when you find her, be sure and let us know," Fletcher called after them, laughing.

23.

Marc didn't stop to raise the top of the car. He climbed onto the wet seat and with Petty beside him, drove as fast as he could through the slashing rain. He was in a race with a murderer, a triple murderer who had a head start. As he speeded toward Hillways, he mapped his course of action. The paper Judge Ladbrooke had left,—the tiger would be after that. But if Petty and he went to look for it first, they would expose their flank and the tiger would seize the chance to get at Barbara and finish her off.

If, on the other hand, they concentrated first on finding Barbara, the tiger would meanwhile destroy Judge Ladbrooke's message,—the only evidence as to the identity of the murderer. And it might take them a long while to hunt for Barbara. They'd have to search those three big houses, the garages, all the shrubbery on the grounds,—and it seemed to Marc he'd seen a summer house, too.

And then if they found her and she was still alive, they might learn nothing more. She probably didn't know the identity of the murderer,—the Judge apparently had not told her that. But even if he had, if they could construe his last words to point to someone, the evidence against the tiger would be destroyed. . . . The lady or the tiger, that was the question. But of course, Marc decided, life had to come first,—even if the tiger escaped them. Barbara would be their first objective.

The slicker-clad policeman at the entrance to Hillways passed them through on Petty's identification. The fanlight over the door was on and light poured from all the first-floor rooms, but Marc noticed that the upper floor was dark. Julia, returned from her day off and vibrating with excitement, let them in.

Marc glanced into the front room and took a quick count. Three of them! Halsey and the Ladbrookes were sitting in there together. He turned to Julia. "Has Mrs. Humber been here? Where's Mr. Minary?"

"They're both in the library. It's this way, sir."

With Petty fairly tramping on his heels, Marc followed Julia into the back hall, toward a room across the passage from the living room. The door was open and Castleman saw that Minary was in his leather lounge chair, looking like a man who has used up his last reserves.

The deadly irony of the situation flashed through Marc's mind. Here was a man who, a week ago, had been suffering from a plethora of wives, confronted by a painful and difficult choice between them. Fate had solved his problem all too drastically. Now he had neither. He had a wife and couldn't keep her; he put her in a pumpkin shell . . .

My God, am I going crazy, too? Marc wondered, curbing his wildly darting thoughts.

Cissie was in there with Phil. She was in a corner bending over a cellarette. As they came toward the room, she turned and crossed to Phil carrying a glass. She placed it in his hand without speaking, bending over him like a ministering goddess of mercy. The soft light, her flowing dark dress and the tenderness in her face lent her for a moment a sort of olympian beauty.

Marc's entrance broke up the little tableau. Phil looked up with a desperate question in his eyes. The doctor shook his head. "No, nothing yet."

As the hope faded from Phil's eyes, Marc said, "I have come back, Minary, because I think there's a bare chance that Barbara is still here. In this house or hidden somewhere on the place. We didn't make a thorough search earlier, because we thought she had been lured away. But maybe we missed a trick."

Phil was on his feet before Marc had finished. "Where shall we look first?"

"We'll start with the back stairs. See if we can trace her from there."

Minary led the way to the kitchen and opened the stair door. Marc saw that the steps were built against the wall at the left, and boxed in on the other side, with a wooden partition that made a dark space to the right, an open closet or a passageway. That was where the tiger had crouched as Barbara came down the stairs. When she started into the kitchen it had sprung from behind, and carried her,—which way? Not up,—either out into the kitchen, or . . . ! Marc stepped into the dark space beside the partition where the tiger had lain in wait. "Is this a closet or . . . ?"

Phillip reached around him to switch on a light and Marc saw that he was standing on a landing leading to the basement steps. He ran down them with the others close behind him. There were three closed doors in the walls of the small pine-paneled hall at the foot of the steps. Marc opened the one at the right and went into a game room. Feverishly they looked into the closets and lifted the lids of the window chests, which contained nothing but badminton and table tennis equipment. They pulled the heavy chairs from the wall and looked behind the bar. But everything was in order.

They hurried on into the laundry. Its drying racks, stationary tubs and built-in washing machinery afforded no place of concealment. The furnace room, sheltering an oil burner, was also as bare as a pin.

It was in the small adjoining room that they discovered the closet door securely bolted on the outside. On the inside they found Barbara lying crumpled on the floor of the shallow airless cubicle.

She was alive, but Marc could not tell how seriously she was injured. He released the scarf which gagged her, her own scarf which she had been wearing decoratively knotted about the neck of her sweater that afternoon.

When he felt the swelling on the back of her head, Castleman gave quick orders to the panic-stricken group crowding about him. "I haven't my medical kit with me and I can't tell the extent of her injuries. Call a doctor and tell him to get here immediately. Meanwhile, I'll treat for shock. I'll need blankets, hot-water bottles and heating pads. Bring them to the living room, Cissie. We'll have to carry her that far."

To the men he said, "I want something rigid to put under her. Find an ironing board,—or take a lid from one of those chests."

Cissie raced for the stairs as Minary and Petty dashed into the laundry. They came back bringing a large ironing board, and helped Marc to ease it cautiously under the unconscious form on the floor. He was taking no chances. The lump on her head felt like a simple contusion, but with her pulse the way it was, her neck or spine might be fractured.

They lifted their burden and carried it slowly and carefully up the narrow stairs, through the hall and into the living room, where they placed her on the sofa, still lying on her improvised stretcher. Marc wrapped her in blankets and placed at her feet the heating pad that Cissie handed him.

She was beginning to show the first signs of returning animation, when Dr. Jerome arrived.

"I think she's coming around all right," Castleman told him. "She was suffering mostly from lack of air and shock. The pulse was weak and irregular when I found her,—but it's picking up nicely, now."

When Jerome began his examination, Marc turned away from the patient and took stock. Phillip was beside

the couch with the doctor. Cissie had disappeared again.
Everybody had been running around fetching things and
now none of the others was in sight. This was the chance
the tiger had sought.

Marc moved out into the hall and looked upstairs. The
upper floor was still in darkness. Julia came through from
the back and Marc asked her quickly—"Julia, what happened to Mrs. Minary's personal things, her clothes and
letters,—I mean the first Mrs. Minary—after she was
taken to Oaklawn?"

"Why, her things are right where they belong, in her
room. I kept Miss Evelyn's room ready for her, just the
way she left it. I always thought she'd come back some-
day."

"Do you mean no one has used that room since?"

As Julia nodded confirmation, Petty emerged from the
back hall in high fettle. He looked at Marc with respect.
"Just phoned the news in to headquarters. Fletcher'd
already left for home. Is he going to be burned? You
were right all the time, doc."

"Julia, will you take me up to Miss Evelyn's room?
There is something up there that will let us know who
killed her."

Julia looked at Marc doubtfully a moment until, convinced by what she saw in his face, she turned to the
stairs. She exclaimed, "That's funny! I left the light on
in the hall up there when I went after the blankets."

She started up first with Marc back of her. He turned
to Petty who was close behind and whispered, "Do you
have a gun?"

"You betch'er life," was the reassuring answer.

They were halfway up the stairs when Julia let out a
cry. "There's a light on in Miss Evelyn's room! Nobody
has a right to be in there."

Marc pushed past her, and running on up, threw open
the door with the light cracks showing around it.

The room was in great disorder, but it was empty. Castleman ran across it and through the door in the far wall. It led into a bathroom which connected in turn with another bedchamber. It was almost dark in here, and as he fumbled slowly across the room, the others caught up with him. Julia switched on the light. Marc saw the other door and stepped through it into the center hall near the head of the rear stairs. The other two emerged behind him. There was no one else in the hall or on the stairs.

Marc turned to the young detective. "Listen, Petty, there's still a chance we can crack this case tonight. Get back downstairs quick. Get all those people together in the living room and keep them there. Don't let anyone leave or get rid of anything—any paper. Don't let anyone get near the fire or light a match . . . or put anything in their mouth. A paper could be wadded up and chewed or swallowed. Use your gun if you have to!"

Petty was already sprinting for the stairs. He called back, "I'll hold 'em for you, doc,—until Fletcher gets here. He's probably on the way now."

Julia looked at the doctor with frightened eyes. "Who has been in Miss Evelyn's room? What did they want?"

"Julia," he explained gently, "Judge Ladbrooke, before he died, left something, probably a letter, in Miss Evelyn's room. Tonight somebody heard about it for the first time and went in there to look for it—while we were working over Mrs. Minary. They had about a half-hour. Maybe they found what they wanted,—but maybe we interrupted the search. Let's go back and see if we can find anything."

Julia wrung her hands in agitation over the mess that waited for them. The bedclothes had been dragged from the bed. The mattress and pillows were in a heap on the floor, and the cushions from the chaise longue had been piled on top of them. The drawers from the chest, dressing table and desk had been lifted out bodily and the contents dumped onto the floor.

Marc looked about him in surprise. The pictures hung straight on the walls, the broadloom carpet was undisturbed and the four books on top of the desk stood upright between the onyx bookends. It wasn't a paper then. But what on earth . . . ?

With his eye he followed the progress of the marauder, beginning to the right of the door, going the length of the inner wall past the bed, turning the corner, along the end of the room to the far wall and stopping beside the open closet door. Marc walked over and looked through the open folding doors. It was a long shallow closet with two-thirds of its length occupied by a metal bar hung with garments in cellophane bags. The clothes had been roughly pushed together at one end and the hat boxes from the overhanging shelf were lying opened on the floor. Marc saw that wide drawers were built into the rest of the closet wall. The top one stood open.

This then was the place where the search had ended. Here the tiger had found what it sought, or had reached this point when they had scared it away.

Marc relaxed slightly. There was no more need for hurry. If the Judge's message had been found,—that was that. It was all over, then. If the note was still in the room, he had all night to look for it now. Petty was holding the tiger at bay downstairs.

"Julia, have you gone through these drawers at any time since Mrs. Minary left?"

"I should say not! Why would I be going through Miss Evelyn's things, and her lying sick up there at the hospital?"

"Well, I thought you might have straightened things out. When you are housecleaning, don't you usually wash out drawers?"

"I put her things away the day after she left here, but

I haven't been in her drawers since," Julia answered, mollified. "Time enough to clean up her drawers when she was ready to come home. I just dusted and ran the vacuum in the room, and kept the curtains and windows clean."

"What are in these drawers?" Marc asked, pulling the top one further out.

"That's where we kept the bed linens."

"We'll have to see if anything has been hidden in here." He lifted out the sheets one by one and handed them to Julia. There were white sheets, and pale pink ones, with pillow slips to match them all, and sheets with tiny pink flowers sprinkled over a snowy background. But Marc found nothing else except small bags of dried lavender resting between the folded linens. The lower drawers contained quilts and white blankets, each in a silk case.

There was a double row of smaller drawers in the end wall. As he turned to these, Julia volunteered, "There's nothing but shoes in there."

Marc pulled open one of the top drawers and saw it was filled by a bundle in black tissue paper. He extricated from the wrappings a pair of silver slippers on shoe trees. Picking one up, he looked it over closely. It was so small it rested upright on his open hand, a high-heeled little concoction of interlacing kid straps with tiny jewels gleaming in the intersections. The silver was dull and tarnished and the little shoe looked like a dusty cobweb with a few glistening dewdrops caught in its meshes. Marc felt himself oddly touched by the mute memento.

He laid it aside and looked into the next drawer, noticing that Julia, too, was moved. Her face was working, and tears gathered when Marc took from the second drawer a pair of black suede pumps, trimmed with large, gilt-edged butterfly bows.

On opening the third drawer he let out a whistle of

excitement, and Julia, drying her eyes, peered over his shoulder. A large shoe box, tied with a coarse cord, was wedged tightly into the compartment. Something was written across the top but the light in the closet was too dim for Marc to make out what it said. He lifted out the drawer, and inverting it, pried out the box with his pen-knife.

He carried it into the light and read the inscription written in a faint shaky hand. "For Phillip Minary. To be opened after my death. J. A. Ladbrooke." Beneath it in weaker, poorly formed letters, Castleman made out the following instructions. "Phil, be careful—fingerprints—use judgment."

Marc hesitated only for a moment. This was no time for scruples. He cut the cord and lifted off the lid. Lying in the box was the smallest pistol he had ever seen,—a blunt nosed, rectangular black revolver.

Julia let out a suppressed scream. "What is that thing?"

"That," Marc answered her with grim satisfaction, "that is the gun that shot Hal Crane."

24.

LEAVING JULIA in the ransacked room, Marc walked slowly downstairs, his brain racing as he fitted the implications of the gun into the puzzle previously pieced together. Petty was standing in the archway, facing watchfully into the living room, his hand on his pistol holster.

Marc called to him in a low voice. "It's all right now,

Petty. Come over here, I've something to show you." He
lifted the lid of the box and exposed again that lethal
little black revolver. "Take this down to headquarters. I
think the ballistics men will find the bullet that killed
Crane was fired from this gun. But first, check for fingerprints. The prints on this pistol are going to match up
with the fingers of one of those people in the room
yonder."

Petty stared at the doctor goggle-eyed. Finally he burst
out with, "God Almighty! Have you busted this case—
or have you busted this case! . . . Wait a minute. I'll have
to let Fletcher know about this!"

Marc stood at the foot of the stairs watching warily
the entrance to the living room until Petty came back,
saying, "I caught Fletcher. He'd just got home and was
going to come out here to get Barbara's story. Now he
says for me to bring the gun and meet him at headquarters."

Minary handed over the precious box, but Petty hesitated. "Sure you'll be all right alone here, doc? With
those people in there? Will they try to make a get-away?"
He thought swiftly a moment. "Say, we have three men
here on the grounds watching the houses. What do you
say I tell 'em to close in on that room?"

"Good!" Marc answered in relief. "They needn't come
in the house. Station them around outside so that nobody
can get away. That'll do it. Get the fingerprints off that
gun, and come right back. You needn't wait for the ballistics test. Bring a fingerprint man back with you." When
Petty nodded and started for the door, Marc called after
him, "Do you have any cigarettes on you? I smoked my
last one quite awhile back." Petty grinned and tossed him
a half-full pack.

As Marc lit a cigarette, Phillip and Dr. Jerome came
out from the living room. "Here you are, Dr. Castleman!
I wanted to see you before I left and no one knew what

had become of you. Our patient is in good shape. She had a slight concussion, and of course there was a good bit of shock. She should take it easy for a day or two. I've told Minary to have X-rays taken tomorrow,—just to be on the safe side. But I'm sure there is no fracture."

He had slipped into his coat as he talked, and now picked up his hat and bag. "Good night, doctor. Glad to have seen you again. . . . You needn't worry about her any more, Minary. She'll be herself in a couple of days. I'll phone you tomorrow after I've seen the X-rays. . . . Good night."

Phil turned to Marc. "Won't you come in and join us, doctor?"

Barbara, displaying remarkable resilience, was propped up on the couch, looking quite normal except for the bandage about her head. "I don't know how to thank you," she said to Marc as he came over to the couch. "It was a terrible experience! I don't think I could have stood it if I'd been left down there all night."

"We should have found you much sooner. Do you remember what happened to you?"

"Not very much. I was coming down stairs,—I'd just reached the bottom, when something hit me and I felt myself falling. When I came to, I didn't know where I was. It was dark and I couldn't get my breath. It was horrible . . . like a long nightmare. I guess I was only half conscious. . . . But why did it happen? Why was I attacked?"

"Because you were telling me something very important. Do you remember what we were talking about when you left to go upstairs?"

Barbara looked blank for a moment. "Oh, . . . yes. I remember now. We were talking about Judge Ladbrooke's death."

"You were telling me about the dictation he was trying to give you. What else did he say besides 'Evelyn's room' and 'Phil?' "

"Why, that was all. I told you. He went into a convulsion before he could say any more."

"Fortunately that was enough."

"What do you mean—enough?" Cissie broke in imperiously. "Enough for what? Do you know who attacked Barbara? What has Judge Ladbrooke to do with that?"

Marc turned from the couch and faced down the length of the room. They all looked questions at him, tense, excited, alarmed. He felt menace reaching toward him, emanating from someone among that scattered group. A little spearhead of chill pierced him and spread through to his nerve ends.

Holding them all in his glance he spoke slowly and carefully. "No one is to leave. This house is surrounded by the police. There are two men just outside these windows. They're watching all of you all the time."

He turned slightly toward the couch, still keeping his eyes on the others. "Barbara, Judge Ladbrooke was trying to tell you he had left something in Evelyn's room for Phil. Something connected with Crane's death. I've just found it. It has been in her closet all these years,—the gun that killed Crane. The Judge was careful to preserve the fingerprints on it. A detective is taking it down to headquarters now for tests. In a little while, they'll be coming back here and they'll want to take all your fingerprints. . . . Because there is a murderer in this room. The murderer who shot Crane and poisoned Eve!"

"My God!", "Who is it?", "What do you mean?" Ejaculations from six throats shrilled into an exclamatory chorus. As Marc walked wearily over and sank down into a near-by chair, Scott's voice cut authoritatively into the babble. "Don't you think we are entitled to some sort of an explanation, Dr. Castleman? Which of us are you accusing?"

"I'm accusing no one, Mr. Ladbrooke. Chief Fletcher

will do that when he has made the necessary tests. I'll tell you as much as I know.

"The truth is going to shock—most of you. I want to mitigate that if I can, give you insight into the personality of someone you all love—and who is now dead."

"Good Lord, Marc," Cissie broke in. "Do you have to go all classic story-book detective on us? Build yourself up to a long-drawn-out climax while we flap on tenterhooks? For God's sake, tell us straight out, who did it?"

"But I don't know that, Cissie. Not yet! There's just one thing to go on. The fact Judge Ladbrooke gave his message to Barbara and left the gun for Phil, seems on the face of it to remove them from suspicion. As for the rest of you,—anyone's guess is as good as mine."

Cissie looked at him unbelievingly for a moment and then tossed off her inquisitorial air. "At the danger of becoming trite, I'm moved to remark for the umpteenth time today that you look like a doctor in need of a drink." She turned to the brandy decanter on the table beside Barbara, poured out a drink and brought it over to him.

"Thank you." He accepted the glass, placed it on the broad arm of his chair, and then carefully knocked it over while lighting a cigarette. "Damn!" he exclaimed, jumping to his feet. He retrieved the glass, and filled it again himself. Cissie gave him a scathing glance, but the others, waiting tensely, apparently didn't suspect his little maneuver. He felt rather foolish,—but there was danger in that room.

He sat down and sipped the liquor gratefully.

"Is it Eve's character you think you're going to explain, Castleman?" Scott was ready for battle. "I don't know what crazy idea you've got hold of now, but I'm not going to listen to anything 'shocking' you've. . . ."

"No," Marc interrupted. "I'm not going to analyze Eve. I'm going to tell you why she was killed." He put down his glass, and began tersely.

"From the beginning I've thought there was a connection between Crane's murder, Eve's insanity and her own death. And I was right! I assumed further that she was killed because she knew the identity of Crane's murderer, and I was right on that count, too. Of course that erases Tilton from the picture. I never believed he had killed Crane."

They were all hanging on his words, staring at him with eyes that were expectant, fearful or anxious. "But at this point I was blocked." He hesitated. "I couldn't discover why any of you had a reason for killing Crane. I thought of a variety of motives,—of passion, revenge or jealousy. I even wondered about mistaken identity. And all the while I turned my back on the obvious thing about his death,—that it must have been connected with his recent activities with the graft ring,—the activities he was pushing right up to the moment of his murder. In eliminating Tilton from the picture, I also automatically eliminated the motive that Tilton was assumed to have had.

"And that was a big mistake. For Tilton was not the only one endangered by Crane's activities."

There was a reaction—a movement, an indrawn breath —from someone in the room that told Marc he had hit on the truth. But, looking around the scattered, tense figures, he couldn't tell who it was whose control had slipped for a second. He sipped nervously at his brandy and continued, "Crane had been working on Tilton that last night and had obtained information from him. Obviously he was killed because he had gotten too close to the truth. But Eve was on Crane's side, and so, I had thought, were all the people close to her. Yet somewhere there had to be a link between Eve and the crowd that Crane and Minary were fighting.

"The link, when I finally found it, turned out to be another one of those obvious things that we failed to see just because it was in such plain sight." He paused for a dramatic moment. *"Eve's father was a judge!"*

Minary's face suddenly tightened. Scott's expression indicated amazement, and then anger. Halsey's shrewd eyes gave nothing away. The women, baffled, looked questioningly at Marc.

"Don't you see what that means?" he asked them. "The political machine had this community and half of the state sewed up tight. It controlled local elections and political appointments. . . . And yet Eve's father held a judgeship."

"Why damn you! Don't you dare. . . ." The Judge's son leaped up expostulating.

"Wait a minute, Scott! Don't jump me yet. I'm not claiming your father was a Dr. Jekyll-Mr. Hyde. It's not that simple." Marc sighed and brushed his hand wearily over his black hair. "I think he was like so many of my friends, business and professional men I play squash with down at the Club. They call themselves realists. They say they have to live with what they've got, and the political machine is too big to buck. So they put up with it, nonchalantly. Further they do business with it. My friend, who sells wood to the city, sells it on their terms. Either he butters fingers, or he goes out of business.

"These realist friends of mine are amused when I blow up at the waste and graft in government. They shrug their shoulders and say it's the price we pay for democracy. They accept it as inevitable . . . and I suspect, take advantage of it when they can. Like getting parking tickets canceled and their tax assessments lowered."

Scott's anger had not subsided. His face was suffused and the tic in his eyelid was twitching again. Marc hurried on, forestalling interruption. "Now Judge Ladbrooke was a wealthy man and many of the concerns in which he had holdings here must have done business with the city. I don't believe he ever took part in a shady deal himself. I'm convinced he was a man of personal integrity and that his conduct on the bench was impeccable. But he must have known what went on, how the companies in which he was a director earned their dividends. And he accepted it as an inevitable accompaniment of the American way of doing things.

"And the politicians understood his attitude, they felt he was a safe man, that he would stick to his knitting and let them alone. So when the Bar Association pushed him forward for a judgeship, the powers that be were agreeable They had to make some concessions to public opinion now and then."

"But that doesn't link my father with the graft ring and Crane's murder. You've made some pretty slanderous implications, Dr Castleman." Scott was a very angry man.

"At first the link was rather nebulous," Marc admitted. "Just the Judge's tolerant attitude toward the City Hall crowd. But when this reform movement began, the Judge, because of his own prominence and his daughter's interest, found himself swept along as one of the sponsoring group. Now, according to Mrs. Ladbrooke, he didn't believe they were going to accomplish anything and he tried to curb Eve's enthusiasm. Isn't that right?"

"Yes." Phil looked like a man who had been in communication with ghosts. "And he advised me against going into the D. A.'s office. . . . But I thought it was because he didn't want me to leave Ladbrooke and Halsey,—I didn't realize that he .. condoned . . ." He couldn't bring himself to complete the sentence.

"He couldn't make his tolerance more explicit without shocking his idealistic daughter," Marc pointed out. "And he wasn't actually opposed to your investigation. He had nothing to fear from it personally. He just didn't believe you could get anywhere. But the trouble was that one of you," he glanced slowly around the room, "one of you who had grown up in association with Judge Ladbrooke, had absorbed his realistic philosophy without his personal probity."

"You mean . . . !" Cissie's little magpie eyes darted curiously from face to face.

"But you. . . !" "That's unwarranted . . ." "What . . ." They all chimed in protesting, yet each looked speculatively at the others.

"I don't suppose any of you were in special need of money, but the pickings were easy." Marc overrode their clamor. "That was back in the depression, too, when panic seized people who were getting down to their last hundred thousand. . . . Moreover there is a lure about playing a secret game, and a sense of power. That aspect would appeal especially to a woman,—a restless, lonely woman."

"I think you're right about father Ladbrooke's realistic point of view." Madeleine's beautiful face was no longer vapid. "But what evidence do you have that one of us was involved with graft?"

"I reasoned it out this way," Marc answered. "The six of you were the only visitors to Eve the day she died. Therefore, it had to be one of you who poisoned her. I started with that. Then I figured she'd been killed because she knew Crane's murderer. Therefore, when I concluded the motive for Crane's death lay in his discoveries about city graft, it led me straight to the fact that one of you must be connected with the graft ring."

They were all silent, mulling over his words, unwilling to believe his accusation and yet unable to find a flaw in his reasoning. "There were other things, too," Marc went on. "For instance, on the day when Eve's mental disturbance began,—presumably because she'd discovered the truth about Crane's murder—her only contacts were, again, with your little circle. She went to town with Cissie, stopped at Phil's office, went over to her father's, entered her own house in a state of collapse. See how it all fits?

And the evidence I found in her room tonight clinches the whole thing."

Marc could see that they were reluctantly accepting his point. They all moved restlessly in their chairs, crossing or uncrossing feet, shifting into changed positions. "I still don't see what my father had to do with this," Scott protested.

"He was the focal point of everything that happened the night Crane was murdered," Marc answered. "He occupied a peculiar position. The various relationships between you formed an isosceles triangle. Phil, Eve, Crane and the reform group occupied one corner, the City Hall gang, secretly including one of you, were in the opposite corner, and the Judge was at the vertex. He was inactive but he had a line running from his position to each of the opposing camps.

"The reformers thought he was in full sympathy with them, but the crowd that viewed him from the other corner, saw only the realistic side of his nature. Those different attitudes were reflected in two lines of action that night,—two converging lines that met at the vertex with an explosion."

The six looked at Marc with varying degrees of incomprehension. Cissie seemed so theatrically baffled Marc wondered if her expression could possibly be genuine. He saw a quickly extinguished gleam of understanding in Halsey's eyes. Madeleine's face was completely blank. Scott remained intransigent, and Barbara and Phil appeared to be struggling to grasp his idea.

Castleman wondered how much time he had left. He glanced at his watch and hurried on. "Let's take what we know and see if we can't piece together what happened that night. Neither the Judge nor the murderer . . . let's call that murderer the tiger—a lethal animal of undetermined sex. Neither the Judge nor the tiger knew that Crane was working undercover for Phil. Under the guise of friendship, Crane had conducted a psychological campaign against Tilton, and, on the night of Jonathan's birth, he had brought him to the breaking point. He left him in Mike's bar and went to Phil's office. Barbara couldn't reach Phil and Crane left, saying he was going to stick with Tilton. At that point we lose his trail.

"The bartender said that Tilton left shortly after Crane did, and he didn't remember seeing either of them again. Now we know Tilton had the wind up, but hadn't decided what to do, whether to turn state's evidence, to run away, or to stick it out in the hope Phil lacked sufficient evidence to convict him. In his indecision he would turn to someone for advice, someone close to Phil and likely to know the direction Phil was taking. In other words, I think he went to the tiger. Is that a logical assumption?"

Phil, tight-lipped and absorbed, nodded in quick confirmation. Halsey, revealing less emotion than the others, had been listening critically, like a lawyer hearing a cross-examination. When in the manner of one reserving judgment, he said curtly,—"Go on," Marc continued.

"The tiger, seeing the shape Tilton was in and realizing he was the Achilles heel of the outfit, would certainly advise him to get out of town. And we know he did leave, that night. . . . But the discovery of what Crane was up to must have given the tiger a bad jolt, and raised the suspicion that Crane was putting pressure on other weak members of the gang. He might even have someone on the point of spilling everything. In this emergency the tiger needed Judge Ladbrooke's help. . . . I suppose the Judge was at the hospital that night?"

"Yes," Phil answered. "We were all there until Jonathan was born and they brought Eve down. They let me stay in the room with her, but they asked the others to leave. I don't know how much longer Judge Ladbrooke stayed on."

"We left him there," Madeleine said. "I was dead tired

and went to bed, but Scott was so worried he went back to the hospital in a little while."

"It was a long time ago," Cissie said. "But it seems to me when they said Eve was in no immediate danger we all left at the same time, except the Judge. I can remember him sitting there all by himself. I wondered if I shouldn't stay with him."

"He was gone by the time I got back," Scott said. "I waited around alone most of the night."

"Well it would have been easy enough for any of you to have gotten the Judge to yourself, then, and told him something urgent had come up. Certainly on the evidence of the pistol, the tiger and the Judge were together that night. The Women's Hospital is downtown, so they probably went to the Judge's chambers, or the firm's law offices.

"Now let's go back and see if we can pick up Crane's trail. He'd find Tilton had left Mike's, and when he couldn't locate him anywhere, he'd think maybe Tilton had already skipped town. He'd told Barbara he was afraid of that. It was urgent to trail Tilton and bring him back immediately, but with Minary out of reach, Nelson, the District Attorney, was the only one who could order direct action. And Barbara had convinced Crane that Nelson wouldn't act on their say-so. He didn't know Crane from Adam, or anything of what he'd been doing.

"Crane had to find someone to vouch for him. Someone in the reform group, who knew him personally, and who was intelligent enough to grasp the situation. It was inevitable that he would think of Judge Ladbrooke.

"Somehow he found him, wherever he and the tiger were Perhaps while hunting for Tilton he saw the lights on in the Judge's chambers or in the Ladbrooke and Halsey offices,—or he may have gone there when he failed to reach the Judge at home or at the hospital. But from the evidence of the pistol again, we know those three had a fatal meeting that night.

"Crane walked in on the conference between the tiger and Judge, explained the situation about Tilton, and asked the Judge to appeal to Nelson. The Judge had just learned that the tiger was involved, and although I don't think he would have deliberately blocked Minary, he'd try to cover up for the tiger and let the ax fall on others, but here was Crane clamoring for immediate action." He turned to Scott. "What do you think your father would do in those circumstances?"

Marc had read about people turning into stone, and now he saw it happen. Scott sat rigidly, grasping the arms of his chair, immovable. Even the quivering in his cheek had stopped. He looked steadily at Castleman with dead eyes, incapable of speaking.

Cissie, the irrepressible, broke into the silence. "There's this about lawyers,—they never rush into things, and they love to compromise. So if you ask me what the Judge did, I'd say he ran true to legal form,—he temporized. Told Crane to wait until Phil was available the next day. Plenty of time for action then."

"Exactly," Marc accepted her verdict with satisfaction. "Now Hal Crane had red hair, and someone described him as a 'convert.' Barbara, you and Phil knew him the best, how do you think he would have reacted to the Judge's advice?"

"Hal wouldn't have taken no for an answer," Barbara replied positively. "He was wild that night, sure he was going to crack the case if he could get action."

"Crane was very loyal to me," Phil said, sadly. "He was young, impetuous, and hot-headed. I don't think he would have been put off easily."

"Add to that," Marc said, "the fact that Tilton had let slip something . . . probably hinted he was protected by somebody in Phil's intimate circle, maybe even mentioned the tiger's name. Crane didn't tell Barbara what Tilton said, only that he had talked freely. Probably, at the time,

Crane put it down as calumny, thought Caesar's family above reproach. But when the Judge tried to hold him back, he would remember Tilton's hints. His suspicion flared up and he probably accused the Judge, outright, of protecting the tiger.

"I get a picture of him,—young, impetuous and filled with the crusader spirit, hurling defiance at the Judge! Telling him he couldn't use his wealth and position to bottle the thing up. That he was going straight to Phil with what he'd heard from Tilton. If Minary wouldn't listen, he'd go to the other members of the reform party! If *The News* wouldn't print his story, other papers would. He would have done it, too. There was only one way to stop him, and the tiger took it. Ten years ago, the tiger was young and impetuous, too. Caught, and in panic!

"When Crane, breathing fire and brimstone, turned to leave, he was shot through the heart."

25.

THERE WAS a gasp, the sound of several sharply in-drawn breaths,—and then a sudden, pregnant silence. Marc looked at his watch again. Five after midnight. He wondered how much longer it would take them to get back with the telltale fingerprints. His own nerves were ready to snap. The tension in the room was terrific.

But Halsey, unmoved, still maintained his judicious

attitude. He said now as though Marc were on the witness stand, and he was summing up for a jury, "All this is pure conjecture—except that Jonathan Ladbrooke was a judge. From that one fact, and the reading you have made of the character of a man you've never met, you have built up quite a house of cards. I admit it's plausible . . . all but this last bit. Aren't you stretching the arm of coincidence a little too far, Dr. Castleman? Just at the moment when this tiger had a sudden impulse, and an unexpected opportunity to kill,—how did it happen that, just then, there should be a gun lying handy?"

"There was no coincidence about that, Mr. Halsey. Don't forget that all the money which flowed back into the hands of the politicians was in the form of cash. The tiger frequently carried large sums for distribution, often at night, and a gun was carried constantly, too. That little revolver I found in Eve's room would fit into a woman's handbag or a man's pocket. The tiger was rarely without it."

"The gun part's reasonable, but I think you've gone off the track on something else, Marc," Cissie broke in. "If Judge Ladbrooke really knew, if he'd actually *seen* Crane killed, he would have called the police. He might have been tolerant about political peccadilloes, but I can't believe he would ever have condoned *murder*."

"You can't get around the evidence, though, Cissie," Marc insisted. "The Judge not only was in possession of the gun later, he knew the murderer's prints were on it,—and intact. He couldn't have that knowledge unless he saw it happen. I don't think he condoned the murder. He was undoubtedly horrified. But when you remember the murderer . . ." Marc looked straight at her, "was an orphaned girl who had been entrusted to his guardianship, or" . . . he turned to Halsey, "a young man in his own firm, the son of his senior partner and lifelong friend, or . . ." he glanced toward Scott and Madeleine, "his own son or

daughter-in-law,—then you can understand why he hesitated to turn the tiger over to the police. And after all that
wouldn't bring Crane back."

Cissie continued to stare at him, unwilling to be convinced. There was a long shuddering sigh from Madeleine.
She held on to her chair arms with white-knuckled hands,
almost as rigid as her husband, and her eyes were unmistakably filled with fear now. Marc raced on confidently.

"We know the Judge didn't report the crime, and apparently no one heard the shot. It was fired in an empty
building in a part of the city deserted at night. Crane's
body was put in his car and the tiger drove it to where it
was found the next morning.

"Tilton was suspected but wasn't apprehended, and
after awhile the thing blew over. Eve came home with the
baby and things settled back to normal. But the tiger must
have wanted to destroy that gun, and the Judge was holding on to it. He probably picked it up while the tiger was
parking Crane's car. That gun stood between an innocent
man and the electric chair. If Tilton, or anyone else, were
ever tried for that murder, it's hard to believe the Judge
would have kept silent. And the gun was his proof.

"Maybe they had many arguments over that gun,—
maybe they had just the one discussion, that afternoon,
there in the Judge's library. For I'm certain they were
threshing things out that afternoon when Eve returned
from town and ran across the lawn to her father's
study."

"So that was it. That's what happened to Eve!" Scott
was jolted from his immobility. The words were barely
audible, half groaned. He groped for his empty glass, his
eyes filled with horror.

His wife picked up his glass, and after a quick, apprehensive glance at him, took it over to the brandy decanter.
Cissie, who was sitting near the table, filled it with a
shaking hand, and then splashed her own glass full. She

drank it down greedily as Madeleine went back to Scott.

"I'd like a refill, too, Cissie," Halsey crossed over to her. "How about you, Barbara?"

"No, thank you." She turned excitedly to Marc. "Dr. Castleman, doesn't that remove Cissie from suspicion? She couldn't have been in the study with Judge Ladbrooke, for she had just let Eve out of her car."

Marc shook his head ruefully. "You forget it was Cissie who told us that story when we began to investigate later. Maybe when Eve left her, Cissie went over to see the Judge, and then a little later, Eve crossed the lawn, came up to the open windows and heard the two of them talking inside.

"Certainly, sooner or later that afternoon, Eve did go over to her father's, approaching by way of the study with the open windows. She probaby caught only a fragment of the conversation, and from the garbled bits she heard she must have imagined her father was even more deeply involved than he was.

"Scarcely able to walk or speak, she stumbled back to her house and in through the side door. Julia put her to bed and she refused to see anyone else. She had to be alone, to decide what action to take. She had to choose between her father and her husband. Phil was being crucified over Crane's death. His whole professional career was at stake. Moreover, Eve must have believed her father had deliberately misled him and betrayed his confidence all along. She could save Phil now,—but only by revealing that her father was an accessory to Crane's murder. She couldn't do that to her father. But if she kept still, she would be feeding her husband to the lions.

"It was a terrible dilemma. Even a healthy mind, a well-integrated personality, would have been strained by such a situation. And Eve was not healthy. Her failure to adjust to the realities of life, her idealized relationships, her fanatical zeal, her periods of withdrawal and depression, all indicated a high degree of emotional instability. The root of her trouble probably lay in her early life. The mother-child relationship is basic, and Eve was deprived of that, of the sense of security given by a mother's care. Then, too, her father and brother centered their lives on her, and their emotional demands may have been too great.

"At any rate, we know that she was mentally ill when she overhead that conversation in her father's library, and the shock induced a rapid deterioration. She lay there in her bed for a week in solitary torment. Her father,—her husband,— her husband,—her father! Without food or sleep, she hunted ceaselessly for a way out, exhausting herself, beating against pinioning circumstance, until the strain became unendurable, and she escaped from the dilemma by denying it. She blanked it out, blanked out reality, all conscious experience."

Scott moaned and dropped his head into his hands. Madeleine leaned toward him, started to touch him, then drew back uncertainly, her face a battleground of conflicting emotions.

"The prognosis was hopeless," Marc went on. "But Mc-Keith accepted Eve as a patient and he tried to find out what had happened to her. The Judge said he didn't know, that he hadn't seen Eve at all the day of her collapse. Then, later, when Cissie described how Eve had gone over to his study on reaching home, he must have realized in a flash what had happened. I think that from that moment he began to hate the tiger."

"If I were the tiger," Cissie interposed, "wouldn't I have been pretty dumb to make up a story about Eve's going across to the Ladbrookes'?"

"If you are the tiger, Cissie, you were caught in a hole and had to make up a story quick, when McKeith got you all together and began to question you about Eve's last sane hours. If you said that Eve went straight into the

house from your car, and if she was in collapse when
Julia met her inside, it would look as though you were
responsible for her condition. You had to think up something on the instant, and remembering how you yourself
had crossed to Judge Ladbrooke's, you said that that was
what Eve had done. It wasn't until you saw the expression
on the Judge's face that you realized the effect your story
would have had on him."

Cissie subsided, the indignation and outrage spread over
her features blanketing effectually any other emotions
stirring within. Marc picked up the thread of his story.

"I suppose the Judge was eaten up with remorse. It
would have been an alleviation to him, at that point, to
have confessed that he was an accessory after the fact and
to have turned the tiger over to the police.

"But he hesitated, because there was someone else to
consider now. His new grandson. If he confessed to com-
plicity in a murder, it would be a hard thing for the boy
to live down. So the Judge still kept silent.

"But he didn't want to pile wrong on wrong. He
wanted to make sure that Tilton would never be convicted
for that murder, and being of a legal mind he wanted to
fix things in such a way that even after his death, Tilton
would be protected.

"We know that he was planning to make a new will,
and he was probably working out some method of pre-
serving that pistol intact as long as Tilton was not apprehended.

"Meanwhile the tiger, seeing the hate and the remorse
in the Judge's eyes, grew desperate fearing the consequences. I suppose we'll never know whether the Judge
was poisoned or whether he died of apoplexy."

"You mean, that Judge Ladbrooke, too . . . ?" Phil
asked in amazement.

"Possibly," Marc nodded. "At any rate, on the afternoon of his death, he was alone in the house except for

the servants. He had a sudden seizure and realized he might be dying. His first thought was of the gun. He couldn't die and leave a murder charge hanging over Tilton. Even before calling a doctor, he wanted to make sure the evidence in Crane's murder fell into the right hands. He used what strength he had to put the gun into a box on which he wrote simple instructions for you, Phil.

"He knew that if he died, neither his safe nor his desk were immune from search. He thought suddenly of the empty, closed-up house next door. He would have a key of course, and he hurried over there. He didn't want the secret disclosed prematurely, and if he lived, he intended to come back and retrieve that box, so he hid it in his daughter's room. No one would have occasion to go through her things in the next few weeks. If he died, the Judge thought Phillip would find the box when he returned, for of course he had no idea that Eve's room would be left undisturbed for ten years.

"When the Judge returned, he met Barbara and seized the opportunity to try to leave a message for Phil. But before he thought out what he wanted to say he had the final seizure, and Barbara didn't mention the episode to anyone, . . . fortunately.

"As soon as the Judge died, the tiger began to look for the gun, and of course failed to find it. As time passed and it remained undiscovered, the tiger hoped that it would never be found. However, even if someone came across it, it would just be taken for a gun that had belonged to the Judge . . . unless a ballistics test were made and the ownership of the gun traced through the serial number.

"So the tiger felt safe on the whole. The Judge and Eve were the only ones who knew the truth. The Judge was dead and Eve would never speak again. But after so many years, when the tiger was lulled into a false sense of security, danger sprang up from an unexpected quarter.

Metrazol came into use. I was experimenting with it, and wanted to try it with Eve. Now the tiger wasn't at heart a killer. It had killed once, unpremeditatedly, in panic. It had possibly killed a second time in self-protection. Now it had to kill again. It waited to the last possible moment. But McKeith was going to start analytic therapy, and he would have gotten Eve to tell her story, especially as her father was dead now.

"So Eve, too, was silenced. But there is no peace for the wicked. I came into the picture, and with what must have seemed to the tiger an uncanny instinct, I immediately guessed at the connection between Eve's death and Crane's. So I too had to be removed. It was only by a lucky chance that I escaped from the tiger's attack as lightly as I did. And I was on the right track. I followed the trail that is ending here tonight."

Marc picked up his glass, drained the last of his liquor and set down the empty tumbler with an air of finality. When they realized he had concluded, they glanced at each other uncertainly, and then all turned toward him again, unbelievingly. It was Madeleine who voiced the question in them all.

"And you really don't know the identity of the tiger even now?"

"An hour ago when I began this account, I didn't know," Marc answered. "I hadn't had time to realize the significance of finding that gun where I did." He paused. The air was electric. "But in the last few moments the remaining pieces of the puzzle have clicked into place. . . . Yes, Mrs. Ladbrooke, now I know who the tiger is."

26.

MARC READ the insistent question in all the eyes focused upon him. But no one had the courage to ask for a name. The air was charged with storm signals. He wondered why Fletcher wasn't here by this time.

Suddenly he remembered, with dreadful misgiving, that Fletcher was one of the gang. Could he be trusted even in a murder case? Maybe the police were all as crooked as hell! And he had given them the evidence,—the gun, the fingerprints, and the Judge's message! His flesh crawled as he looked into the tiger's eyes.

Phillip Minary put the question. "Well, Dr. Castleman?"

Marc, shifting his gaze from the tiger, looked around the circle of faces. "Remember," he began slowly, "that I'm not the only one who knows. The police have the gun, and the prints. There's no use trying to make a break for it. This house is surrounded.

"All right," he yielded. "I'll tell you who it is. . . . But haven't you figured it out for yourselves? Even before I found the gun, I thought it unlikely that the tiger was either Phil or Barbara. I didn't see how either of them could have had the opportunity to get on the inside of things at City Hall.

"And of course Mrs. Ladbrooke was a newcomer. She'd been here about three years. . . . But a beautiful woman, with a gift for intrigue, can go pretty far in less time than that. I couldn't eliminate her, and the other three of you had lived here all your lives, had been closely associated

with the Judge, and had wide connections in the city. I
was sure the tiger was one of you four people, but there
was nothing to indicate which of you it was . . . until I
found the gun! Judge Ladbrooke put that gun where he
did to insure that the tiger could not get at it. His choice
of place is a sign post pointing directly to one person.

"He expected Phillip to make some disposition of Eve's
belongings when he moved back into his house. If going
through his wife's things were too painful an ordeal,
Phillip might very well ask someone else,—a woman, to
do it for him. He would have chosen either Madeleine or
Cissie. And Scott, who was torturing himself over Eve,
was likely to visit her room, to handle her things, to
grieve over her up there. . . . But the one person, who
under no circumstances would have been expected to go
into that room, was . . . !"

All eyes turned swiftly to the man in the chair by the
window.

It was then that they heard the approaching siren, faint
as yet, coming from the distant boulevard. Halsey heard
it, too, and stiffened. Crouched down in his chair with his
hand in one pocket, he looked into their accusing eyes,
and they knew they had a tiger at bay.

He leaped to his feet, and Marc was aware of a flash of
movement at his side as Cissie sent the brandy decanter
hurtling down the length of the room. Halsey ducked, cut
around behind Madeleine's chair and plunged into the
hall. Marc had been braced for a shot, but he saw that
Halsey's hand came empty from his pocket as he raced
out of the room.

The sound of the siren was close and insistent now, as
they ran after the fleeing tiger heading for the back of the
house. The side door on the right burst open and the two
plain clothes men rushed in from the grounds. The tiger
turned to the left and sped for the other door at the end
of the cross passage. He had a head start and he nearly

made it. But Scott's fury gave him superhuman speed. He sprang with a wild leap and caught Halsey by the ankle as he went through the door. He fell headlong, half inside, half out. They heard his head crack on the doorstep, as Scott sprawled after him.

Fletcher and his men were crowding pell-mell into the hall. The two who had been left on guard pulled Halsey to his feet. He looked around him blankly with dazed eyes, his hand against his head. Scott, winded by his fall, pulled himself slowly upright.

Halsey's eyes cleared. Suddenly tense and alert, he glanced about him desperately, and his captors tightened their grip on his arms. As his shrewd mind analyzed the situation, the discipline of years asserted itself. The sea-soned poker player accepted the fact of his loss, and turned stoically to the Chief of Police.

"All right, Fletcher. I'm the man you want. I'll go down to headquarters and dictate a confession. Let's get it over with quickly."

At the door he turned back and looked for a moment at the little group who were watching him, wordlessly. One corner of his mouth curved into a bitter smile. "I'm not sorry . . . that it's over. It hasn't been pleasant living, you know . . . these last years." He raised one arm in a fare-well salute and wheeled out into the night, surrounded by the law.

Scott stumbled into a chair in the living room. "Oh, God, why did he do it? Why couldn't he have let her live? She was so nearly well again!"

Madeleine was instantly at his side in anguished pro-test. "Oh, Scott, don't! Don't start that again. It won't help now. . . ."

Marc stepped up with professional authority. "Listen to me, Scott. . . . There is no place in the world today for people who cry over spilt milk . . . Churchill and Roose-velt and the people they lead aren't sitting down wringing their hands over the mistakes of Chamberlain and the French and the isolationists. They are in there fighting with all they've got."

Scott looked at him with tired, sad eyes. "I know. I know that,—it's easy to say, but . . ."

"But you've got to face it like other men do," Marc commanded. "Millions of men have lost sisters, and wives, and children. They've lost their homes, and their limbs, and their countries. But they're still fighting for the living,—the dead belong to the past!"

Scott turned slowly and looked up at his wife. His eyes grew tender and he reached up, put his arm around her and pulled her down on the arm of his chair.

"What I can't understand," Minary remarked, "is why he sat there and let us trap him. Jeff Halsey has always been a fighter. He never gave up. Not even after the verdict was in. He always appealed an adverse decision. Why didn't he make a break for it earlier?"

"He had too shrewd a brain to fool himself," Marc answered. "He knew he had one chance in a thousand with the house surrounded, and that if he ran for it he'd be throwing in his hand. He tried to bluff it out. Even with the gun, we'd have to explain the motive, tie in all the circumstantial evidence to get a conviction. He hoped I hadn't a convincing case, that he could find a flaw somewhere. So he heard me out.

"I think he did have a plan," Marc went on. "I think that for years he was prepared to disappear the way Tilton did, if that gun turned up and he found himself in a tight place. The trouble was events moved too fast for him.

"He didn't have a gun with him when he came out here to Hillways this afternoon. He'd probably been chary of carrying a gun since Crane's death and he didn't dream he was in any immediate danger of discovery. He knew I had nothing to go on, but a hunch about Crane,—and I was on the wrong track on that. He saw my car and slipped up to eavesdrop on my conversation. As soon as he heard Barbara telling me Judge Ladbrooke's last message, he realized where the gun was,—but he didn't think I could make anything of those few words. He knocked Barbara out for fear she had more to tell, and since he couldn't get at the gun then, and since he didn't want to be seen on the premises, he hurried away. He must have just reached home when Phil called and told him to meet us at the courthouse.

"As soon as Fletcher let you go, Halsey came back here with you hoping to get a chance to look for the gun. But you all stuck together. There's a lavatory here on the first floor, and he couldn't think of any excuse to go upstairs. He got his chance during the confusion following the finding of Barbara. He dashed up to Eve's room and started looking, but before he found the gun, Petty and I came up and scared him off. He ran down the back stairs and joined you in here, but Petty came right down and kept him here until I took over. By that time I had found the gun and the house was surrounded. He didn't have a chance."

"He was the executor of Judge Ladbrooke's estate," Barbara reflected. "That is why the Judge didn't leave the gun in his library safe or put it in a safety box. He knew that if he died, Halsey would be the one in charge of his affairs. He was writing a new will—and I bet Halsey wouldn't have been the executor."

Cissie rose with a reluctant decisiveness. "Well, boys and girls, I don't know about you,—but me, I'm going home and have me a nap before breakfast."

They all got up then and moved out into the hall, Phil supporting Barbara, Madeleine and Scott clasped arm in arm. At the door Minary offered his hand. "I'm not going to attempt to express our appreciation to you, Dr. Castleman. You know what we feel. . . . I can only say, thank you."

"Well, I'm glad we've finally gotten everything straightened out," Marc answered in embarrassment.

He *was* glad, of course, he thought as he went down the front steps. But,—bcpped head and all, he'd enjoyed the thrill of the chase.

Now the clock had struck twelve, and the detective was a doctor again. The routine of Oaklawn was waiting for him. McKeith . . . Ward five . . . Shivelly . . . Potts. He smiled remembering Shivelly that morning,—her radiant face against the pillows as she hugged the baby doll beside her.

And what the devil was the meaning of that last dream of Potts'? It wasn't consistent with the theory he'd been going on. The roc with the queer expression in its eyes,— there was a mystery for you! Of course, it was possible, . . . yes, maybe he hadn't paid enough attention to the cliffs that were always the background of Potts' dreams. He'd have to revise his interpretation. But there wasn't much time left now. He'd have to hurry if he were going to crack Potts' case, too, before his commission came through.

www.ingramcontent.com/pod-product-compliance
Lightning Source LLC
Chambersburg PA
CBHW050421260626
47156CB00003B/1101